23 Degrees South

A Tropical Tale of Changing Whether...

By Neal Rabin

Copyright © 2015 by Neal Rabin

All rights reserved, including the reproduction in whole or in any part in any form without the written consent of the author.

ISBN 978-0-9970468-1-6
Library of Congress Control Number: 2015957578

Published in the United States by
Ponderosa Publishing, LLC

This is a work of fiction. Names, characters, places, and and incidents either are the product of the author's imagination or are used fictitiously. Any resemblance to actual persons living or dead, events, or locales are entirely coincidental.

Climate is what you expect; weather is what you get.
—Dominique Gingerblast, Meteorologist

Prologue

Salt clumps; especially in humid weather. You reach for the shaker, tip it over, yet nothing emerges but frustration and disappointment. The problem dates back to Babylonia where the salt shaker was first discovered. By 1911, The Morton Salt Company figured that modern man had suffered long enough at the hands of insidious, invisible water vapor. They dispatched Prescott and Milo Proctor, two of their finest minds, to the lab. They were granted an unlimited budget along with a career-threatening one-month timeframe. Thinking grand, the scientists requested a custom-built fifteen-foot blackboard, ten boxes of the highest quality chalk, plus five hundred pounds of mounded salt for testing. They floundered for weeks.

During one particularly lengthy all-night session, exhausted and under pressure from their approaching deadline, a slap-happy Milo Proctor tossed a mountainous pile of chalk dust in the face of his sleeping brother Prescott. The dust floated everywhere. Prescott awoke screaming and furiously rubbing his stinging eyes. Suddenly guilty Milo grabbed a pitcher of water and threw it in his brother's face. The rest is inadvertent history. Chalk, or magnesium carbonate ($MgCO_3$), was all they ever needed. As Prescott toweled dry, he noticed that a nearby pile of chalk-dusted, water-soaked salt had not clumped.

Adding a few thimbles of $MgCO_3$ to the signature saltbox absorbed every single drop of water before the salt had a chance to take its first clump-generating sip. Morton ran an ad featuring the very first Umbrella Girl, carrying the round blue container under her arm in the rain.

Below her image rests the iconic slogan:

"When it rains, it pours."

And so…

Chapter 1. | A Simple Breeze

Feeling rather full of himself, Hart, the newly minted Senior Manager for the Maytag Corporation in Sao Paulo, Brazil sat comfortably ensconced within the safe confines of his palatial new office. He rocked back and forth, slowly checking out the deep lean of his stylish, graphite black, Aeron chair. On his faux oak desk lay an old guidebook covering all things Sao Paulo. Not even on the job one week, he still puzzled over the uncomfortable fit of his title. "How the hell can I be a senior manager at twenty-two?" He felt very much the impostor. "How did I rate an assistant too?" Carmen dos Reis sat at her desk a few steps down the hall. Slight, curvaceously built, dark skinned, with stunning blue eyes, and dark lustrous hair. She gave a lilting, intoxicating Brazilian rhythm to everything she did. Hart spoke three languages and none of them adequately described Carmen's beauty.

He'd been thumbing his way through the dog-eared guidebook, studying up on his new city. São Paulo was founded by the well meaning, goal oriented Jesuits way back in 1554. It sits on a plateau precisely 2,493 feet above sea level, forty-five miles from the Atlantic coast. For Hart, who grew up only a few miles from the ocean, he may as well have been in Iowa. He felt sure at some point he would grow to enjoy his new surroundings, but still had nagging doubts. Putting down the book for a moment, he swallowed hard against the depression he had battled from an early age. "It's called a Dukkha, and you're lucky to have it," that was the unsolicited advice from his Buddhist Studies professor at UCLA. Depression sucked. It wasn't a gift from the gods; it was a scourge that arrived at all the wrong times. He hoped his luck would hold since he hadn't suffered a bout in quite a long time. Learning about his new surroundings helped keep things on an even keel. He never enjoyed surprises; they forced him off-balance.

Once again he paged into his new distraction. Back in the early days the Jesuits ruled all things. Jesuits were famously regarded as the Pope's Paratroopers, his First Responders, the Vatican Seal Team whose mission profile directed them to splash down amongst the unsuspecting in all corners of the world and show them the one true way of all things. These stout-hearted foot soldiers of Saint Ignatius Loyola were nicknamed Jesuits by the folks on the other side of the door. If your Renaissance doorbell rang, and the guy on the stoop wore all black, you could trust that he was not there to sell you the latest Michelangelo print. Jesuits wanted to talk about Jesus. Jesuits translates as "one who uses the name of Jesus with relentless frequency." Let us say "Jesus" at breakfast, lunch, dinner, tea time, on the way to the mall, waterfall, or nightclub. Jesuits prefer Jesus over tiramisu, mud pie, filet mignon, and any fresh fish including rare, seared Ahi. The infamous acronym—WWJD—What Would Jesus Do—originated with the Jesuits back in the darkening days of the late Renaissance.

These road warriors conceived Sao Paulo as the mission center for their frequent traveler club members: participating nationally affiliated early settlers and, reluctantly, the local heathens. If you were not a Jesuit, or well-connected royalty, then you were lumped into the category of godless nuisance native or heathen. As far as Team Jesuit was concerned, heathens served no productive purpose unless they could be converted to the right side of the holy ledger. Those that would not buy in for whatever reasons were simply designated as road kill. They squatted in the middle of the progressive highway, disrupting the missionary victory drive towards the Holy Trinity: civilization, salvation, and incorporation. The Jesuit advance guard brought the Holy Spirit, but they also traveled with their calculators. New World Wealth Management, or the upside of global colonization, occupied a large chunk of the Jesuit mindset whether they landed in Borneo, Boston, or Brazil.

Looking out his window at the street below, Hart considered this history. He hadn't seen many black robed Jesuits cruising about the tragically hip streets of modern Sao Paulo. Perhaps they were horrified by how far modern Brazil had strayed from the marquee they hung up way back when. Perhaps they considered the country a job well done and had simply moved on. A quote at the top of the next page in his guidebook stopped him cold:

"That which you are seeking is always seeking you."

Hart uttered the phrase aloud to no one in particular. He unconsciously retooled the adage into a personal question of reflection. How in the holy landslide of Roman-numeral-numbered Popes, he wondered, would a 17th century, twenty something Jesuit priest on an obligatory recruiting pilgrimage know anything about his circumstances? Logically, of course he wouldn't, but the saying still applied to his personal life. For some time Hart had realized how much of his time had been devoted to passively hanging a line over the side of his metaphorical rowboat and waiting for a strike. His paralytic life strategy had centered on aggressive anti-seeking, at least until he fell into Brazil. Now he was simply afraid that he might have let the big one get away. He pushed those thoughts deep down into a cavern of his brain marking them for later exploration. Internally, he labeled the quote enigmatic and mysterious, but mostly too damn irritating to dwell on for longer than the two seconds he had given it. He thumbed to the next page.

It was at this precise moment of uneasy reflection that Hart's best friend Simon burst into his office, knocked over the luscious Carmen, and to the best of his recollection, shot him point-blank in the neck.

Chapter 2. | Fuck if I know

A phone came to life amidst the sound of spinning blenders at the Janiero juice bar in the tony suburb of Vila Olimpia.

Carlos dos Reis had a mantra that served him. "Fuck the fuckers that fuck you before they fuck you again." Had Carlos realized what chaos had begun bearing down on him at that moment, his life might have voluntarily veered in another direction. According to Einstein's theory, Star Trek, and all that worm hole science stuff, Carlos might have had time to execute a pre-emptive strategy, and make his way to the nearest exit before the doors were cross checked and sealed. As far back as he could remember, life had backhanded Carlos, not once but many times. Most of those knuckle slaps he created himself. Those first few rips surprised and hurt him, after that it became a matter of expectation and pain management. Like the phenomenal athlete we all knew in grade school who somehow stepped on a waist-high landmine at exactly the wrong time, Carlos fulfilled the wrong destiny. He had two choices and consistently, even redundantly, selected the worst of all possible worlds. Dark skinned, with high cheekbones and thick dark hair like his mother, Carlos also possessed a genetically chiseled body inherited from his maternal grandfather, the legendary Capoeira master known only as Mestre Bimbo. He was small, about five feet six. His height only exacerbated his anger.

The Favela jungle line had reached out a tentacle for Carlos. The line incorporated a variety of sophisticated modes. Simply put, it was a phone call from the neighborhood house of horror, Carandiru, Sao Paulo's largest prison. A call was placed to a rotating collection of telephones ranging from private homes, to decrepit, pond scum phone booths, to police headquarters, to lunch counters. Someone answered, took a message, and then set about the task of fulfilling the designated request. Beginning at the juice bar, the vine caught up with Carlos through the hands of a random eleven-year-old boy on the streets of Heliopolis. Heliopolis—one of the grand slums that dot all Brazilian cities. Chewing on a Ghirardelli bittersweet chocolate bar with hazelnuts, Carlos recognized the kid approaching him from the city's soccer pitch. The boy handed him a piece of scrunched up paper. Carlos flipped the kid a Real coin and opened the balled mass.

The only words written on the paper: "Get stupid."

He tossed the two words around in his brain. For a moment he tried to pretend that he tossed them out the virtual window of the nearest fifty-story building. Whoosh, they sailed out, smacked into gravity then headed straight down and crashed onto the pavement disintegrating into a zillion unrecoverable pieces. "Damn!" He said it aloud, then in his head, then out loud again. Not now, he whined to himself.

The last two years had been the most productive of Carlos' chosen career. His most recent accomplishments included boosting a wide assortment of luxury cars parked at various branches of the Brazilian Savings & Loan Bank, exploding multiple hand-crafted bombs placed near various telephone switching stations, plus his most recent escapade—a late night clean out of the recently opened Sega Super Store. Carlos had been building a reputation. Welcomed back to the favela from a stint in prison by a cadre of PCC (local crime mob) members, they celebrated their mutual disdain for the present government and its growing list of inequities, alongside their love for their still-imprisoned fearless leader—the Shadow.

Carlos' shoulders drooped as the reality of the message sank in. Parolees walked a tightrope with their freedom. Carlos knew what needed to be done. It wouldn't take much. He paid his rent for the next six months, strolled down to the nearest bar, drank half a bottle of Calypso Dark Rum, marshaled his nerve and walked out of the favela.

Recently crowned junior detective Jorge Rosado had just unbuttoned the collar on his thick rayon blend uniform. He hated being hot. Sao Paulo police uniforms sadistically captured, retained, then perversely amplified the tropical heat. He also hated walking a beat. He figured that life was left in his rear view mirror until his replacement patrol officer, Paolo Girardo, called in sick with a rapidly moving case of tainted street food. Rosado had filled in one last time. His feet walked the beat while his mind wandered off to organize his new metal detective's desk and its three slightly off-track drawers. Contemplating where to put his pens, stapler, and scotch tape dispenser he entirely missed Carlos dos Reis Machado making a beeline towards his exact position. Carlos promptly smash-mouthed the unsuspecting Rosado with a roundhouse left to the jaw. Surprisingly Rosado maintained his balance, but lost his cool and came rushing back at Carlos while reaching for his gun. Carlos crouched low, like an attacking tiger, then placed his left arm down on the ground as a pivot point and windmilled his legs. The motion upended Rosado at his knees sending him crashing to the ground in a moaning heap and a permanently aching tailbone. By this time two other policemen, guns drawn, flew across the street tossing their half-drunk passion fruit smoothies into the fast lane of oncoming traffic. The first smoothie hit the windshield of a Kwik Copy delivery van, entirely blotting out the driver's vision. The driver slammed on his brakes. The van fishtailed over the median line into the opposing traffic, where it came to a stop. The driver let out a long sigh of temporary relief. Temporary, that is, until Mrs. Jaio Gilberto placed her 1984 Toyota Camry solidly into the van's midsection. The precise and potent hit launched the van and its contents skipping back onto the highway median. The gentle Sao Paulo breeze lifted and stirred the day's paper output into a Mardi Gras frenzy of ticker tape, giving the whole intersection an oblique feeling of seasonal celebration. The streets were littered with an eight-by-ten inch flyer trumpeting a speaking engagement by a Jesuit priest by the name of Lazarus. Lazarus Knows appeared in bold print across the top of the flyer. "Come Sunday morning you will too" read the rest of the now well-disbursed ad.

    No real injuries, plenty of insurance claims, definitely no Mardi Gras party, and six months inside for Carlos dos Reis. But then he knew that sitting at the barstool. Once returned to the fold and re-inserted back in the starting lineup of the prison futbol squad, Carlos made the customary rounds of re-acquaintance. The Shadow, aka Julian Coelho, waited patiently.

    Coelho, your standard hard case criminal boss, controlled his empire from inside the walls of Carandiru Prison. His cell came equipped with a phone line from which he maintained constant contact with the outside universe. When necessary, any direct order from the Shadow moved from thought to implementation in a matter of hours.

Carlos found Julian watching the soccer team practice game from his usual perch high in the yard. He walked up the bleacher stairs to sit down next to him. Julian sat alone. No cadre, no other inmates within twenty yards of him. He looked weathered and older. It had been two years, but seeing Julian's condition, it felt more like ten.

"Greetings Ram Dass," Carlos said.

Julian laughed. The new Che Guevara tattoo on his neck crinkled its eyes and appeared to be laughing along with its host body, "See, you have skills after all."

"I'm here for six suffocating months. What's so urgent?" Carlos made his annoyance clear.

"I'm going to get the shiv in here before too long. Sadly, the PCC is no longer the organization I'd like it to be. Too concerned with economics over cause. There is a selfish, vile, greed obsessed element that has emerged to try and dominate the old guard. There's resistance, but not enough."

"What resistance?"

"Just me, I guess."

Carlos took a deep inhale.

"I heard this priest last year." Julian smiled, sensing Carlos' surprise.

"You listened to a priest?" an incredulous Carlos asked his mentor.

"I didn't say I heard the angels singing the holy word of God and took a knee! He came in here to talk to us about the world; a guy about your age. He made sense. You should have a listen, make something more out of your own life before you end up like me."

"What's his name?"

"Father something. Just give him a listen and you'll figure it out."

"I'm confused with all this. You spent years teaching me to be like you. Now you're having second thoughts. What the hell Julian?"

"Life is unpredictable. Be aware."

"I'm doing six for that pearl of wisdom?"

"It's not all about the money. I want you to carry on the fight when I'm done, but not the same fight." Julian communicated the news with little emotion.

"That will never work. I don't want to be the heir apparent. All the fuckers that want your ass will be after mine too."

"What have I taught you?" Coelho rallied a smile.

Carlos recited the lesson by rote: "Fuck the fuckers that fuck you before they fuck you again."

Julian gave a surprise chuckle, "Not exactly how I put it, but I like your spin."

"Why don't YOU follow your own damn advice?"

"I've run out my string. There's no respect for age anymore. It's a real tragedy. See if you can do something about that sometime." Julian smiled, then got up to leave. He left a Lindt bittersweet 73% lying on the ground.

Carlos scooped it up and put it in his pocket as he walked back to the pitch, sad, irritated, and as always, angry.

Chapter 3. | Oh Yeah...

Prior to making his course-altering jump to Brazil, life had not been firing on all cylinders for Hart. He'd fought a constant battle, side stepping out of his own way long enough to shake a relentless feeling of despair. He knew there was more but had been settling for less. He knew it was less because it always rolled back around to the despair thing, which ignited the whole circular slip and slide for yet another ride around the same damn block.

Three months earlier, Hart stood with a towel wrapped around his waist after a late afternoon shower. As he had for the past year he'd spent his morning teaching tennis on the public courts near his flat. He was vigorously drying his wavy brown hair half listening to the TV droning in the small living room of his Westwood, California one bedroom apartment.

"Looks like another beautiful day on tap for tomorrow: a few large, puffy clouds and not much else to get in your way. Highs looking like the low seventies through the end of the week."

"Really, Dominique?" an incredulous anchorman questioned. "Because it's raining pretty hard outside the studio right now, and those clouds look kind of fierce, so the whole beautiful day thing..."

Perpetually cheery Dominique, giggling while dismissively waving her arms answered, "Going, going, gone by tomorrow Roger. No worries."

Roger added with a half grin, "Well folks, we sure hope Dominique knows best. Moving onto other news, the International Olympic Committee meeting in Lausanne, Switzerland announced today that Brazil has been awarded the Summer Games, beating out the combo bid from Boise and Walla Walla. Too bad Idaho, but I bet they're dancing in the streets of old Brazil town tonight! Right Brittany?"

Brittany Hammond, the busty, brunette co-anchor condescendingly bit back, "Thanks Roger, and I'm sure wherever 'Brazil town' is, they are dancing. In other news..."

Hart's telephone rang.

"Hart?"

He instantly recognized the voice. It triggered a wave of childhood memories reaching back from Chips Ahoy and milk to college graduation.

"Leice? Hey, long time." The voice of his best friend Simon's mom made Hart smile. A small bead of sweat magically appeared on his forehead.

"I haven't heard a word. Have you?" Leice was using her concerned mother's voice.

"Once, a few months back." Hart offered no details, since he didn't know any. He had received a post card from Rio, specifically from the Carmen Miranda Museum. A beautiful black and white portrait shot of Carmen wearing a classic fruit salad headdress. Simon had written a terse three lines on the back. "Weird place. Didn't know she did a movie with Jerry Lewis. You should have come with me. Simon."

Leice continued, "He was teaching tennis in someplace called 'Boat to Katu.'"

"That's more than I got."

"I'm worried."

Hart had considerable history with Leice Jovenda, but at that moment he could not figure out what to do or how to help her. He promised to let her know if and when he heard from Simon. He remembered eating a chicken drumstick and unexpectedly saying goodbye to his best pal twelve months prior. For as long as Hart could recall they told each other everything—well almost everything. That bastard had kept something from him, which he discovered while chomping on a mouthful of backyard barbeque. Two months later Hart had an answer, but he had to put his ass on an airplane to Brazil to find it.

Folded into his window seat set for the ten hour flight to Sao Paulo, Hart had nothing but time on his hands to reflect on the trail of events leading up to his here and now. Before the doors were shut, and with a little assist from an Ambien, he drifted off.

THWACK!

"Fuuucckkk!"

Deep in his dream, Hart dropped his Wilson Blade racket, grabbed his balls, and crumbled to the hard court. He reached in vain for the net to brace himself. The little fluorescent green ball rolled innocuously away, its' task completed. His best friend from age seven, Simon, collapsed on the opposite baseline in paralytic laughter.

"Sorry!" Simon shouted a disingenuous apology.

"Real funny asshole." Hart clutched his groin, as if that would squelch the instantaneous nausea.

Simon strolled up to the net. "That was a legitimate shot. You're supposed to use the racket not your dick."

"Give me a minute, you bastard."

"You're not hurt that bad."

"I can't breathe."

"You're talking which means you're breathing. Quit being a pussy."

The only child of a single mother, the perpetually enthusiastic Simon Jovenda was tall and dark-complexioned, an angular, sharp-featured Brazilian kind of handsome. Hart got used to craning his neck upwards talking to Simon while they walked. To school, from school, around school, the two of them constantly hung together. Because of his early height Simon could drive his own Autopia car at Disneyland by the middle of second grade. Even though Hart generally suffered from carsickness, and could always be counted on to hurl during the family Sunday drive, Autopia was entirely different. While most kids had to strap up with their Mom or Dad, Simon and Hart cruised the Disney highways solo. They liked it that way: wind in their hair, independent and free. The salient fact that the cars were on a one way track never struck either boy as confining.

Simon's mother, Leice, spoke Portuguese, which from the first moment he heard it, Hart equated with sex. This was further complicated by the fact that in Hart's eyes, Leice could've easily passed herself off as a Bond girl of the first order. Portuguese sounded like someone whispering a soft secret into his ear: smooth, delicate, steamy, and addictively mysterious. Strangely, although he understood it, Simon never spoke it. He wanted to learn Hebrew. Hart had to for his Bar Mitzvah, but Simon's choice was a puzzle. Leice cast it as a demonstration of his bond with Hart's family and an indirect way to disown his own fathers' abandonment. If Portuguese stood as the language of sensual pleasure; Hebrew pulled up the rear, riding quad with Afrikaans, Flemish, and Dutch—four languages as mellifluous as a jackhammer ripping up the sidewalk outside your bedroom window at two in the morning. At twelve years old, Hart didn't reach for a deep-dive on meaningful answers. He chocked it up to simply Simon, and was happy to have his pal along for the ride in Hebrew school.

The Jovenda house vibrated with a subtle invisible rhythm, whether or not music played on the turntable. Leice made Hart crazy. Simply walking in the door triggered three responses in his adolescent body—sweat, drool, and a complete loss of the power of speech. Hart could feel the dew forming on his face and under his arms before the front door even opened. He tried to hide this as best he could by keeping his arms pinned to his sides and by lightening quick brow mops. Then the slaver; from the corners of his mouth—an unending pool of saliva—would congregate threatening to spill over into public view. Finally, and most bizarrely, the dislogia took over. Like a computer freezing at the most inopportune moment, the speech center in his brain simply froze solid. The sudden halt meant a complete loss of his ability to articulate thoughts. Yet despite this abundance of humiliations, Hart was overcome with a surge of well being and unexplained contentment around Leice. He would walk into Simon's house, brace for Leice's kiss on the cheek, perform his personal prevention routine, and then let the rush of warm feelings wash over him. Wearing a stupefied grin, Hart gingerly made his way back to Simon's room to flop on the bed and recover. He never grew tired of the phenomenon. The triggers receded, but still followed Hart throughout his romantic life.

Simon spent great swaths of time at Hart's house too; so much so, he considered himself part of Hart's family. Hart's mother, father, and even his surly older brother shared the sentiment. Hart's dad, a former Air Force pilot, even taught both boys to fly an airplane when they were fifteen. Hart got his license, but Simon never did. Having a single mother who worked meant Simon had a lot of time to himself. Simon voluntarily went to Hebrew school with Hart every Monday and Wednesday afternoon. When Hart asked him why, Simon replied with his favorite aphorism—"Because you gotta grab life by the fucking balls."

"With Hebrew representing the actual balls of life? How's that?"

"It's not that literal. Just grab hold of something and yank away." Simon laughed at his miserable pun.

Beside the fact that Leice's work kept her away from home until dinnertime, Hart figured Simon attended out of friendship tempered by boredom. Eventually, while actually paying attention, Simon ended up fluent in Hebrew. Hart went through the motions, mouthing his way through the whole ritual. They both enjoyed the Jewish sport of posing paradoxical questions to their teacher. Why doesn't glue stick to the inside of the bottle type inquiries, except more Jewish. Does God have a weekly 'to do' list? Who wins a three-way cage match: God, Buddha, or Jesus? Why was God so hard-core on Sodom and Gomorrah? This culminated with penultimate question: If God is all knowing with reasons for everything then why did He allow the Nazis to kill six million Jews? Simon paid particular attention to the Nazis. He could not fathom that depth of evil. To Jews, the Holocaust is a genetic inheritance. It exists in the bloodstream like red and white corpuscles. The Nazi corpuscle generates a cornucopia of emotional content from outrage, to hatred, to pity, to sadness, to Hogan's Heroes. To the uninitiated, like Simon, it blew the lid of their ethical and moral naïveté concerning humanity's grievous limitations. Jews created sitcoms around the horror; Simon found no humor in it at all.

Fortunately, their Hebrew School teacher, Mr. Goldman, had a sense of humor, plus a great looking daughter. All religions and philosophical viewpoints were fair game for Goldman. By not shielding them from other religions and spiritual beliefs, he hoped his students would organically attach to Judaism. Surely it would have been a gigantic shock to him to know that Simon was a Jew-postor. On Hart's twelfth birthday Mr. Goldman made him a gift of the classic Herman Hesse book Siddhartha. He read it then loaned it to Simon, who never gave it back. Simon always believed Hart possessed something he did not. He could never solidly identify what that mystery something was, or decide if lacking it made him jealous, disheartened, or relieved.

"I'm going to marry your mother. I love her, and I'm pretty certain it's mutual."

Hart decided that it was his destiny to marry Leice Jovenda. He was twelve. Although Hart never witnessed Leice display any of the same physically debilitating signs, he concluded that if he felt the chemistry then so must she. He recognized the age difference, but knowing that in just five years he'd be seventeen and legally eligible to marry, with parental permission, he concluded there were no deal killer obstacles. He anticipated his parents would approve of the match without hesitation. Hart's flawless logic—they loved Simon, and Leice begat Simon. Hart knew in his heart that his fatherless best pal would have no problem with his brilliantly conceived master plan. It happened walking home from school one day. Hart, while chomping on a Mounds bar, and after holding his tongue for almost a year, let loose his plan. Simon did not accept the news as joyously as Hart had imagined.

"Shut the hell up. Never say that shit again, or I swear to God Hart, I'll kick the living shit out of you!"

"I thought you'd be happier? I'm grabbing my life by the balls, right?" Hart wedged his Mounds wrapper into a nearby chain link fence.

"Oh my god. You idiot, it's MY MOTHER! My Mother! And pick up that wrapper, you pig!"

Simon accelerated away, turning only to shake his head, and wag an index finger in Hart's direction.

Hart shouted after him, "Jesus Christ, Simon, calm down!"

That surprising display of anger changed Hart's thinking. It upset his carefully conceived life path. Simon remained pissed off for a good week, maybe two. Hart decided not to mention the concept again while remaining confident he'd figure out some other way to realize his dreams without involving his buddy. The plan eventually evaporated when Hart met Marjorie Goldman at Hebrew School. Marjorie walked into the class one afternoon, and Hart's nervous triggers appeared. She sat next to him and the familiar warmth of well being washed over him too. Their relationship, though brief, proved less complicated than his previous master plan.

Simon grew to 6'5" by the summer of tenth grade. As an excellent tennis player, he fit quite well into Hart's family system, which was ruled by the racquet. When they played tennis together Simon would often come over in between points to talk strategy, or more often to sling a stealthy insult about the other team's caliber of play. As he tilted his stretched frame over Hart's, it felt like they were in a secret chamber apart from the world. Simon blotted out the sun and any other distractions.

Hart felt safe in that shadow of friendship. And so it went until the graduation barbeque.

Hart was a pretty sad guy when he showed up in Leice's backyard for the Father's Day party celebrating Simon's graduation from college with a degree in Humanities. He had been admittedly treading water teaching tennis for a living, and teetering on the fence over a decidedly murky future. He lurked apart from Simon's family and other friends in the back of the yard, chicken drumstick in hand. Hart stared over at the empty swimming pool behind him, feeling like a seven year old clutching onto the side while trying to navigate his way safely into the perilous deep end.

Simon could quote Chaucer, Tennyson, Keats, Socrates or whomever with equal dexterity but he never did. He could be gregarious, the life of the party seemingly open and on display with more bravado than inhibition. He had a private side too, a side Hart never entered. Not because he didn't want to, but more because he was not invited in. Hart reasoned that growing up without a Father certainly leaves a hole, but balanced the equation by figuring if you never had that piece to begin with, how big could it be? Simon held onto his own tiller and steered a course unfettered by an Alpha male at the head of the dinner table. Although his Dad's whereabouts remained an unsolved mystery, it never appeared to be a source of emotional upheaval for either Simon or his mother. It was just Leice and Simon against the world. He did not complain about the hours he was left alone to fend for himself. He rarely bucked his mother's desires. He integrated, cooperated, and navigated life to avoid any rough waters. He got along. Over all their years together, Hart could only recall that one occasion when Simon took a firm stand. Still, Hart knew that Simon's brain constantly churned. His stealth, skunk works factory, worked twenty-four seven on top-secret strategies to be deployed at some future date of need. Many times, like right now, Hart envied that existence with one exception: did life always have to be snagged by the balls?

After a toast from Leice honoring and congratulating her son for making it through college, mostly on his own, Simon stood up and faced the crowd.

"Thank you all for coming." He let go a huge sigh of relief. Hart immediately sensed something coming from the skunkworks. His face turned blank, waiting.

"I have no obligations left. That is a heavenly feeling." Simon smiled and took a huge inhale. "Mom, I love you. The time has come for me to step out. I am heading off to Brazil in a couple weeks for an open-ended stay."

The look on Leice's face told Hart that she had been forewarned. The crowd reaction, an uncomfortable smattering of hesitant applause and cursory well wishes, confirmed that everyone else had reached the same conclusion that he had. Brazil? Simon's eyes scanned the crowd and zeroed in on his best friend's expression. Oh shit, Hart thought, did Simon just read my lips? Hart rapidly generated a supportive smile and even a half-assed fist pump. Then he got that queasy feeling of envy in the pit of his stomach, thinking he had just been leap-frogged on the road of life. Hart knew that in Simon's mind he had had opted for a deep ball grab, yet opted not to share it with his best friend. Hart shook his head and thought about what a selfish bastard Simon had become! Why was he going to Brazil? Why hadn't they talked about this? Was he going alone? What questions did Brazil have the answers for? Maybe he was off to Brazil strictly to avoid all the questions entirely. He had never spoken or even thought much about his homeland, at least not to Hart.

Hart fumed. The crowd thinned out. Pretty soon it got down to just the two pals tossing out half-eaten BBQ, assorted salads, plates, and cups.

"Your Mom sure looks good." Hart started it off.

"Oh come on. Don't do that shit." Simon smiled, but did not laugh.

"Really?" Hart declared, catching Simon's gaze.

"Don't start on me." Simon shook his head and gathered up more partially munched chicken parts.

"I'm waiting on the story pal," Hart balled up a plate and hoop tossed it ten feet, hitting nothing but can.

"You have not been listening to me." Simon pointed an index finger at Hart in frustration, then shook his head. "You see this?" He pointed at his own head. "You know what this means. I'm using my mind to make my choices. Should I speak slower for you?"

"Why are you so angry at me?"

No reaction from Simon other than to continue cleaning up the backyard.

Figuring he had overlooked or ignored some lingering hurt, Hart sorted through a hundred conversations between the two of them searching for the origin of Simons anger. He stuffed his own feelings of abandonment and doubt down in favor of a softer tack. "It's okay man," Hart said.

"That's exactly what pisses me off. I don't need your compassion. I'm great! I'm not lost, misguided, or melancholy. I will not be joining your non-stop journey on the woe is me train."

"Screw you! That's what you think of me?"

Simon realized he had gone too far. "Too harsh. I'm sorry. But dude, look in the mirror," Simon countered. He plucked a half eaten BBQ drumstick off a random plate and bit down.

"That's gross man. I'm not a puritan, but half eaten cold chicken? Even at a family BBQ, that's pushing it."

Simon tossed the bone in the garbage.

"It's from my O.C.D. Uncle Felix. He never touches anything with his hands. He brings his own silverware, cuts one bite of everything and leaves the rest. It's cleaner than you are."

"Brazil?" Hart blurted out. Enough preamble with someone he had known virtually his entire life.

Simon smiled and tossed another plate in his hefty bag, then moved to another table. He flipped it over and began to fold down the legs.

"I know you're pissed because I never mentioned it." Simon tossed his own balled-up plate ten feet further back than Hart, hitting nothing but can. He shot Hart his black mamba glare.

"Hell yes, I'm pissed off."

Simon looked down at his hands as he spoke. "Hart, my friend, it's about destiny." He turned his hands palms up one at a time. Looking first at the right, then the left, he offered his thesis: "Destiny and adventure." He clasped his hands together to emphasize his point.

"Balls. You're talking about the balls thing." Hart mocked.

"I am not going to park my life in the same garage for the whole run. I have to get out of here and see something. What's the difference where I go? I have a lot of questions without good answers and I have some answers with no decent questions."

"Exactly," Hart agreed, "that's your suffering talking."

"Christ Hart, this is not some kind of deep seated Buddhist suffering. It's called CURI-FUCKIN'-OSITY! I've heard you say my exact words."

"You're talking poison man." Hart felt like Simon was reaching for something outside of himself. His closest friend was desperately grabbing outside the box for the elusive feather in the wind. Hart viewed it as his obligation to save him from a terrible mistake.

Simon glared, "We're not going to talk about the six poisons. I love you man, but I refuse to engage in the six poisons theory over this trip. You took a couple classes on Buddhism and you've become the holy Emperor Imhotep?"

"Imhotep was an Egyptian architect, moron."

"I'm mocking you."

"Not funny. I'm just saying," then in rapid fire order, "anger, desire, greed, envy, sloth, and DELUSION!"

Simon pushed aside a table and sat down on the lawn, folding himself into an awkward six-footer Lotus position.

"It came out angry, but I'm more frustrated with you than pissed. I don't want to be judged. I just want to get out of here. If you knew what was good for you, you'd do the same."

That stuck to Hart's ribs, "You know what's good for ME now? Fuck you!"

Simon shook his head yet again, "I don't like this side of you. This eye glaring, Babel speaking Religious studies major crap wears me down. It wears at me mostly because you don't have a clue where you're going, and you won't admit it. Why don't you come with me?" Simon offered a genuine invitation. "We'll do it together like we used to. I have family there."

"No you don't." Hart fired back. "You have no idea if that's true or not. How can you leap down there without a plan?"

"That is my plan." A Simon smile.

"How existential of you."

"Actually I have two plans. One is to look for my father's family. The other is to do some work for the Simon Wiesenthal Center and find some Nazis. They have a list and some guesses on the whereabouts of some really despicable old Germans who need to be caught. I figure I owe it to the Jewish people."

Hart's open jaw hung there for two minutes, picturing his best pal as a bonded, Wiesenthal endorsed, Nazi hunter on the prowl for decaying armbands in the wilds of South America.

"Sorry?" Hart laughed at the prospect.

"I know it's bizarre and possibly psychotic, but I'm mostly serious about it. You know they're still down there."

"Simon, do you want to be an ox driver or a Buddha?"

"I don't even know what that means."

"An airplane ticket away from home, does not guarantee you will be any different there, or for that matter, even when you come back."

"Why don't you just say 'same shit, different day,' instead of being all cryptic religious philosophy major dude?"

"Can I take you to the airport?" Hart decided not to continue arguing with Simon. He realized a significant part of him actually did want to go. The Nazi hunting scheme made him nervous, but determining he had no real rational reasons other than betrayal, jealousy, and envy to rain on Simon's parade he capped the argument. Who wouldn't like to see a few more Nazis, no matter how old they may be, nailed to the global retribution cross? Knowing that his best pal was going off world Hart suddenly felt very alone.

Chapter 4. | When the Rain Comes

The amount of rain pounding the streets of Vila Olimpia confounded the forecasters and almanac geeks who had recently proclaimed the Brazilian rainy season officially over. Historical data will only get you so far in life. 'Trust your heart.' That's what Manuela Dos Reis' grandfather had always told her.

Tall and lean, with soft boyish features, and an aquiline nose inherited from his saber-toothed grandfather, Florante Greve, third edition, headed for the office of the grand old man. He wore his light brown hair fashionably slicked back, creating an appearance more severe than his true nature. His combination of slick and soft pronounced him an early model of today's metrosexual modern urban man. He knocked once. Grandpa Greve, the family vituperate asshole, never took the grandkids fishing, to the park, or for ice cream. He worked. Gauging and decoding love from the old man depended upon how much he gave you to do and when the work needed to be finished. Florante III had adjusted to his style by the age of ten.

Florante Greve the First, clutching a pile of papers in his liver-spotted hand, grunted, signaling that his entrance had been approved, "Only an idiot could fuck this up, so don't!"

In this touching display of grandfatherly love, and with that supportive admonition, the newly minted lawyer received his first case as a practicing attorney for Greve Almeida & Son. GAS, as it was known in the trade. The firm had a reputation for driving in the fast lane of Brazilian corporate politics. Its tentacles had been wrapped around every power seat of Brazilian commerce since the turn of the century—the newest one, and the previous one. True, the young Florante III had agreed to a power marriage between Sabrina Almeida and himself, but he still considered himself a self-made man. As self-made a man as one can be, given his pronounced head start on the opportunity escalator. Florante III was never handed anything except a college tuition check. His father and grandfather made sure that the meaning of hard work was not lost on their heir apparent. Florante spent many years at GAS performing anything asked of him from floor mop, to fetch detail, to law clerk, and eventually, inevitably, to Managing Partner.

On this pro bono case Florante would defend a pregnant woman by the name of Manuela dos Reis Machado or, as she was known in her favela, Mistress Bimba. Allegedly Bimba had attempted to rob a small branch of the Brasilia Savings & Loan Bank by putting on a fairly lethal demonstration of Capoeira. Unfortunately and unbeknownst to Ms. Bimba the bank had not yet opened for business. She ended up squaring off against three construction workers, a visiting aid worker from Portugal, and a Human Resources representative from BS&L posting an employment opportunity sign on the front door. Florante invited Mistress Bimba to the GAS offices for a conference.

Living in a favela is a lot like living in a gated community, except the metaphorical lock keeps folks in not out. Favelas are the Brazilian equivalent of South African townships like Soweto, Mexican slums like Tijuana, virtually any street in Calcutta, and any other zero opportunity shantytowns on the globe fixed in poverty and riddled with hopelessness. However, even the hopeless seek hope.

Capoeira combines opposites like fighting and dancing, violence and aesthetics, truth and justice. Way back in the day, that day being the 1600's, Brazil—a Portuguese franchise country—grew lots and lots and lots of sugar cane. The triple "lots" required a like amount of slaves. The work had no upside for the slaves who lasted at most five years in the fields. The choices for them lay between work or die, or die pretty soon anyway. Many slaves thought they ought to create some additional options, including a longer life. They rebelled. The use of Capoeira became a deadly alternative for escaping enslavement and hitting the road to opportunity. After a sufficient number of soldiers, police and other government officials had received a Capoeira-fueled ass kicking, quite naturally the government banned it altogether. Spin forward a few centuries to the razor's edge existence in the favelas, and one can see why the art of Capoeira made an easy transition to the modern era. You were your own best security force.

Mistress Bimba was a descendant of Brazil's most legendary Capoeira master practitioner—Mestre Bimba. Manoel dos Reis Machado started training at the very tender age of twelve. A gifted athlete, he soon was crowned Mestre Bimba—the Brazilian Bruce Lee. He founded the first official training academy in 1932 and lifted Capoeira out of the underground without the benefit of a personal public relations firm, television, radio, or film appearances. Florante learned all of this history during the ninety minutes he spent interviewing Manuela, the ironically demure, slight figured, dark complexioned, green-eyed beauty with the rather distended belly housing her twenty-eight week old fetus.

"I needed a cushion for the baby," she confessed to Florante.

It seems that taking in laundry and delivering it barely kept Manuela fed, clothed, and under her roof, "What was I going to do when the baby came? I panicked, I have the wrong friends, I was just trying to survive."

Up until the point that Manuela began tumbling out catch phrases culminating with the Gloria Gaynor inspired "survival" line Florante felt his heartstrings vibrate. The woman appeared much too savvy to rely on the basic "someone, anyone, please help me" defense. Something simply did not add up. After all, she had handily delivered a substantial ass kicking to three grown men. The facts said she was hardly a damsel in distress. However, he was not a detective; he was lawyer and a new one at that. He was also not an idiot, nor did he want the grand old man to think otherwise. His directive had been "don't screw up." That dictated the straightest possible route to acquittal.

As he listened to Manuela he began to conjure up a defense strategy. It centered on her desperate struggle for survival. Her circumstances had chased her right into the corner branch of the Brasilia Savings & Loan Bank, embarrassingly ahead of any meaningful deposit of actual money. Seven months pregnant and living in the Favela created pressures she had never experienced. Since the bank had not actually opened, and no money had been taken, he thought the case could easily be reduced to simple assault. Remembering that Brazil remained a classically machismo culture, he asked himself if the three battered construction workers might prefer to shield their humiliation at having their asses kicked by a seven months pregnant woman from prolonged public viewing. He then asked Manuela to take him to her house in the favela, for background research.

They took a taxi to the now-opened Brasilia Savings & Loan Bank, sitting like an oasis in the desert across the street from the northern entrance to Heliopolis. Manuela walked confidently into the mix, oblivious to the surrounding swarm of life in turmoil. She moved easily equipped with an invincible confidence only seen in women sporting a fetus. She didn't seem to see anything other than the weaving path lying directly ahead of them. Brick block buildings no higher than three stories crowded narrow streets of rubbled asphalt and dirt. Cars, carts, and people including an abundance of children of every age, size and color competed for walking, driving, and rolling space for themselves and their collective tales of personal struggle.

They passed a dirt and weed soccer field along their path where two teams of ragged pre-teen boys raced back and forth with uncanny skill. Somehow they all seemed to know who was on which team. Florante marveled at how they had magnificently managed to escape the boundaries of struggle for at least a little while—a random spot of joy.

Manuela kept a steady pace and a glaring gaze seemingly unconscious of the teeming life encircling them. They turned left, right, left, winding their way deep into the bowels of Heliopolis. The streets were flooded with all kinds of commerce, ranging from fruit stands and haircuts to prostitution and drug dealing. There were tiny shops, poolrooms, and lots and lots of bars. Florante had never been so deep inside the favela in his life. His sweat seeped through his designer suit jacket revealing a state of mind that belied his firm jaw and steady gait. The steady din of sounds, the narrow alleyways, and the mass of people all combined to suffocate Florante. Each breath echoed unfamiliar in his ears like a scuba diver on his first dive.

What little money existed in the favela moved freely from place to place, palm to palm, like a steady flow of water from a mountain stream. No one except the landlords owned anything in Heliopolis. Everyone squatted and existed in and out of the shadows. It all played like a waking nightmare for Florante.

"I'm sorry about the aid worker." Manuela tossed over her shoulder. They rounded yet another corner in their weave towards her home.

"Uh, huh," Florante responded abstractly while leaving mental breadcrumbs every fifty feet just in case he had to find his own way out. He thought about his wife, he thought about his new young son. He continued to sweat inside his tailored suit.

"Not those other bastards. They deserved it."

He'd only been married three years. His child was not even one.

"We're almost there."

"Almost there? Good." His response was an out of body acknowledgment that they were still walking.

The further they traveled into Heliopolis the steeper the rise in Florante's levels of fear. After another few minutes the scuba-sound of his breath finally receded to autonomic background noise. He told himself to focus on the task at hand; concentrating on Manuela's story. He knew that little of her comments were useful in creating a solid defense. Sifting through and understanding her emotional state of mind would be helpful in generating sympathy in the event of a jury trial, but the burden of explanation would rest on his abilities.

Gathering a bit more of his fluctuating poise, Florante asked, "At least it was over quickly, but why didn't you run? I mean, there was no money in the bank after all."

Unfortunately, at that precise moment, while taking yet another breadcrumb glance behind him, Florante turned his head just in time to narrowly avoid bumping into the back of a now frozen Manuela. Two large wild-eyed Brazilian men wearing cutoff shorts and wife beater T-shirts had abruptly blockaded their path.

"What's this?" He whispered to Manuela.

"Sshhh," she stood relaxed and poised, hands at her side.

Both men sported a healthy coating of favela grime, which dusted every inch of their dark-skinned, rippling muscular six-foot-plus frames. Looking around Florante thought, not a single friendly face, no place to run, a fate of certain dismemberment or worse—never making it back to the safe streets of Vila Olimpia. Never making it back to the arms of his wife, who, he just discovered in this recent millisecond of thought, he had grown to love deeply despite the convenient arrangement of their marriage. No legal career, no summers in Europe. He would never learn to play the piano—not that he wanted to, but he would not get the opportunity to want to; no fame and no family fortune. Worst of all, worse than all of this imagined shattering of his personal hopes and dreams, he would leave a fatherless baby boy. He sank, then retrenched himself. No time for these thoughts.

The fractionally larger of the two men spoke first, "Straying a little far from your neighborhood, aren't you friend?"

Two taunting laughs bounced off the walls of the small alleyway, supplanting the sound of Florante's own breathing.

"Get out of our way; we have no business with either of you." Manuela extended her greeting a moment before Florante had decided to step in front of her. She displayed absolutely no fear.

"Gentlemen," Florante offered a congenial voice of reason. "I am escorting this woman to her home. As you can see she is quite pregnant. Simply allow us to pass."

The smaller man chuckled as he looked at his friend collegially. "It's all so simple."

"I can make it worth your while," Florante tried again.

"It will be," came the reply.

Both men smiled and began their approach.

Florante inhaled deeply and readied himself for combat. He had not a single insight into his ability to defend himself against one assailant let alone two. Manuela had no such issues. She immediately coiled down to the ground, planting her two hands on the uneven pavement. She launched herself into the air like a springing cheetah pouncing on defenseless prey. Her legs scissored in the air as she spun heading straight for, and in-between, the two surprised Faveladores. She caught one man with a direct heel shot to the groin and the other with a simultaneous heel to the neck. Both crumbled to the ground. In another instant, she had pounced on the back of the first man, slamming his head into the jagged pavement knocking him cold while the other grimaced and watched in frozen disbelief.

Florante did not know whose defense to come to—Manuela or her next victim. His thought process lagged considerably behind her ability to act. Performing with lightening quickness, she subdued the other man with a swift elbow to the back of the head, knocking him out cold as well.

"Oh my god!" Florante exclaimed. He immediately followed up with comically misplaced "Are you okay?" He knew that he was more shaken than Manuela, but his chivalry gene forced the question anyway.

Manuela busily dusted herself off and straightened her blouse with a subdued look of satisfaction.

"I'm fine. Time to go," she said, walking away.

"We're just going to leave them here?"

"It's Heliopolis; they'll be fine, eventually. It's no longer our concern."

Florante glanced back over his shoulder as they continued walking down the street. He already saw some of the local residents opportunistically picking the pockets of the unconscious dusty duo. No screaming for help, no ambulance, no police; just the jungle absorbing its own detritus.

The entire episode from fear, to confrontation, to dénouement took a robustly economic seven minutes. Seven minutes from crime to punishment—an amazing display of efficiency in conflict resolution. Nothing in Florante's professional life had ever taken seven minutes, except perhaps the conversation with Grandfather Greve briefing him on this case.

Maestra Bimba was poetry in lethal motion without the burden of an upper class social conscience to disturb her internal sense of justice and balance. Florante could not help but admire the strength of this woman, but it only added to the mystery of her predicament. He could most certainly follow his mental breadcrumbs and escape from Heliopolis, but finding his way around the life of Manuela Dos Reis posed a much larger problem.

It took another snaking fifteen minutes to reach Manuela's home. She lived in one single room down a creaking hallway on the second floor of a crumbling brick building off a dirt street. Florante felt uncomfortable violating her private space. Manuela cut through his hesitancy with her graciousness.

"Come in, sit down please. There on the bed."

"Manuela, how can you raise a child in this?" Once more he found himself sympathetic to her obvious circumstances.

"You will find a way to help me and my child. I have faith in you."

A sudden and unexpected burden dropped onto his shoulders. He set it uneasily aside for the moment.

"Please forgive my question, but where is the father? If I am to help you I need to know everything I can about what created your desperation."

Manuela sat gently on the floor; legs crossed and smiled, "Then I must tell you."

Chapter 5. | Snowball

As she began her tale for Florante, Manuela recalled the phrase she heard her grandfather recite on many occasions. "If we have hope, good will find its' way out of bad, eventually."

Manuela went about her work cleaning the GAS offices on the 12th floor of the brown brick office building on the high rent exclusive Avenida Paulista. Manuela had a wispy, lithe frame, perfectly proportioned with a dark coffee complexion; a gift from the blending of slave ancestors and European colonists over hundreds of years. At twenty-two, she already held down two jobs to make enough money to support her life in Heliopolis. Cleaning and taking in laundry sustained her tenuous existence. Despite the tightrope she walked, Manuela did not feel the pressure of falling into the abyss of poverty. Her self-confidence and fearless faith in her unseen future provided all the internal light needed to guide her path.

Manuela held the mop and the broom. She wheeled the cart; she folded the rags, she moved easily from room to room focused, yet far away. A secret smile appeared on her face, then vanished. She was both here and gone, traveling easily wherever her thoughts wished to go. Her green eyes glowed as if backlit by a bright inner sun beaming her soul into the world.

Manuela looked over the hill of her daily life. She saw endless possibilities for herself. Manuela loved Carmen Miranda. Certainly not for the cultural stereotype she represented, but for the opportunity she created for herself and Brazil. By the time Manuela was thirteen, Carmen was twenty-six with a skyrocketing career in film and recording. Manuela adored Carmen Miranda beyond the tropical fruit wear, beyond her bulging bosoms, and beyond her sex kitten smile. She saw more because there was more.

The older man working late that night saw only the radiant beauty and magnetic sensuality of the girl mopping the offices. He had seen her before. He had imagined himself lying with her. That perfect, taut, coffee skinned body opening up to his desires freely. Giving herself to him, wrapping her legs tightly around him and holding him still while she moved beneath him. He had worked late for several weeks at a time, hoping to gather the courage to speak to her, to act on his desires. In his mind, they were perfectly suited: he—masculine, virile, handsome, wise, powerful; she—youthful, ambitious, eager, beautiful, desperate for opportunity. All of this occurred in the privacy of his mind. The mind of a seventy-two-year old man cresting the hill towards his mortality.

Life had caught up with him. It grabbed hold of him by the tail of his tuxedo jacket on a random night out with his wife. On his way up a set of marble stairs on the way into the opera he stumbled. No one saw it, no one commented, but he recognized the moment. Had he simply not seen the step? Did he lose his focus for a single untracked moment? That could happen to anyone. Not to him. He bobbled. It wasn't a small trip, more of a buckling of the knee; his higher brain functions had underachieved. He had lost the proverbial step, but it had not been a physical step. Much, much worse, it was a mental step. That worried him and branded his mind with the unthinkable realization of his own demise. He encountered more: a misspelled word not caught; a court brief read over completely but without comprehension. He isolated his feelings and buried them deep within his mental parking garage. Unfortunately the parking ticket kept illuminating itself bright neon RED in his pocket: a pulsing, vibrating RED light, reminding him of the eventual fine coming for an expired meter.

After the Opera, he and his wife came home. Moments after they walked in the door of their high priced mansion in Vila Olimpia he grabbed her. Violently he took her in the entryway. It had happened once before that way and it frightened her. She asked him what was wrong. "Nothing," he said.

Esmeralda, a large full-bodied gal with a pet Pomeranian that never left her side, chose not to mention the affairs she always knew about. A willingness to smile and look the other way has supreme benefits that countered the loneliness. She did not want to know. Acknowledging them threatened her blithe existence. The last time he had grabbed her that way had been at the ending of another affair with a younger woman. The woman had grown bored, as they all did. Esmeralda suspected nothing more than the end of yet another affair, and lay still as he burst into her and spent himself into sleep.

Mortality wears a skintight wrestlers leotard, with a fierce matching mask, and comes ready to rumble. Florante Senior knew the bell had rung. No matter how fierce the struggle, the outcome was pre-determined. Anything else was strictly for show.

He grabbed Manuela from behind before either of them realized it had happened. She could have easily fought him off and most likely killed him with a single blow. They fell in a heap, knocking over her cart of cleaning supplies. At 2:30 in the morning, no one heard the noise. Manuela's head hit the side of the cart on the way down deflecting, off the steel corner and striking the floor at a hard angle. She awoke in his office on the couch, a cold cloth wrapped around the side of her head, but already able to feel the hardball-sized bump and splitting headache rising in pitch.

"Let me get you some water," he said mawkishly rushing out from behind his broad Brazilian rosewood desk.

"You attacked me Senhor?" she hazily charged rubbing her head.

"I have done nothing of the kind. You fell and I ran to catch you, but I was too late. You've been unconscious for at least an hour." The consummate lawyer's tone was firm with just the right hint of compassion. His unending reservoir of well-rehearsed perfumed lies filled the air like the Viennese Philharmonic on a summer night. How seamless the deceit; he had already contemplated his strategy and simply executed it with a practiced cold calculation.

Manuela looked down at her dress and saw the rip in it. Her underwear felt slightly askew, bunched and tucked in around her honor. She reached beneath her dress to rearrange them and felt the wet spot. She held back her tears, but the light behind her eyes dimmed at the understanding. A thousand thoughts coursed through her mind at once—the end of her dreams, the fear of the unknown, the dread, and the revulsion. She wanted to get up and beat the living shit out of this violent, deceitful old bastard standing in front of her holding a glass of water.

"Senorita, not all things are as they seem. You have taken a hard blow to your head which can cause serious side affects." He took out his checkbook.

Observing her disbelief, anger, and sadness, the emotions streamed past him like so much tickertape dispassionately delivering stock market updates. He wrote out a check.

"Please, you must get yourself to the hospital so a doctor can examine that injury. May I take you? I will pay for it. I feel terrible. I should have caught you before you fell."

Manuela did not speak. What could she say? Who would believe a girl from the favela over a celebrated and influential mainstay of the Sao Paulo political and social glitterati? A simple answer; the color drained from her face as tears rolled down her cheeks and onto the brown leather couch. They both watched the steady flow pool on the leather then cascade in a slow trickle to the carpeted floor. The plush pile, beige carpet drank them up as if they never were. They made a silent agreement.

Florante took her to the hospital where he left her in the care of the Emergency Room staff. She kept her job for another six weeks; until she discovered the worst of her fears had come to pass. GAS gave her an extraordinarily large severance check and sent her back to Heliopolis. She had enough money for six months of no work. But it didn't last.

Chapter 6. | More than appliances

A whiplash moment before his head met the faux oak desktop, Hart's shiny new universe abruptly vaporized into unconscious indigo. He now found himself hanging off the side of his Channel Islands twin fin surfboard, peacefully relieving himself in the vast, relatively warm Pacific Ocean.

"Outside!" the cry went out.

The collective group of California surfers bobbing in the line up at Malibu's Surfrider Beach had spotted an incoming overhead set of waves. Why is nature in such a hurry to screw with me? thought Hart.

His parents said he grew up in the ideal neighborhood at the ideal time. Upper middle class homes where life moved easily from one day to the next, without unmet wants or needs. His parents were joyous, proud, and supportive—his friends the same. Contentment permeated the air.

Hart felt none of these things. Not joyous, not proud, not content. He dragged around a deep internal misery, secreted away from everyone. A dark space existed inside that he could not seem to fill up. A private, almost deceitful, place where all things appear possible yet hang impenetrable, simultaneously. All roads remain surely passable, but only under the perfect weather conditions. Living in limbo, he teetered beneath the constant strain of determining a "go" or "no-go" countdown. It gnawed away at him, undermining random moments of contentment, like this one in the ocean he loved. He temporarily pushed it to the side, but the feeling of dread never fully receded. It was permanently his, and like the moon tides, it kept coming around again, and again, and again. 'You will learn to make this spiritual trumpet work for you,' Dr Segalove often reminded. Hart wanked to himself, easy for her to say, she didn't have to deal with the headaches and nausea.

Quickly reclaiming his board, he scratched hard to paddle over the first of four waves, hoping to avoid getting hammered as they crested and broke. He was woefully out of position behind the pack of surfers making their way over the top of each passing building-sized wave. 'Paddle, paddle, paddle,' the autonomic mantra repeated itself in his head, crowding out all the other thoughts spinning around in his brain. 'I should turn around and take one of these.' He posed the challenge to himself as other surfers turned and paddled into each successive roller. "Too big, maybe too crowded, what's the worst thing that could happen? Death by drowning would suck. Do not panic." The jumble of conflicting upset passed through him as he kept up his paddle. Without warning, Simon appeared in his brain, 'Turn around you pussy. It's only water!' Hart flipped his board around. He saw two other surfers match his pivot. Timing his paddles with the speed of the water he stroked one, two, three. He felt the surge grab hold, pushing his board in and down the face. He pushed up to his feet with exquisite timing. He saw a perfect wave unfolding before him. Life was sweet.

"Coming down asshole!"

Aaahh, Malibu. He was not alone in this brief moment of grace. The surfer behind him technically had the right of way, and to prove the point, shoved Hart off his board into the waiting arms of the churning surf. In a series of underwater gyrations reminiscent of a Romanian gymnast, Hart surrendered to the wave. He had spent enough time in the oceans grip to recognize a life-threatening wipeout versus a mere life-shaking one. Routine completed, the wave spit him out in a jumble of foam. He swam over to his surfboard and refilled his lungs with air. He sat peacefully on his board out of the impact zone, pondering the notion of paddling back out.

The Brian Wilson classic, "God Only Knows" popped into his head freezing the moment of solitude. If only life unfurled itself like a classic Beach Boys song. Hart figured everyone held onto their flaws in one form or another for the duration. Maybe a trumpeting Dukkha had some advantages he simply couldn't see just yet. Taking any sort of true corrective action required a level of self-awareness that had eluded him until recently. As a steward of his own mental health, Hart had begun to contemplate his own travel options. He had scored a truly bizarre interview at the UCLA Placement Center for global player, the Maytag Corporation. The exotic lure of appliances had not been the quality that attracted his interest. Checking his watch, he decided against another go-round in the lineup. He pulled himself out of the water, dried off and headed for Westwood.

"People call me GoGo," Head Placement Guidance Counselor Gloria Arosha said as she motioned for Hart to follow. She speed walked down a long hallway and ushered him into her corner office. A human dynamo, she was a small, round gal with wide brown eyes, a Middle Eastern skin tone, prominent nose. Wagging his school transcript in her hand she said, "You're too smart to be treading water."

Hart squirmed in his chair, not knowing how to respond. "Well," she pressed, "This is a great opportunity for someone. Is it you?"

"Sincerely?" Hart asked. He had resorted to the Placement Center out of a perpetual fear that his life might veer off the tracks without some form of conventional stability. He knew teaching tennis would not carry the long day, but hadn't clue one for what would. A drip of ocean water leaked slowly out of his right ear. What else might be abandoning his body and heading for the hills, he thought. Am I sinking? He felt a wave of nausea. How do you know when it's your last chance, your moment of truth; do alarms sound, are there flashing lights? When does your inner genius get off its ass and kick in?

Gloria was waiting for an answer. Her no-bullshit manner acted like a truth serum for Hart. She leaned across her desk and looked him in the eye, "Kid, you are my job description. I look for kids like you every day, but I don't take my time screwing around with floaters. If you want to bail out on your life, do it somewhere else."

"GoGo," he said seriously, "I definitely need to change my address for more than a few reasons."

"Don't smart-mouth me. There are ten other kids that want this job for legitimate career reasons."

"Wait a minute, I'm not done yet." he shot back. "You are right," he blurted out, "I have absolutely been using my life as a flotation device. I've been depressed; not clinically, but in an Eastern philosophical kind of way. I'm confused and disinclined to make a decisive choice for my future."

"Please." GoGo wagged her hand at him. "Hardly anybody gets it right the second time, let alone the first time. It's a merry-go-round, and you just have to buy a damn ticket. I'm not a therapist. I'm a pragmatist. I deal with

3 by 5 index cards and cases like you." She leaned back in her chair.

"So I'm not unique? That's a blow."

"I'm not here to be your mother," she rattled on. "This job takes you outside the norm and drops you in the third world—like electro-shock therapy in a mild climate. It might be exactly what you need, or you might be bailing on your life. Only you know the answer. I can see by your GPA that you have a functioning brain. You just don't seem to want to —"

Desperation shook Hart on the shoulder as he cut her off, "What do I need to do?"

Gloria put her hands on the desk and stood up. "We're done. Get yourself ready because I've already made a recommendation for you with the interviewer. You've got one hour. Think Maytag. It's about more than appliances."

Hart got up to leave. It was time to think poetically, because thinking about appliances was simply, unthinkable. As he headed out Gloria admonished him, "Remember, this next interviewer isn't looking for the same things we are. We, being you and me."

One hour later Gloria Hart walked back into her office. "I've got some good news. The Maytag rep didn't hit it off with the other two applicants I sent." She sounded pretty happy which meant she was more in Hart's corner than he'd thought.

"Why not?" Hart asked.

"He's a no-nonsense guy; maybe a hard-ass, maybe a misogynist. I'm not too sure, but you've got the last shot at the job. And so…" She escorted him out of her office pointing to an open door down the hall.

"The strange truth is, I want the job." He didn't realize that fact until, like the water in his ear, it leaked out of his brain.

GoGo smiled. Hart paused before the doorway to center himself and quietly clear his throat. A large, firm, calloused hand reached through the doorway, latching onto his with a firm, single downward shake. One of those calibration shakes where the intention of the grip attempts to take "the measure of the man." Hart recognized the increasing pressure as a no-nonsense, NFL watching, boxing fan, possibly even a WWF kind of man's man. A tactical strategy appeared in Hart's brain. He tabbed through the options in a millisecond: return the crunching grip, matching the exact intensity coupled with a cold eyed James Bond stare; exceed the force with his own, displaying a highly competitive nature; relax into it in order to make the antagonist secure in his dominance; or, the most unthinkable suicidal tactic of all, go docile and allow him to completely squash the hand coupled with a possible grimace of mock pain? Hart chose the Mexican standoff with matched intensity.

"Hart," he boomed, "Bruce LeVitta. Nice to meet you, son. Grab yourself a seat."

Hart sensed the pop quiz coming around the bend. He could see the words forming in LeVitta's brain, the brain dialing the vocal chords, and finally, the words floating out of his mouth. "Você fala português Hart?"

Hart tossed out, "Quero meu bife mal passado," and chuckled.

LeVitta's face went blank. He tilted his head like a mystified German shepherd trying to decide between attacking, or simply padding away. Hart had told him that he preferred his steaks cooked rare.

Hart quickly smiled, adding, "Falo, falo. Não tem problema. I just wanted to make sure you were paying attention. Besides what if we go out to eat later? Don't you want to know how I like my steak?"

Either the interviewer's exterior would crack and make everything easier, or Hart would be back on the tennis court tomorrow morning as usual. Opportunity squandered, but no real harm done.

LeVitta laughed and pointed at him from across the desk, "Got it. Nice. A sense of humor in a foreign language; that works for me Ace. Your transcripts say you're pretty smart."

"I can hold my own." Hart pushed up straighter in his chair.

"Gloria pretty much told me I'd be making a big damn mistake not to hire you. Why do you suppose that is?" LeVitta rocked back in his borrowed executive chair waiting for a response.

"Gloria recognizes my potential." Another puzzled look from LeVitta; not so much amused as questioning. Hart knew it was time to deliver the goods or leave the room.

He started again, "Mr. LeVitta, truthfully, I hope you are looking for someone outside the envelope. I'm not a Business School guy. I've got common sense and an urge for something challenging and new. I'm a quick learner and pretty damn quick on the uptake. If that works, I'm in, if you are looking for some button-downed junior wing-tip-wearing, double-breasted suit to float down to Rio, that's not me."

LeVitta scooted up to the desk as if to feign putting an arm around him. His demeanor shifted. They were confidantes now, fast friends, best buddies, pals who leveled with each other. "Ace, we don't need a Harvard MBA for this job. You nailed it exactly right. Someone with common sense fits the bill. Hell, you don't even need to speak the language fluently, although I'm countin' that as an asset in your favor. Maytag loves opportunity, son. We crave it! And that's exactly what we've got going down there. We want to carve it out and stake our claim to Brazil in a big way. For now we need someone to go down there and place hold the geography until we conjure up the right strategic plan. Course we do have product down there, but we'd mostly like to clean up the gray market first, get some eyes on the country and go go go."

"Gray market?" Hart said puzzled.

"We're Maytag. A Maytag Washer is the world's gold standard for clean. We invented dirty just so we could create the solution!" He chuckled out loud to himself. "Who doesn't want to get next to god damn godliness?" He beamed.

LeVitta sustained his monologue of triumph, "Maytag rules the planet. Even if we're not there, we're there. Cleaning up the planet one washer at a time, it's missionary in scope."

"Ace," he pontificated, "Your job is to reconnoiter the conditions on the ground. Suss out the lay of the land, keep your eyes open and report back to HQ. Specifically report back to me. I'll be down there too. When we figure out the right plan of attack back at the home office, you'll be in a great position to advance through the ranks as a junior executive. Besides it's Brazil!"

"You're selling me?" Hart was surprised that the tables had turned so quickly.

"Hell yes. I'm a salesman. Gloria's right. You ARE MY guy. We're a little behind the gun on this one Ace, so I'm gonna need a quick decision on your part," Levitta stood up in anticipation.

"Uhhh, I'm in." Hart gripped his theatre chair once again and watched as his outer body delivered the yes. As they power-crunched hands, Hart's very next foreboding thought air dropped in on him, like an unwelcome surfer on his perfect wave. He then had an immediate impulse to write Simon a letter.

Chapter 7. | Can't trust chocolate

One month later, good on his prediction, Julian Coelho lay dead in the prison showers, his neck sliced from ear to ear. Carlos woke up to the news and knew exactly who had done the deed. Everybody knew the guard who pulled the knife, but not everyone knew that Julian's right-hand man inside, Jobim, had given the order. Carlos peeled back the wrapper on the last Lindt bittersweet Julian had left him, and remembered their first meeting many years ago.

Growing up, Carlos was the unstoppable kid, a superb natural athlete in any sport. His mother held a job as a live-in nanny for a wealthy family from Vila Olimpia. The family had a son about his same age, but the two children were galaxies apart. Excluding Sunday, when he was forced to attend church with the family, Carlos spent most of his time outdoors and alone. He felt neither welcomed, nor accepted by this affluent family. His athleticism opened opportunities to play at a level well above his age. Exposure to the older boys, even the wealthy ones, pushed Carlos faster and further than a watchful parent would want. He kept pace with the older boys by doing exactly what they did plus some.

"Hey Carlos, Jao and I bet Ben that you could throw a rock from here and break that blue car's windshield. Ben said you're too much of wimp to even try it." Two of the older boys enjoyed challenging the diminutive all-star.

Carlos thought to himself, 'I can do that easy, but I don't think I should.'

The boys continued to egg him on, "Come on little man. How good are you? Don't be such a pussy."

'I'll show them,' Carlos thought confidently. He picked up a baseball sized rock and hurled a frozen rope. The windshield of Jesuit priest, Father Xavier's 1979 Honda Accord exploded into thousands of bite-sized pieces spread about the hood and front seats of the well-weathered car. In a split second everyone vanished from the futbol field leaving Carlos as alone as he felt. He stood still for a moment of regret, before following their example and running off.

Give me a child until he is 7, and I will give you the man.

Jesuits live for a good solid axiom, something they can sink their considered religious zeal and intellectual prowess into bringing to fruition. They love them as much as a calculating politician loves a handy baby. This particular classic was mentioned at the previous Sunday's sermon Carlos had been forced to suffer through. The kindly Father Xavier had delivered the message. Whereas his adopted family counterpart had enlisted in the Jesuit doctrine hook, line, and Jesus, Carlos realized that his ship had already sailed in a different direction.

"I'll be my own damn man," he said to his mother after the service as she hustled both boys into a waiting car for the ride home. His mother heard the remark, shook her head, but offered no corrective comment.

Too embarrassed to admit the rock to the windshield, his guilt simply slow danced its way down a slippery path. It finally, comfortably, evaporated and became the simple pride of just getting away with it. Carlos' bravado won him many friends who surrounded him with massive quantities of poor judgment and destructive encouragement. The older boys celebrated his deeds by ratcheting up the ante each month.

When the other boy's mother abruptly died of cancer, shortly after their twelfth birthdays, Carlos suspected things were about to change for him. His mother and the head of the household, who had a strange bond he had witnessed from an early age, married only two years later. Lazarus, now the official 'step brother,' opted out of the home. He shifted to a completely submerged life as a Jesuit novitiate. Carlos felt like the odd kid out at a private party for two. One night after turning sixteen, without a word to either his newly minted stepfather, or his mother, Carlos returned to his roots and found a place in Heliopolis.

Carlos survived on petty crime. He moved from the basics like stealing a cash drawer when the clerk looked the other way, to stealing cars during broad daylight. He got popped the first time for practicing his pick-pocketing skill set on an undercover policeman right in front of the newly remodeled corner branch of the Brasilia Savings & Loan Bank. He began his first year in the Brazilian penal system at the impressionable age of nineteen.

Carlos spent his next twenty years in and out of the system—on parole, off parole, in jail, out of jail. His circle of friends along with his opportunities for mayhem grew at an alarming rate. Carlos learned the ins and outs of prison life. He learned that, even though he was stuck in prison, life's opportunities were not limited by cracked concrete and iron bars. During a two-year stint for robbing a sporting goods store in his old neighborhood of Vila Olimpia, Carlos met Julian Coelho.

Carlos had scored three goals as the undisputed star of the prison soccer team's monthly match against the guards. He ran through the defense, barely breaking a sweat from one end of the dirt field to the other. Coelho was a founding member of the all tattoo prison team and leader of the infamous Brazilian gang, First Command of the Capital, the PCC for short. Known as "the Shadow," Coelho lived a life encamped in extremes. His role at the helm of the PCC made room for no other alternative. His reputation for unprovoked violence and cruelty created a safety zone around his prison 'stay-cations.' A prison guard let Carlos know that the Shadow had requested an audience with him. Carlos, well aware of Coelho's reputation, approached him cautiously. Coelho sat surrounded by a cadre of well-inked inmates.

Coelho started, "Nice game." Handing Carlos an elegantly packaged bar of chocolate he carefully unwrapped an identical one of his own.

Carlos stared at the bar not knowing how to respond other than a hesitant, "Thanks..?"

"Call me Julian."

"You're the Shadow," Carlos acknowledged.

"Kid, if I wanted you to call me the fucking Shadow, I would have said call me the fucking Shadow, right?"

Carlos nodded his head as Julian continued. "Winning matters." He broke off a small piece of bar, popped it in his mouth savoring the taste.

Still staring at his bar, Carlos didn't respond.

"Carlos, that's a Cote d'Or Noir de Noir Intense 74%. It ain't no damn Hershey bar. That's Belgium chocolate. It's for winners. Eat up."

Carlos peeled back the black and red elephant logo from the Cote d'Or and bit into the bittersweet chocolate. Aside from a life filled with violence, Coelho's personal vice was bittersweet chocolate. He took it very seriously. Carlos had been tapped. As head of the most vicious gang in the country Julian had power that extended far beyond the walls of the prison.

He beckoned Carlos with a waving hand. "Sit here."

Carlos worked his way between the tattooed Coelho honor guards who cleared a space. He took an uneasy seat staring at one of the more extreme members of the Shadows' sycophants. The burly Jobim, smiled back at him with perfectly filed white teeth. His smile was not comforting.

"Tell me, what are you doing in here?" Julian asked.

"I've got a really sad personal history I'm trying to overcome. Sometimes I get stupid." Carlos kept his head up and held Coelho's gaze with an unflinching eye.

Coelho stared right back, "That so?"

Carlos asked, "What the hell do you want with me?"

The honor guard thought Carlos must have been a complete moron. Four men, each missing their third finger, quietly but quickly moved twenty feet away just in case Coelho blew a fuse. Jobim stayed put. Carlos figured Julian must have had some need for his unique skills. He had only one problem with that theory that stumped him. Excluding his exceptional prowess on the soccer pitch, Carlos had absolutely no unique criminal talents to crow about, unless getting caught counted as a skill.

"Some people prefer 80% bittersweet, some people lean to the milk. These assholes in here have no fucking idea about the differences. I like the 70 to 74% bars. You know why?"

Carlos eked out a nervous smile. "Uh, more chocolatey?"

"Don't say that. It makes you sound like a fucking moron. Never say chocolatey."

"Okay."

"Answer is, just enough sweet to temper the bitter." Coelho smiled back and continued his prison philosophy lesson. "You get it, don't you kid? It's all about the bitter."

Carlos took another bite of his bar, which to him, tasted like compressed dirt. He watched Julian, but kept a wary eye on the large man with the filed teeth. Unlike most of the other men sitting around the Shadow, Jobim had all of his fingers.

"We get angry, we fight back. We ALL get stupid. We get caught. Occasionally it can taste sweet. You hang with me and learn some things before you leave next time."

Carlos contemplated a "thanks, no thanks" reply, but then thought better of it. He realized it was actually more edict than offer. At a clear loss for options and seeing no glaring down side, Carlos simply said nothing at all. Coelho either didn't mind, didn't notice, but more likely didn't care. Turns out Julian Coelho wanted a legacy. He had no wife, no children, and no family of any imaginable kind. A vicious and powerful man locked inside Brazil's penal system with no hope of freedom in his foreseeable reproductive future. Lacking great genetic alternatives, the Shadow selected the Shade, as Carlos became known, for his heir apparent. Angry, bitter, physically gifted, sad, fatherless, desperate Carlos involuntarily got himself adopted. He spent the next several years with Julian Coelho. When Julian got a tattoo, Carlos got one too. Julian believed a man should have a theme in his life displayed proudly in pictures.

"You can't run away from tattoos. Pick a path and stick to it."

While Coelho featured classic revolutionaries like Che and Marx, Carlos chose famous rockers of the seventies—a raw and independent bunch that had no fear of raising their middle finger to social conventions, political correctness, or hotel mini bars lacking an ample supply of Johnny Walker Blue Label. Carlos periodically added the logos of Deep Purple, Black Sabbath, Led Zeppelin, Aerosmith, and in a singular moment of emotional reflection and space available, he added fierce Willie Nelson to his left elbow.

Carlos moved in and out of prison with amphibious dexterity. The Coelho blessing followed him back onto the streets, where he enjoyed a renewed standing in the Heliopolis crime community. Although not consciously aware of it, each return trip to prison, with the extended Coelho exposure, substituted as an extended academic masters program specializing in vocational skills for the budding crime boss. Carlos developed a taste for finer chocolates, along with a skill for constructing fairly robust explosive devices out of everyday materials—batteries, detergents, soda, gasoline, and hydrogen peroxide, among many options. He learned about stealth and style. He learned how to select appropriate targets and how to cover his trail. What began with the simplicity of a waxy, pedestrian Hershey bar blossomed into a refined appreciation for Lindt over Nestle, bombs over bullets.

Carlos finished his chocolate bar, knowing he had some unfinished business to attend to before his six months ended.

Chapter 8. | 23B

Descending through a pre-dawn overcast cloud deck after the ten-hour flight from Dallas, the American Airlines triple seven jet made its way towards runway number nine at Guarulhos International Airport. Gliding over the outskirts of the city, Hart looked out his window to a sea of red-tiled roofs separated by islands of huddled thirty-story buildings. The clustered high-rises that populate the Sao Paulo skyline appeared in the distance like round-tipped stick pins on a wall map. Sao Paulo holds over ten million people sprawled across its girth. They exist in various states from indigence to indulgence. Living in everything from modern steel and glass structures, to cinder block tenements, to the crumbling corrugated metal found in its sprawling chaotic favelas. Guarulhos International sits fifteen miles from the center of this metropolitan jungle. With the density of cars and hordes of people it all resembles one giant throbbing amoeba poised to divide. A place that has become a far, far cry from anything ever imagined by its Jesuit forefathers.

Hart took it all in. He shook himself and thought about Simon. Then he thought about Leice. One year already passed and Hart had only heard from Simon once during that entire time. He had virtually vanished. His emotional mindset coming down amidst all of this controlled bedlam bounced from phlegmatic to panic. "Shit! I've made a terrible life altering miscalculation. Shit again! I guess I'm stuck with it now. Shit, I've bailed out on my life. I'm not even supposed to be here." Another quick glance out the window and his inner dope sprang free.

'Oh my god, I can't live in this crime-infested, poverty riddled, hyperactive third world city. I don't know anyone. I can't do the job; I don't even know what the job entails. I'm about to be swallowed up by a Portuguese-speaking ant colony. Look at that traffic down there, thousands of cars seemingly frozen in place. How long have they been there, stuck and suffocating in a blanket of toxic air? I'm drowning. I can't find my way in this chaos. Mister Wizard please get me the hell out of here.'

The plane's intercom sprang to life and delivered a reprimand from a disembodied voice, "Will the passenger in 23B please remain seated!"

It can be hard to hear over the heightened roar of the jet engines descending down the final approach path. Hart's anonymous seatmate elbowed him in the deep thigh motioning to the loudspeaker. Hart thought to himself, 'why did my neighbor elbow me in the deep thigh? We've barely spoken the entire ten hours.' He rubbed the rising bruise on his leg mixing it in with his ongoing inner panic.

The loudspeaker erupts again, more forcefully, "Sir! Please remain in your seat."

The firmness of the voice over the PA system, coupled with the number of eyes rapidly turning his way might have clued him in. Hart, a moment behind the full complement of airline passengers, now suddenly realized that his internal idiot had gone over the wall. The Idiot squirted out and made himself known to a dispassionate, but justifiably paranoid outside world. Hart reeled him in and shrank. He buckled. He rubbed his thigh. Hart sat down and aimed his humiliated face out the tiny porthole window to the sky, staring into a long line of consequences.

The wheels squealed and screeched against the runway as the jet touched down at Guarulhos. Hart silently huddled his things together and prepared to disembark. He would step off the plane and move from one known world to the unknown next.

The airplane PA erupted once again, "The Local Time in Sao Paulo is 7:00 AM. We realize you have a choice in travel and thank you for flying with American today. We hope you have a pleasant rest of your journey."

Hart sat frozen in his seat contemplating the future lying outside the pressurized crosschecked airplane doors. The upside down time zone change had made him bleary eyed. He lapsed somewhere in that middle zone between numbing fatigue and oblivious sleep.

"Dude, you are a real mess. Get out of my way and let me off." His fed up seatmate pushed past him into the aisle.

Hart snatched his half filled plastic water bottle, his backpack, and merged into the passenger exodus. Emerging from the jet way, he rapidly skulked away from his fellow travelers towards customs. Crowds lingered everywhere. Hart felt the crush. The place looked like it might explode with one more person crammed into the building. Even if everyone were assigned a single floor tile as personal space, he'd still have someone standing on his shoulders. Lines formed whenever anyone stopped anywhere. Lines to pick up a luggage cart, lines for the bathrooms, lines for magazine stands. Hart inadvertently started a line while bending over to retie his Jack Purcell tennis shoes. He looked up and found seven people waiting single file behind him. When he moved off, they stood alone, seven against the world for a moment before each wandered away to find a more meaningful queue to wait in.

The sign for Baggage Claim pointed through another crowded connecting hallway. Hart slogged his way between the throng towards his waiting bag. Picking up his luggage he once again weaved his way between the human traffic jam headed to Customs. Weary and unfocused he bumped head-on into a short tattooed man navigating in the opposite direction.

"Check yourself asshole! Watch where you're going!" The man shouted.

Hart noticed what looked like a wrinkled Willie Nelson face staring at him from the man's left elbow.

"Sorry, I just got off a flight from the States," he apologized.

"Fuck off." The man stomped away.

Welcome to Brazil thought Hart. Nice folks. Arriving at the Customs switching station, he followed the action of the passenger in front of him by pushing a solitary silver button. It illuminated a dorky looking miniature yellow traffic signal post—Red light for STOP, Green for GO. Pulling the dreaded Red light meant the customs officers had the right to rip through your luggage in a random search for contraband. Fortunately, Hart scored the Green and headed out the double doors to the sardine can main-terminal.

Exhausted, he scanned the throngs for a sign with his name on it. Wedged in the form of a perfect ninety-degree letter "L" for fifteen hours, in a cold aluminum tube, with two hundred and fifty other grumpy "L's" had worn Hart down. He was beginning to regret each forward step deeper into the nightmare of his new reality. He felt glum, greasy, and distinctly unprepared, especially at eight o'clock in the damn morning.

Outside Customs, Hart saw Carmen holding the sign: Maytag welcomes Mr. Hart. He had never had his own personalized sign; it made him feel substantial. Carmen delivered a gloriously warm and convivial straight-toothed grin. Her smile was a virtual B12 shot in his aching plane sitting ass.

"Hello, Mr. Hart. Welcome to Brazil."

His bleary-eyed response, "Just Hart."

Carmen had the distinct air and clipboard of a person in absolute command. Her mind consistently focused two steps ahead of the next question. Hart's response unexpectedly threw off Carmen's precision. "Really? But he told me," she paused to recompose, "I apologize. We got that incorrect."

"It's not incorrect," he offered, "Hart is my first name, not my last. You got the name right, we just don't need the whole deal."

"I'll get your bag," she grabbed it.

"Thanks. I'm beat." He stared into her day-glow green eyes catching their intensity.

"Don't check me out," she flipped over her shoulder.

"Huh? I wasn't doing that," His answer was a defensive reflex; he was most definitely checking her out. Busted within the first thirty seconds of their introduction. Hart began to mentally page through his Maytag employee manual, searching for company policy on fraternizing with fellow employees. The Classics IV tune "Spooky" began spinning up on his internal stereo as Hart relaxed into the care of his new corporate mate. Carmen's coffee-colored beauty pushed the fear and paranoia to the back of his personal thought queue, at least temporarily. Suddenly, he felt sweaty, and noticed a welling of saliva in the corners of his mouth. He took the final sip off his complimentary American Airlines water bottle and propped it on a nearby bench.

"You're not going to leave that sitting there, right?" Carmen frowned.

"Course not." He grabbed it up and stuffed it in his backpack.

Carmen set the pace in front of him, dangling the Welcome sign as she walked toward the parking lot. "Our car is just here." She pointed as they passed yet another giant "Welcome to Brazil" sign. Including the Welcome sign coming through customs and the sign Carmen held up, he counted three welcomes.

"What's the story on all the greetings?" He asked Carmen, who stopped and turned to face him.

"Sorry, I'm not clear on your question." She understood it, but chose politeness.

"Why all the 'Welcome to Brazil' signs?"

"Ah, because you're in Brazil, and we're happy to see you."

"But, you don't know me. How do you know you're so happy to see me? As a country I mean."

"We're willing to give you the benefit of the doubt. How's that as an answer to your not serious question? The car is just over here." Carmen was now done with that particular topic.

Hart knew he had slipped up, "Yeah, never mind. I'm just over-tired, I guess."

Carmen rolled Hart's bag to a waiting sand colored Toyota Landcruiser equipped with an early twenties slender Mestizo—a genetic milkshake of Portuguese, Indian, Euro heritage named Bolo. Bolo grabbed the bag from Carmen and tossed it into the back. Hart's brain fog began to lift as he oriented to the new surroundings. He thought about calling his folks to let them know everything was okay, but figured that would have to wait until it actually was verifiably okay. His bags loaded, they set out for Sao Paulo.

"How long's the ride into Sao Paulo?" Hart asked, getting comfortable in the backseat.

Bolo had the most unique speaking characteristic Hart had ever heard. The fun began right after his lips started moving, yet produced absolutely no sound. Like a satellite broadcast or a poorly dubbed spaghetti western, Bolo's speech somehow emerged with a one-second delay. First the lips moved slightly, and then the words arrived at the ears a split second later. He must have said 'hello' three or four times before Hart even responded with his question.

"lo." Bolo smiled to no response.

"lo," Bolo kept smiling looking Hart straight in the eye through the rearview mirror.

"at ong im?" Bolo asked Carmen

"Tired," she answered.

"What'd he say about me? I only asked how long to the city." Hart asked.

Hart's frustration rose to the point where he had to choose between banging the side of Bolo's head or his own to fix the problem. Determined, but still tired, he doubled down on his concentration and tried again.

"ill bow an get," Bolo offered.

"Sorry, what?" Hart turned his head giving at least one ear a better shot at deciphering him.

"itari," Bolo fired off another round.

"Yes," Hart answered, "it certainly is."

Bolo looked at him sideways, then tried again, "itari."

"Absolutely," Hart shrugged his shoulders glancing at Carmen for some guidance. She laughed signaling that he had most definitely gotten it wrong.

"tea en are."

Miraculously, the light went on in Hart's fading brain, "We're driving for an hour?" He then glanced at Carmen who nodded.

"Yes, that's right. It's about an hour to Sao Paulo." Carmen finally fully translated.

Bolo nodded too and kept driving. Apparently less than ten tries to decipher his language skills made him happy.

Carmen continued, "We've got everything sorted out for you. I'm taking you to the Fasano Hotel in Jardins. It's in the best section of town and very elegant. The Jardin is very much like your Beverly Hills." Carmen glanced at her clipboard to confirm whatever notes she had on her schedule.

"I'm a simple guy," Hart mildly protested, "just a tennis player from California."

"I know what you're thinking, but don't worry about it. It's on the company."

Hart watched Bolo darting in, out, and around the traffic before nodding off.

Forty-five minutes later they cruised up Avenida Paulista and turned on a small side street. The Landcruiser pulled up at the curb of Hart's new temporary home. The morning clouds had lifted and dissolved, revealing a beautiful azure blue day to share with our hero and his eighteen million new Paulista pals. The elegant Fasano Hotel lay strategically positioned between the two hippest streets in Sao Paulo—Avenida Paulista and Faria Lima. Designed for South American high rollers, the hotel sat in the dead center of the headliner-shopping zone. Armani, Bulgari, Vuitton, and

Cartier all awaited the fat wallet crowd a mere stone's throw from the hotel front door.

Hart and company entered the post-apocalyptic, retro-hipster zone that was the Fasano lobby. The Hotel mixed the 1930's speakeasy style with a contemporary chaser. English brickwork on the façade in the lobby combined with smooth bare walls, and matching androgynous, tight-lipped, slick haired, tragically hip staff. Hart plopped down in one of the hard-as-rock period leather oversize chairs to wait for check-in. A Caetano Veloso song softly drifted out of the hidden speakers in the otherwise stark lobby.

Carmen walked over to his chair, accompanied by a mystery sex staff member. The androgynous being wore a skin-tight brushstroke Berlin black jumpsuit, sported tightly varnished skull-embracing black hair, and a Botox frozen facial expression of indeterminate emotional content.

It dangled a room card in front of Hart then spoke in a flat monotone, "Your suite Sir; Nineteenth floor, Room 1922."

A left arm extended from its side, palm skyward, "The lifts are around the corner and to your left. Your luggage has been brought to your room."

With its human interaction completed, it turned and melted back into the décor.

Carmen and Hart walked over to the lifts together, "I'll be back at one o'clock for lunch, if that's okay with you?"

Hart decided right then never to refuse a meal or any other interaction with Carmen. One o'clock gave him plenty of time to shower, unpack, check the lay of the land and get his bearings.

"Great idea. See you." They headed off on their separate missions.

Hart walked to the elevator feeling a huge uplifting sense of both independence and loneliness without the weight of being alone. He felt a strange freedom from youth. "No one within a geographical range of at least eight thousand miles knows the who, what, or why of me," he thought. He pondered his options while depressing the nineteenth floor button in the lift. As the Otis built lift sprang into action he thought, "Maybe this was a good idea after all. I've been a subject for so long—subject to my parents, my friends, schools, jobs, obligations, and always expectations. The lack of all of that leaves only one question for me to wrestle to the ground: Who am I anyway?" Hope and horror rolled into one simple question, "I know less about myself than anyone else I know. How can that be?"

The elevator doors parted silent and smooth. Hart headed down the austere hallway to room 1922. His room revealed a breathtaking sky view of Sao Paulo. It lay before him, a jungle of skyscrapers and snaking streets, like a teeming insect colony. People and cars moved everywhere in every direction all at once. He held a single silent IMAX view of his new life. Hart threw off his travel clothes and stood naked in front of the specter of Sao Paulo's eighteen million people. There he stood perched precariously on the most tenuous of tightropes. It stretched over the gulf between the invincibility of the supremely self-assured and the despair of the hopelessly moronic. 'Here I am,' he thought, 'what's next?' The knock at the door prematurely answered his question. Frantically, Hart searched for pieces of clothing. Too late, the door opened and a startled black clad maid wandered into his solitary universe uninvited.

"Fresh towels for you, sir." Looking more amused than embarrassed, she dropped a stack of white Egyptian cotton towels by the door, then gracefully tucked a smile, and backed out of the room.

For certain the word would pass rapidly amongst the staff. Hart would simply be ordained by those in the know as the naked preening idiot in room 1922. Tossing his clothes into a couple drawers, he leaned deeply into a hot shower and then tried to lie down for a quick nap. After restlessly tossing around the bed for twenty minutes, Hart soon realized the exquisite futility of an under achiever. He got up and headed down in the elevator to explore the fabulous Fasano hotel.

Somewhere between the 14th and 12th floor he heard what sounded like a gigantic sonic boom. Had an asteroid made an unscheduled low pass over Sao Paulo? The elevator rattled on its tether banging loudly against the walls, then stopped dead in its tracks. Hart waited afraid to move for fear of triggering the precipitous drop to the bottom of the shaft. One breath at a time he un-weighted first his right leg then the left. Using his best Brian Boitano skating technique he began sliding his feet gingerly towards the elevator control panel. Three small slides and one small pirouette later he reached the doors. Pressing floor buttons proved useless. Opening the emergency phone box located above the button controls revealed the photograph of a vintage 1967 dial phone sitting on a hotel bed. Helpful. He felt calm, slightly nervous, but not truly petrified; yet. Channeling his highest being of sanity he sat down, crossed his legs and waited.

Chapter 9. | We are what we carry

Six months after the layoff from GAS, Manuela shifted gears as best she could. As the only remaining living relative of Capoeira Master Manoel dos Reis Machado, she felt a silent genetic tug to return to her roots. She began to teach Capoeira to children in Heliopolis while continuing to take in laundry and sewing. She made ends meet as best she could, dreaming of better times.

As her pregnancy progressed, so did her reputation. People in Heliopolis referred to her as Mestre Bimba in deference to her heritage. She thought of someday re-opening her Grandfather's Capoeira training academy. Life inched forward. As Manuela sat back on the bed in her one room flat, she glanced at the poster of Carmen Miranda smiling down above her. She rubbed her belly, and took a long slow relieving exhale.

The knock on her door startled her back to reality.

Romo Medicos, her landlord, picked that opportune moment to deliver the news.

"I'm raising your rent," he grumbled.

"Why?" she said softly.

"You make more, you pay more." Romo had other properties in the favela, and around Sao Paulo. His empathetic concerns were limited to the depth gauge on his bank account.

"You can't be serious. That's not right."

"Consider it doubled as of next week. If you don't like, it move out,- Mestre Bimba!" He threw out the sarcastic taunt, then walked away without further discussion.

Manuela shut the door and wept. Her heart formed a protective coating shielding her spirit from the actions she had to take. By the time she finished telling this tale to Florante Greve, the naïve, hard working grandson, his determination to repair the damage done by his family was set in stone.

"This will not stand, Manuela. Just do as I say, and we will get you out of this."

"Thank you, Senhor Greve."

"I will be back tomorrow." Powered by a righteous resolve, Florante Greve III left Manuela's home and followed his breadcrumbs back to the GAS offices. He thought about confronting the old man, but realized his grandfather could never admit such a thing. The old man's parting words, "only an idiot could fuck this up," meant he already knew the truth and expected his grandson to figure it out. Florante surmised his grandfather wanted protection.

Caked with sweat from the day's adventure, Florante walked deliberately up to the twelfth floor corner office, knocked once, and then without waiting cracked open the big oak door. The old man sat rocking back in his chair, phone to his ear. At the sight of Florante, he motioned him to enter as he wrapped up his conversation.

"That's right; I said fuck those fuckers that fucked you before they fuck you again. Talk to you later." He hung up the phone, chuckling to himself.

Florante had heard his grandfather's anthem on many occasions.

"What can I do for you? You haven't screwed up the one case I gave you, have you?"

Florante chose his words carefully, "There is no case grandfather. No more than a few broken bones with some bruised testosterone. Nothing was stolen. I thought if you knew the presiding judge, we could get a plea of no contest, pay some damages to the bank, and get the whole business dismissed. What do you think?"

The old man knew every judge of note in the country. He also made it a point to never waste time or money. Pro-bono work was for desperate, second-rate hacks looking for a quick public relations coup. GAS never bent to that level. Its exclusive clientele did not require a stoop down to help the self-perpetuating rabble. In keeping with his Darwinian philosophy, Grandfather Greve never donated any of his considerable fortune to social causes either. Anyone living below the line obviously had no desire to raise themselves out of their self-imposed pit of despair. He reserved his charity for works of sustained glory—art galleries, train stations, theatres, and museums. Anything where the name Greve might be featured prominently bathed his ego in the contentment of his own legacy.

Barely raising his eyebrow, he said, "Good work, agreed. Get me the judges' name and I'll make the call today." He began to review some briefs lying on his desk as a tacit form of dismissal.

Florante walked slowly to the door then turned back, "One more thing, sir."

"What?" Senior grumped impatiently.

"I'd like the firm to pay all the damages as a pro-bono gesture." He watched the expression on his grandfather's face shift from gruff to guilty, then to remorse.

"Of course, let's make this thing right for all parties. Well done, Florante."

Florante's mouth hung open for a split second. Manuela had told the truth. That old bastard had truly committed a despicable act, and now they both knew it.

He pushed one more time, to be sure, "Do you have a limit on the funds, or can I use my discretion?"

The old man now looked up with an icy stare of acknowledgment, "Your well advised discretion. Now get the hell out of here." He grabbed his stack of papers and swiveled his leather chair towards the wall.

Florante closed the door, uttering "Ho-ly shit!" aloud to no one in particular. From that moment on, Florante's fortunes at the firm, already assured by birthright, zoomed ahead at an accelerated pace. The old man slowly ceded the most significant clients and control of GAS to Florante. Florante's life merged into the fast lane of Sao Paulo's affluent Amex Black Card set. No expense was too much, no request denied. Did he take advantage of the guilt associated with his grandfather's crime? Naturally. Did he feel complicit in that guilt? Not exactly, but he certainly cohabited with it.

Florante moved Manuela and her newborn child into his house as a nanny for his own newborn boy. Some of the guilt was assuaged, yet he carried the burden of it with him for his remaining years. He also carried something else: his love for Manuela. At twenty-three, Manuela began her new life as mother to Carlos, and live in nanny to Florante's rather stoic young son.

Florante Senior died less than five years after the rape as a result of an innocuous client conference with the soon-to-be-divorced for the fifth time, Mrs. Domingo Geoffreys. While kneeling down to pet and patronize Mrs. Geoffrey's recently imported, soft-coated Wheaten terrier, the poorly disciplined, high strung pooch leaped up and attached itself to Mr. Greve's considerable nose. The collective screams of the conference room participants penetrated all twelve floors of the GAS building. Some recalled it as a dissonant Stravinsky inspired chorale. By the time an ambulance arrived poor, aging, Florante Greve Sr. had suffered not only the loss of his prominent proboscis, but copious amounts of iron poor blood as well. While in the hospital, he contracted a rabid staphylococcus infection that hastily spread throughout his guilt-ridden body. He lay dead within forty-eight hours.

Manuela and Florante flourished in ways that Sabrina Almeida and Florante never could. Theirs was a relationship built on complete and total honesty; each one knowing the bare truth of the other. Arranged love cannot compete with consuming romantic love supported by two people willing to fight for each other. Years later, Manuela received the white belt of a Gran Mestre—the only one in existence - shortly after the birth of her daughter. The Bimba Institute for Capoeira opened next door to the ubiquitous touchstone in her life, the Heliopolis branch of the Brasilia Savings & Loan Bank. Location, location, location governed the choice for both Florante and Manuela, who reveled in the irony. Her school served both sides of the opportunity ladder. She paid special attention to her students from the favela who had the tougher road to travel. To them she imparted her experience navigating the unpredictable paths of the street: how to be shrewd, when to be clever, how to read an opponent, and how to walk through the rain.

Chapter 10. | Count me in

"Guillotine wants a word."

One of Jobim's lieutenants brought a request to Carlos on the prison futbol field.

Two days after Julian's body was discovered, Carlos scored three mad man goals in the daily futbol game. He dribbled the length of the field for two of them, knocking down anyone in his path. By the third goal, the competition essentially parted, giving way to the certainty of a score.

"Fuck off," Carlos answered toweling off with his shirt.

Absolutely no surprise that the former number two had ascended to number one. Jobim had given himself the nickname of Guillotine. He had selected infamous slashers as his personal tattoo motif. His body sported a host of ruthless killers from Jack the Ripper to Hitler to Charles Manson. At an even six feet tall, and almost as wide, Jobim presented an imposing roadblock. Carlos said nothing, but accepted that a confrontation was inevitable.

"Don't be like that cuz. He just wants a word." The man had two full sleeves of tattoos. A host of labeled faces all based on a family motif—Uncle, Cousin, Bro, Sis, Mom, Dad.

Carlos relented, figuring he might learn something that could serve him at a later date. He turned and walked towards Julian's old perch above the yard. The Guillotine had taken over the exact spot occupied by Carlos' mentor. He smiled his perfect white-toothed Cheshire cat grin as Carlos approached.

Jobim wasn't given much to conversation because of an incongruously, high-pitched voice coupled with a lateral lisp. "Carloth," he chirped happily.

The fearsome Guillotine opted for one or two word conversations. Most of his commands consisted of nods and grunts to his new lieutenants.

Carlos smirked and walked away. Jobim's lieutenants looked at their boss, awaiting the decisive action grunt. The Guillotine obliged and life lurched another step forward.

One month to the day after Julian's unsolved death, Carlos and Jobim both pulled shifts in the prison laundry. Within thirty minutes of his shift's start, Carlos noticed a distinct level of quiet. Acting on some hidden cue, he and Jobim suddenly had the laundry facilities entirely to themselves: no guards, no other inmates.

Taking Julian's advise to heart and, being the consummate survivor—a man of little sympathy, patience, or cowardice—Carlos grabbed the nearest hot iron. He turned, and at a hot walk, headed directly towards the Guillotine. Jobim was feigning busy, loading clothes in an industrial dryer. He looked up, pulled out a deer hunter's luxury buck knife, and prepared to meet Carlos' oncoming assault. Nothing like advance planning to make the days go smoother.

According to Winston Churchill, "planning is essential, plans rarely work." Jobim however, was not a student of history. He badly miscalculated Carlos' next move. Jobim had expected Carlos to use the iron as a weapon. Carlos, remembering Father Xavier's smashed windshield, broke into a run. Then, like an Olympic Javelin thrower, he wound up and hurled the hot iron on a frozen rope straight into the dryer door. Jobim's reaction time could be measured with a sundial. All he could do was watch as the door shuddered then slammed shut on his right hand, cracking his wrist bone. He grimaced in pain, but Carlos had not intended it to be a deathblow.

The door pinned Jobim's hand just long enough. Carlos grabbed a pile of wet clothing in his right hand, then dipped his left shoulder into a perfect forward roll. He sprung out of the tight tuck into a full two-legged kick to Jobim's knees. The big man let loose a high-pitched scream while crumpling to the floor. Though down and wounded, the Guillotine still managed to hold onto his knife. He countered with several frantic waves of the blade. One of his thrusts providentially found Carlos' left thigh. It sliced cleanly into his skin just as he made his way out of the kick. A thin line of blood oozed from the wound.

The slice did not slow Carlos down. He hurled the pile of wet clothing at Jobim, covering the knife hand and Adolph Hitler. He then grabbed the now-tepid iron from the floor and swung a full force roundhouse blow to Jobim's head and Genghis Khan. The skull-crushing impact shepherded the Guillotine directly into the afterlife.

After several deep breaths, Carlos loaded Jobim's lifeless body into the industrial dryer along with all of the wet and dry clothes he could find. He shut the door and started the cycle. Grabbing a random t-shirt Carlos, tied off his injured thigh. Then he mopped the blood off the floor, grabbed another fresh shirt from a pile of washed clothes, finished his shift alone, and returned to his cell. There were no repercussions, and no one bothered Carlos during the remaining three months of his six-month stay.

Carlos did not ask for leadership knowing that was not his calling. His skills did not extend to strategic planning or personnel management. He had no large vision, no inspirational worldview, and no regrets about his lack of talent in any of those things. Carlos told himself he held nothing beyond a simple fatherly allegiance to a dead convict, now avenged. Excluding his formidable genetic skills at Capoeira, and a reasonable expertise in creating and exploding small homemade devices, Carlos enjoyed nothing more than being left alone to process his considerable anger towards society. His vengeance took form through small petty crime attacks on random targets. Unfortunately Julian's last recommendation had saddled Carlos with an agenda well outside the narrow boundaries of his meager skill set.

Carlos' release date arrived. Upon exiting the prison he ran into a slight snag. A group of four fugitive PCC members waited outside the gates holding a cardboard sign labeled with his name.

"Who the fuck sent for you guys?" he said to no one in particular as he slid into their 1984 Diesel Mercedes.

The three in the car sat silent.

"You're picking me up from prison in a stolen car?" Carlos shook his head.

The only girl, a pale, freckle skinned, spike haired ginger sipping on a maracuja smoothie, a pineapple and passion fruit juice combo shot back, "What makes you so sure it's not ours?"

"Which one of you sells the Mary Kay cosmetics? Sure as shit not you. Your damn car is pink." Carlos handed the driver a scuffed CD from his pocket. "Put this in and turn it up."

Willie Nelson's, 'If you've got the money, I've got the time,' blared out of the stereo as they headed back towards Sao Paulo. The group pleaded, first to change the CD, but more significantly for Carlos to take charge of their splinter brigade. Even though Carlos had almost literally lopped the head off their newest leader, the PCC had carried on without either the defrocked and dead Shadow, or the recently crowned, but also dead Guillotine.

Singh, the tall, muscled, dark-complexioned Indian sitting in the back seat summed up the recent changes in the Brazilian underworld landscape, "A few months ago, some shit happened. Shadow got rolled, then Guillotine disappeared."

"He knows this already. Skip ahead," an impatient Dot, as they caller her, pushed Singh.

"Right. Now there's two factions; one carrying on for the Shadow, and the other side dedicated to, um, not doing that."

"You're such a douche, Singh," spat Dot.

Carlos already knew the Shadow's manifesto. Julian had a somewhat murkily defined idea for the mission of the PCC. Level the playing field, and hold the government accountable for screwing over the common man with fierce regularity at every opportunity.

Dot tersely summed up the group's point of view. "Poor people get fucked whenever possible by everyone who can. We're not for that."

Jao, the lanky, sallow faced driver with a swerving Mohawk, added, "Pretty much. I mean we've got expenses too, so we gotta cover those, but Shadow..."

Carlos waved a hand and cut him off. "I'm familiar." Carlos noticed Jao's color and asked, "What's up with you? Are you sick? If you're sick, let me out right here. I'm not catching shit from any of you."

"Thanks for noticing. I've been down with jaundice, so I'm trying to eat more fruits and vegetables."

"What the hell? Shut up Jao. No one cares." Dot was as impatient as Carlos.

"He asked." Jao truly believed Carlos was concerned.

The more dominant PCC faction was content to rob, steal, and operate a profitable narcotics ring. Their mission mimicked a corporate shareholders equity distribution model. The enterprise created wealth through its activities, then split the profits amongst themselves according to a seniority system, based upon years spent in prison.

"Your haircut is for shit. How many still support the Shadow?" asked Carlos.

"Counting us?" Jao ran a sheepish hand through his hair.

"Okay, counting you guys."

Jao clarified, "Counting us, there's three. We're not counting you yet. You're the unknown."

"What if I say I'm with you, but don't want to be the leader?"

"I don't know. We didn't go over that option. We figured given your relationship with the Shadow, you just would. I guess we could beat the shit out of you, dump you off somewhere then forget the whole thing." Jao was absolutely serious as the two others in the car nodded in agreement.

Carlos offered a solution, "Why don't we all lead together?"

"A democracy? That never works. You gotta have a leader." Singh, sitting in the passenger seat, chimed in.

"Besides," added Jao, "you're older than us. You're supposed to know more."

"That's a load of crap. I have no problem leading," offered the youngest member of the group.

"Not going to happen, Dot." Singh was adamant.

"You guys are fucking idiots," fumed a fed-up Carlos.

"That's means you're in." Jao looked around the car nodding. "He's in."

"I'll try it out for awhile, but I reserve the right to take a fast walk away from this shit parade if it's not working." Carlos realized he probably was the only real choice. He'd bide his time and figure out how to make an exit after he got himself sorted out in the favela.

"Where to boss?" asked Jao.

"Heliopolis. I need some food and a lot of sleep."

Carlos gave Jao directions to his place as 'Fuck the fuckers that fuck you before they fuck you again,' echoed in his head. Would that mantra truly be enough to sustain him outside of the mainstream? He had carved out as much time in his brain as he could to make a decision. What else did he really have to do? Maybe he'd find Julian's "Father Whatever" at some point. His choice made, he pushed everything else circling his mind into a dark alley and turned away.

The group dove deep underground. They began a series of strikes with

Carlos' signature tool—the small explosive. They planted the devices near government buildings, high-end retail outlets, and always at the latest electronics stores. Video games held the highest street value, and were the gang's singular group distraction passion. No one could resist a new Gameboy, or the latest Xbox version of Halo or Call of Duty.

Fencing the high-end goods stolen from an Armani, Gucci, or Prada stores helped to raise funds needed to support the organization. They kept the pink Mercedes around, but painted over everything except the trunk. They left the Mary Kay bumper sticker with its "Life can be good" slogan centered on the rear bumper. Branding their crimes with a mocking, ostentatious tool of its own conception left a bitter taste in the mouth of the always-one-step-behind authorities. It also kept the general public constantly amused by government ineptitude. Most of their crimes were blamed on the PCC—a sword that cut both ways. It dramatically increased their odds of not getting caught, but they got little recognition for their own movement.

Taking a page from the Shadow, Carlos decided he would only go out at night. He wanted to cultivate a shadowy reputation of his own to enhance the fear factor of any rivals.

"So you don't want to go out for lunch anymore?" asked an incredulous Dot.

"You can bring me my lunch."

"That's messed up, Carlos. I'm not bringing you lunch like some slave girl. Jao can get it," She flopped on a dilapidated, coffee-stained couch in what passed for the living room in Carlos' two-room flat.

Offended, Jao replied, "I've got a job sister. Besides, I ain't no waiter. I drive the car. That's it. Lazy-ass Singh doesn't do shit; he can do it."

"Okay Carlos." Singh sat calmly on a moth-eaten couch zoning out.

"Shade," Carlos corrected him.

"Shade? What's Shade?" Dot's incredulity was wearing thin on Carlos.

"It's my name from now until I tell you it's not." He glared at her.

"I get it now—Shade. It's your tribute to the Shadow." Singh was a well-practiced kiss ass.

"Okay Shade." Dot patronized Carlos but, luckily for her, he had already tuned her out. She slumped onto the couch next to Singh, giving him a 'what the fuck is this' glance.

The Shade was born, and never looked back until a surprising two years had ebbed past. Carlos discovered that he enjoyed his role. He commanded a level of respect he had never known. Granted, it came courtesy of a solid collection of jerk offs, but it still felt good. Shade learned to strategize and plan his assaults on Sao Paulo's infrastructure with a modicum of precision. His team appeared happy enough to go along with whatever he decided. Shade's star as a local folk hero ascended. Favela residents realized someone had taken up their banner of frustration with the inequities of Brazil's class divide. Mary Kay's marketing slug line began to show up in the favela. 'Life can be good' made its way to the streets. Through no shrewdly calculated plan, Carlos' small gang of four grew into a favela-supported, notorious, dark champion of the oppressed. Besides 'Life can be good,' Carlos noticed his name appearing on the streets too.

Shade Saves – Shade Knows – Shade Sees – Shade Does – Life can be good in the Shade

The notoriety did not go unnoticed. A sudden surge of violent crimes from bombing to robbery against established Brazilian companies and government organizations swept Sao Paulo. Many of them stamped with the false signature of the Shade. Even the staunchly commerce-focused PCC added a few random bombings of government agencies to its existing business model. It kept the authorities guessing. Some perpetrators even created leave-behind marketing materials. Crime scenes were littered with 'Life can be good' swag—hats, t-shirts; even business cards emblazoned with the slogan. The Sao Paulo Police Force was drawn in a million different directions. Carlos had inadvertently propelled himself into a nightmare scenario—a box canyon of blame with no escape. Anyone who could fashion a bomb and set it off credited Shade with the attack.

Holy shit, thought Carlos, I've created a damn snowball that's chasing my ass down a dead end hill. He continued his struggle to find decent targets in Sao Paulo that would make Julian proud of his efforts. It now seemed to him that the copycats had better ideas than he did.

One late afternoon, Dot walked in, holding her usual passion fruit smoothie. She delivered the breaking news, "Someone blew away the Governor's Mercedes, at the same time they bombed the Gucci store on Avenida Paulista. Ripping great!"

"The Governor's car? Whoa." Singh's mouth hung open in awe.

"He was in the Harley Davidson shop two doors down. The car shot fifty feet in the air first, then blew to shit. That's a statement." Dot's enthusiasm was hard to ignore.

Carlos felt like a complete failure. His inability to keep up with the Joneses on a mission that he invented irked. This diminishing confidence did not go unnoticed by his frustrated cadre of followers. They thought of themselves as folkloric heroes stuck sitting on the sidelines.

"What's the deal, Shade? We gotta get busy. We haven't been out in weeks," Dot voiced her displeasure.

"Yeah, what's the deal is right?" Jao slugged back a bottle of Bohemia beer.

"Shut the hell up the two of you. I've got some ideas," In truth, Carlos had zero ideas and had been treading water for weeks.

"You've been saying the same thing for the past month. We gotta go bigger. Crank the explosion. Use more blow-up shit. Think what the Shadow would do," Dot shot back.

Jao gave an imperceptible nod in Dot's direction. Carlos caught the movement from the corner of his eye. He reached across and slapped Dot hard across the face sending her smoothie half way across the room and scrambling her senses into silence.

"Jesus, man, she's a girl!" Singh offered up a meager defense while Dot wiped a spontaneous tear away.

"Oh, gee, I'm so sorry. Now shut the hell up all of you, and get the fuck out of here. I'm trying to think."

"Trying," quietly mocked Jao. He walked out beer in hand dragging Singh and Dot along with him.

Stuck on empty, Carlos took a rare late afternoon stroll through the comfortable chaos of Heliopolis, trying to clear his head. His eyes caught a steady stream of wall graffiti displayed in alleys and on peeling concrete building sides—the usual 'Life can be good' plus 'Safe in the SHADE', 'Cool in the SHADE', 'Shade saves', 'Free Shade'.

"Free Shade?" thought Carlos. What the hell is that? I am free. Then he pondered, contemplated, and reminisced. His mind wandered back and forth from childhood to prison. Then, like a high-speed bullet train, launched itself fast forward to the present and beyond. Life passed by his window at a blur—without detail. It occurred to Carlos that his life had spun and evolved on its own volition until the whole thing had grown beyond his ability to control it. Finally braking to a stop in the now-dark streets of Heliopolis, Carlos had no illusions about his decisions along the way. But at this moment, in the privacy of his own thoughts, he wished he had made different choices.

LAZARUS KNOWS

He noticed a disconnected piece of graffiti—a wooden cross painted on the bare brick side of Gil's Liquor and Snack Shop. 'LAZARUS' was written on the vertical stake and 'KNOWS' chalked horizontally on the cross bar. He walked another few blocks, noticing more and more of the same graffiti appearing along the sides of buildings, in the cracked pavement of the streets. He guessed it had been there all the time like the Sao Paulo ocean breeze, but he'd never noticed it. What did Lazarus know that he didn't?

His mind circled back to his own universe. He pulled a chocolate bar from his pocket and bit down on the Lindt 83% Dark, tasting its bitterness. He had no desire to be a folk hero, a political hero, even a reluctant hero of any slice. He pictured himself lying face-up in a prison yard with his neck filleted ear to ear, just like Julian Coelho. Crap! The image chilled and sobered him. It simply did not match the one lodged in his deepest desires; not even close. Carlos paused. He waited for something to rise up. Not that he lacked dreams; he just suffered from a lifetime of vapor lock. Like a car with a full gas tank; too much heat vaporizes the gas, preventing any hope of ignition—all potential, but no execution. Carlos had always suffered from way too much heat. He could never successfully drive forward for any extended period of time without a stutter, a pop, a backfire, or a halt. Cooling down and patiently waiting escaped his awareness. No images appeared before him. The way forward remained a hazy, obstacle-ridden, fog perpetually difficult to navigate. This particular quiet moment revealed nothing more insightful about his deepest desires than not to bleed out in a prison yard. 'Okay,' he thought, 'I may not have a clue what I do want, but I damn well know what I don't.'

The moment to extract himself from the beast he had created had arrived. It hit him square in the face like a hot iron in a prison laundry room. A new urgent burden to bear along with the trailing balance of his entire lifetime sat down in his crowded lap. How to get out safely, and where to go loomed large over his psyche. Two perplexing dilemmas he would have to solve, and solve quickly. He passed another fresh graffiti sign that made him feel marginally better—FUCK SHADE—PCC RULES.

"One more and I'm out," Carlos mumbled aloud before heading back home to bed and the forgiveness of sleep. He passed back by the Lazarus cross and thanked it for the inspiration to change. He made another mental note to find out what 'Lazarus' actually 'Knows' at his earliest convenience.

The next day, a breezy late fall Sunday afternoon, Carlos gathered his troops. "I've got something in mind."

Chapter 11. | Otis

'*Nothing's happening sitting* on my ass in here. I should at least try and open the goddamn doors.'

Hart got anxious. He had spent over fifteen minutes doing absolutely nothing. Scooting over to face the doors, he leaned over and placed his hands in the space between them. He summoned his best Man of Steel grip to part the metal doors, save Lois, and reach freedom. They moved less than an inch. He pumped up for one more try by taking in a gargantuan, lung-splitting breath. The elevator suddenly lurched down and banged hard against the shaft walls. Hart froze holding his breath until his lungs were bursting. "Holy Shit!" he exhaled, "am I really going to die in a third world elevator?" He looked up at the ceiling, and shook his head. 'God, please not another San Blas!'

Hart was recalling the one other potentially life threatening moment in his brief life. Simon, Hart, together with their pal Jackson had gone on a surf trip to the legendary perfect wave break off San Blas, in central Mexico.

They were three guys with surfboards compressed into a beat up, rented, VW Thing. The Thing that classic German engineered ode to minimalism; designed as nothing more than a corrugated tin bathtub on bike tires. Half way on the journey they ran into a classic seasonal Central American monsoon. Nature generously provided enough blasting rain to re-float the Queen Mary. A U-turn being the only sensible option, they kept driving.

After two hours of pounding rain they finally found the turnoff. A small, cracked, wooden sign pointed the way. The crew headed down a narrow, winding, mountain road leading from the interior valley to the

Pacific coast and the famous surf spot of San Blas. By this time, the force of the rain had increased to that of a full-throttle fire hose. The feeble aluminum windshield wipers on the car wheezed in overwhelm. As they rounded a blind corner, a massive eighteen-wheel Pemex oil tanker truck blotted out the road. Diesel smoke belching, it barreled up the very hill the boys were heading down. Hart swerved to avoid a nasty, certain-extinction collision. The proximity of the truck and the suction created by the high-speed pass literally pulled the pathetic wipers out of their sockets and off the car. One second they were anemically scraping the windshield, the next they were airborne over the cliff, headed into a watery ravine. Jackson began a steady screaming mantra of "oh shit, oh shit, oh shit" over and over.

As the driver, Hart decided zero visibility on a twisting blind curve roadway was too great a challenge. Collectively Simon and Hart decided to take advantage of the VW Thing option package and drop the collapsing windshield for better vision. Simon, possessing the longest arms reached outside onto the hood to unlatch it. "Oh shit, oh shit, oh shit" continued Jackson's refrain from the back seat. "Shut the hell up," Simon shouted as he strained to unbolt the windshield.

Unfortunately, at the precise moment he began lowering it the wind went schizophrenic and shifted its direction 180 degrees. It blew the windshield out of his grasp crashing it down onto the hood of the intrepid, struggling Thing. The glass shattered, crumbling into a thousand pieces. "Oh shit, oh shit, oh shit," Hart and Simon now joined in Jackson's chorus. The adventure-seekers were headed down a narrow, winding road virtually blind and losing layer upon layer of precious skin to a sandblasting non-stop rain. Hart donned sunglasses, hoping they would provide some hint of visibility through the downpour. All of them were so undeniably frightened they laughed themselves into gasping fits of hyperventilation. Death could have come in any infinitesimal instant over the course of the preceding hours. They laughed in the face of their own, very plausible demise; never truly buying into their proximity to personal extinction. After all, nothing feels inevitable when you are nineteen.

To their relief, and astonishment, the rain stopped in a sudden reprieve from Thor the Norse God of Thunder, or some other random benevolent deity. They survived. Three things remained in Hart's memory from that experience: the laughter, the knowledge that life hangs tethered by a thread of dubious tensile strength, and finally, that the surf in legendary San Blas that day was absolute shit.

Stuck in the frozen elevator, Hart reminded himself of that tenuous thread stored in the great parking garage of his mind under "S" for 'Where the Hell is San Blas?' Once again the elevator lurched, but this time it moved up no more than a foot, maybe two. Hart stood, prepared to do whatever was necessary to extricate himself from elevator prison. Deciding he hadn't truly used all his strength on the first two tries he hit the doors again. Mustering his most Herculean effort, he eked the doors open a solid two feet. A black-sleeved hand appeared reaching inside. Hart grabbed hold of it, boosting himself firmly onto the fourteenth floor.

"Obrigado." Hart offered the Portuguese word for thank you. Looking around, he saw that a couple of the windows in the elevator foyer had been cracked due to the concussive sound wave.

"What happened?" he asked the strangely calm employee.

"A bomb sir." Noticing the blank look on Hart's face, he embellished, "just a few doors down at the Harley Davidson Boutique. Are you okay?"

"I am fine," Hart says. His rescuer does not appear shocked by the bombing. "Is this a common occurrence in Sao Paulo?"

"Regretfully, of late we have seen a spate of attacks in the various affluent areas of the city."

"Regretfully?" Hart repeated the word while looking out the huge glass window at the ground below.

Hart scanned down the hall and watched the various guests milling about in an existential group pinch. Each person silently asking, "Are we really here? Did that actually happen?"

"I'm sorry Sir, but I must continue checking the floors for damage. Please excuse me." The staffer bowed his head calmly, and continued through the corridor towards the stairway.

Hart called out once again, "Regretfully? Really?"

"Most likely the Jesuits, sir," the staffer answered before disappearing down the stairwell.

Chapter 12. | Elephant code

"Opportunity must be shared." The black robed Jesuit priest struck his passionate chord. "Desperate poverty, breeds desperate faith, fed on by deliberate evil."

Tall like his father, the dark satin eyes of his mother, with an aquiline nose all his own, he stood at the center of a modest crumbling building. Father Lazarus Greve held the space with a transformative and magnetic charisma the equal of any modern rock star.

"Why don't we change?" He loved posing the apparently unanswerable question before traveling the great circle route to his eventual answer.

The first congregants came out of local neighborhood curiosity. They wondered what the new Priest in the favela had to say that might be different. They wondered if there was any cause for hope. Usually they had heard it all before. Rehashed, reconditioned, grey water words offering nothing but patented comfort. But Greve had no interest in stock quotations or the status quo. Word traveled rapidly downstream in Heliopolis, and more people came. Those who came brought others. The crowds grew, filled with the desire to be part of something. Soon his message percolated throughout Heliopolis, then the other favelas and corticos in and around Sao Paulo. People who were petrified to miss something that might shift their present day reality from hopeless to hopeful now filled every seat, every Saturday and every Sunday.

"Brazil is disintegrating. We are losing our values as a community, as a nation, and as a people." Greve shook his head showing his dismay.

The frailty of the building, an improvised assemblage of bricks, stucco, plaster, drywall, corrugated metal, anything that would stick onto its neighbor, belied the strength swelling within its tenuous walls. Greve's chapel sat as a borderline barrier built just strong enough to hold it in place against the elements of the tropical third world. The occasional drifting breeze moving westward off the Atlantic Ocean, forty miles away, trickled through the generous spaces. It acted as a limp air conditioning for those Paulistas crowded inside each weekend morning.

"Brazil believes in the national soccer team T-shirt: our international symbol of hollow victory. Why don't we change? Rich forgets poor, powerful forgets powerless. Why in a nation two hundred million strong do we suffer the spaces between us?"

Father Greve formerly preached his conscience only once on Sundays, mostly to his parolees and their extended families. After two years it had evolved into one sermon on Saturday and twice on Sundays. The chapel sat only a few doors down from the old Brazilian Savings & Loan and a few blocks away from the half-way house he had been running for the same time period.

"Why in a world of billions can we only hear the voices of the few? We have a minority that must open their hearts and yes, their pockets, to lift the misery. We need more jobs, more education, more caring. God cannot legislate changes. Men must rise up and respond to the challenges of equality and opportunity. We must be our own stewards. We must lead and shadow, we must carry, push and pull our way forward. Why don't we change?"

By the time Greve made the walk back home in the late afternoon, he felt the exhaustion and burden of his day. He spent hours looking down upon a sea of faces staring up at him for celestial guidance, not to mention deliverance. His spirit bounced between invigorated and drained. Bringing hope to the hopeless will drain even the deepest of wells. He wondered to himself if he was truly on the right path.

He remembered the story his first priest, Father Xavier, told him after a sermon one Sunday morning. Greve was a stoic, serious little ten-year-old boy with a heaping tablespoon of quiet sadness. He had let go of his mother's hand, walked up to the priest, and announced his intentions, "Father I want to change the world."

"Life," Father Xavier said to little Lazarus, "can change in a heartbeat. Be careful what you wish for."

"I don't understand." A quizzical expression had appeared on the young Greve's face.

Father Xavier like many Jesuit priests was a joyful intellectual. He often reveled in his own arcanum to the exclusion of all else; even the understanding of a ten-year-old boy.

"My curious son, when we look for answers, the journey is most often long and the road will rise and fall many times all along the way. Let me tell you a story abut a modern man, a writer of some significant fame and fortune." With that preamble, Father Xavier began his tale.

"'Be careful what you wish for,' is a simple phrase first attributed to George Orwell. Have you heard of him?" Greve's expression turned blank. "No I suppose not," Father Xavier answered his own question.

"No matter. You will run across him at some point. He derived the phrase we are discussing when summing up his experience in Burma shooting an elephant.

Orwell was born in India, but raised in England by a modest civil service family. As any forthright, socially conscious, nineteen year old might, Orwell held a strong conviction for protecting the lives of the working class. People like his own family. As a normal teen, Orwell sought the road to glory—for god, country, and absolutely for himself. Equipped with the impatience of youth, he set out on the path to achieve it with as much haste as possible.

"From age nineteen to twenty-four George Orwell served as an Assistant Superintendent in the British Imperial Police in Burma. That's a fancy name for a policeman. Obliged to enforce British laws on the tranquil Burmese people, Orwell's actual experiences flipped and jumbled his views of the British Empire. Living with the Burmese he suddenly saw his home country through a local lens. The peace loving Burmese viewed the British as an imperial power unfairly wielding its might as it pleased. The longer he stayed in Burma, and to his great personal disappointment, Orwell found that he agreed with them. The British sucked!"

It was at this moment that Father Xavier, caught up in his storytelling, fortunately caught the vacant look from Lazarus. He adjusted his style, at least a bit.

"Sorry, Lazarus," he apologized, "I know some of these words are confusing for you."

"No Father, I understand 'sucked,'" answered the boy.

"I'm sure you do. As you can see a disillusionment had crept into Orwell's road."

"As a policeman in Burma, and even though his sympathies lay with the Burmese, the local population still considered Orwell nothing more than a mostly powerless cop walking a beat. He faced a constant hazing, teasing and harassing from the locals. He steadily learned to ignore the mocking and abuse passing his time in Burma doing the best he could to avoid any conflict—the old British "stiff upper lip" thing.

On a random Tuesday morning he receives a somewhat frantic call about a normally mellow elephant suddenly going on a rampage. Duty calls! Orwell grabs his .44 caliber American made Winchester rifle, hops on his horse, and hoofs over to the local bazaar to search for the elephant. He encounters the usual crowd of vendors, shoppers, and indigents tossing out mocking insults and catcalls but sees no crazed pachyderm."

"Lazarus," asides Xavier, "Pachyderm is another word for elephant."

"Thank you Father."

"Figuring he has once again been had by the locals, Officer Orwell is quite ready to roll back to headquarters and return to his peaceful morning cup of coffee. Just then he spots a slightly frantic village woman standing in the middle of the marketplace. She is chasing away some children who are looking at the corpse of an Indian woman lying in front of a fruit stand. Orwell approaches her body. There she lies flatter than the ubiquitous Burmese banana leaf. The elephant has evidently trampled her, God rest her soul, to death. After some hesitation Orwell concludes that he unquestionably needs a bigger rifle. He sends his faithful orderly to fetch the proverbial elephant gun. Once in firm possession of the new gun, and followed closely by a crowd of at least one hundred now screaming, taunting Burmese, our reluctant hero heads toward a nearby paddy field. There he spies the elephant who has stopped to casually munch on a fresh grass buffet lunch.

To Orwell, the elephant looks perfectly content and quite at peace with the world." Father Xavier now puts his hand on Lazarus' shoulder, "Here is the time to pay close attention Lazarus." The boy nods.

"At that moment, in an instant of reflection, Orwell knows in his heart that he should not kill this beast. Perhaps the market crowd had riled it, or perhaps someone else had killed the woman and blamed the elephant, or perhaps a million and one other scenarios. There was no way for Orwell to truly know the absolute truth during the moment of time he would have to make his fateful decision."

Father Xavier looks hard at Greve to make sure the boy understands the point, "You see where this is going right Lazarus?"

"um.." an unsteady, shivery reply.

"Orwell," continues Xavier, "was keenly aware, that the increasingly mangy mob fully expected him to shoot and kill the rogue elephant without hesitation. They wanted it dead, and right now! Standing alone, holding the gigantic rifle, Orwell feels trapped by the expectations of a surly mob, not to mention trapped by his own eagerness and quest for honor."

Father Xavier checks the look on Lazarus' face once again. He knows the boy has intelligence and also knows he has wandered into language that may confuse him.

"You understand Orwell's dilemma?"

"I think so Father. Sometimes the things we think are right turn out to be really, really wrong?"

"Very well put," but Xavier can't resist adding, "All things sought become elusive when the game is on. Clarity easily gives way to doubt and uncertainty when confronted with fear and apparent necessity."

"I don't understand that Father, but the first part I said was right. Right?"

"Sometimes fear sends us down the wrong path," Xavier added.

A curious Lazarus asked, "Does he shoot the elephant?"

Xavier continues, "Orwell's awareness led him to conclude that the delivery of freedom and democracy to the unwashed can be a greater burden of enslavement than those we seek to serve. To be a tyrant is to actually be cataclysmically un-free. In an invisible moment, Orwell had become the tyrant he despised—involuntarily trapped in a box built with his own hands."

"Does that mean he didn't kill it?"

Xavier looked around to see if anyone was within earshot, "Orwell summed up all of his thinking in one word. 'Shit!'"

"Father!" exclaimed Lazarus.

"Sshhh! I know," he said in a conspiratorial tone to Lazarus, "But that's exactly what Orwell thought. The word can actually be quite concise for such complex moments."

"and," urged Greve, "the elephant?"

"Oh yes. Realizing the only road out was through the poor elephant's brain, Orwell shouldered his gun and fired a shot that brought the beast to its knees. Orwell turned to leave—sad but triumphant. Then he heard the crowd groan and watched them begin to drift backward away from the elephant. Turning around he saw the great beast had regained its footing and begun moving towards him. He planted his feet, aimed, and shot again, and then fired another. The elephant was still alive but this time mortally wounded. He approached the dying elephant and emptied his remaining two rounds, plus a clip of regular rifle rounds into the beast. Sadly it continued to heave great wheezing breaths. Out of bullets and seeing nothing more to be done, Orwell left the scene. Meanwhile the crowd of watching Burmese stood and waited for the elephant to die so they could strip it of its meat and carry on with their day."

Tears trailed down Lazarus Greve's cheeks, "He should have left him alone."

Handing the boy his handkerchief Xavier asked, "Did Orwell serve the public good that day, or did he serve his country? Did he find what he was after in Burma, or did he learn,"

Lazarus interrupted, "to be careful what he wished for?"

"Now," said Father Xavier nodding his head, "read this."

He pulled a non-descript, weathered brown book from his robes, and with a slight bow, handed it ceremoniously over to Lazarus. Lazarus, somewhat overwhelmed by the good priests' well-intentioned instructional guidance, took the book back home. He devoted the next two months, just shy of his eleventh birthday, to completing the story of Ignatius Loyola, founder of the order of Jesuits.

Greve smiled at the memory. It provided some relief to his day, but he knew more was needed. Something physical. He needed a tennis game. The holder of a profoundly ample intellect, he was blessed with very limited physical skills. Having no tennis partner in proximity he chose the next best thing for himself. To free his mind he turned to the ongoing painting of the house. He and his charges had been at this project for over a month, yet it remained mostly unfinished.

Greve never noticed the short powerful man standing in the back of the chapel during his sermon. He hadn't noticed the same tattooed man shadowing him on the walk back to the halfway house.

So that's Lazarus, Carlos thought to himself. The Shade pocketed his smile, made a mental note of the house he watched the priest enter, then slid back into the favela.

Chapter 13. | Red Card

Sirens wailed away outside, as Hart decided to head back to the relative safety of his room. Thirty minutes later his phone rang; Carmen was downstairs waiting. Hart took a look at himself in the mirror one more time before leaving the room. He gripped, steeled himself preparing for some unknown battle. He rounded out of the bathroom and out the door. Unwilling to be struck by lightening twice; he jogged the stairs nineteen floors down. Exiting the stairwell, he spotted Carmen who waited expectantly at the elevator door.

Walking up to her from behind, he posed his burning question, "Carmen, what's the story on the Jesuits?"

She answered tersely looking down at her watch, "They have strong convictions."

"You don't think bombing runs are somewhat north of strong convictions?"

"Did Mr. LeVitta reach you?"

"Nope, but I haven't been in my room much."

"He wanted to make sure you arrived safely."

"Don't I look safe to you? Especially now that I've been pre-bombed." He extended his arms for a body check.

Carmen gave a clipped smile. Hart persisted. "Couldn't your Jesuits write a fiery opinion article in the Sao Paulo Daily News, or some other wholesome inflammatory outlet? They could even go on talk radio preaching the end of whomever and whatever, whenever."

"This is Brazil and you are American," Carmen impatiently shot back as she headed for the revolving hotel front door.

"Pardon me?" He asked defensively.

"Americans are insulated. You over dramatize events you don't understand," she tossed her comments over her shoulder and rolled outside.

Hart skipped up shouting after her, "Random bombings are hard to come by in suburban Los Angeles." He caught up to her, "We tend to try and use our words when we don't like things. It's called civilization."

Now on the sidewalk together Carmen tolerated him with an empty stare. She turned again and picked up her pace down the street.

"Oh come on," he called after her, "Slow down!"

She paused to wait, "You can be as smug as you please, but it just affirms your arrogance." Her green eyes filled with disdain.

Hart thought to himself that their lunch ought to be a real blast, "Carmen, I'd love to understand it from your point of view. Right now I think that your Jesuits have developed a strong case of Fertile Crescent insanity."

Carmen had a mission, which could not be deterred by a little bombing run. She ignored his mini rant. "I'm going to take us by the office before lunch. Mr. LeVitta requested it."

Hart knew that he had just scratched the surface on Jesuits in Brazil. "We can do that, but I'm starving. Would it be okay if we got something to eat first? Holy shit?!" They both stopped in their tracks about twenty yards before the corner.

Hart glanced at Carmen, who was already on her cell phone. All of the streets had been blocked off beginning at their corner. There were a collection of police barricades and the tell tale yellow crime scene tape strung from one side of the street to the other.

The area was flooded with investigators taking measurements and looking for odd pieces of story. Hart spotted a cluster of police circled around a lanky, sallow faced younger man with a curving Mohawk. They had him cuffed and were busy folding him into a parked squad car. It looked like something off a typical television police drama.

Bolo appeared behind them in the idling Landcruiser. They climbed in then headed off in the opposite direction. They rounded a corner in a U-turn landing on the busy, bustling Avenida Paulista and headed north towards the jungle of sky rises. A large banner strung across the highway had a picture of the five interlocking Olympic rings coupled with the logo of three figures—orange, green and blue—embraced at the arms in a flowing dance. It included the phrase—O mundo está chegando para nós em 2016—"The world is coming to us in 2016."

"Bomb." Bolo got the entire word out with no two-second time delay, or maybe Hart was just acclimated to his speech. His voice held no emotion. It could've been any word: urinal, phone, brick, or trapeze. Bombs were a normal occurrence in Sao Paulo unless you happened to be standing next to one.

Bolo turned off Avenida Paulista onto a small street called Rua de Mestre Bimbo, named after Brazil's legendary Capoeira Master Manoel dos Reis Machado. The Maytag building nestled inconspicuously behind its closest neighbor, the post-modern, undulating, skyscraping Copan building. The multi-national behemoth Maytag had selected an absolutely obscure, demure, modest eight story basic rectangle as its third world base of operations. Glamour does not necessarily portend success. Maytag kept its profile steeped in the pragmatics of the workingman. They parked. Carmen asked Bolo to wait with the car, as they were going to get something to eat nearby.

Back on Avenida Paulista, Carmen led Hart to The Montana Grill, a churrascaria restaurant. "This is a typical Paulista place to eat," Carmen held the door open for Hart.

"With that name?" said a skeptical Hart.

A man dressed in an impeccably pressed white shirt, tuxedo tie, and a full-length apron escorted them into the restaurant. He was holding a foot long glistening carving knife and a two-foot long skewer stacked with two roasted chickens missing various body parts.

"Please," he said pointing to a pre-set table for two located five steps from a gigantic salad bar.

"I recommend the fried bananas with churrasco. They are famous for this," Carmen flipped over a bi-colored card on her place changing it from red to green.

Hart followed her lead. A Churrascaria translates as a festival of meat—grilled anything from beef to lamb to pheasant to chicken and even rabbit. They also had the world's largest salad bar with items both familiar and alien to Hart's palate. The card on the table sends the signal to the floating carvers that the diner eagerly awaits their services. Carmen and Hart are immediately barraged with skewer carrying, knife-wielding waiters rotating every twenty seconds. They receive pieces of grilled rib eye, rabbit sausage, chicken, and lamb. Hart stacked his plate high and headed for the salad bar where he grabbed mostly lettuce and returned to the table.

Finishing a bite of sausage Hart offered Carmen an olive branch, "I apologize if we got off on the wrong foot."

"I apologize too. I didn't mean to attack you for being an American."

Hart picked up the salt, struggling to get some of it onto his food. "I guess I'll get used to that at some point over here. What's up with this salt?"

"It's the tropics. Most places put rice in it to absorb the water."

"That sucks. Say, If you think I'm an ugly American how do you deal with LeVitta?."

She paused for a long second. "I haven't formerly met him yet. I'm a professional, and I do my job because I know I'm fortunate to have one."

"So, do you live around here?"

Carmen's eyes widened. "That's your conversation starter? A pick up line?"

"Strike that. How about I ask you a question about Bolo?"

"Better," she answered, smiling.

"Where's he from, with that bizarre speaking thing?"

"Hard to say. It does take some getting used to. I know he sends money somewhere every week like clockwork."

He smiled, "I'm going to have to dig into that mystery at some point, for sure."

"Tell me," Carmen turned serious, "you don't seem like the adventurous type. What are you doing here?"

"Because I'm not the typical Junior Maytag executive?"

"Not necessarily, but I'm a quick study and this seems an unnatural place for you."

Hart thought about not answering the challenge. He thought about forgetting he even heard it and distracting Carmen with some innocuous small talk. He could fend her off with some witty repartee, and then move on to a harmless topic like architecture or laundry. Does she truly want the answer to that question? Hart aggressively avoided disappointment in life. It terrified him. Not his own disappointment, but others in him. He figured it was the thread to unravel all he was or thought he might become. Had he already disappointed Carmen? So quickly too; they had only just met.

Channeling a piece of Simon, he forced himself to give Carmen a real answer. Looking into the green eyes staring at him, he blurted out the synopsis of his recently shifting universe. "A little over a month ago I was a fact checker for Rapidly Rising Films. Don't be impressed; it was a porn house. I was mostly teaching tennis, dating random girls, and wondering what happened to my best friend who disappeared in Brazil. Now I'm here."

Carmen took a long moment to inhale the list. She cocked her head first to one side then the other, like a border collie wondering if you are truly going to throw the tennis ball to her, or if it's all a tease. She sifted directly to the element that invoked the strongest question.

"You worked on pornographic films?"

"I was desperate for a different anything. I found a listing for the job at UCLA. The card said 'Entry Level position at rapidly rising film company.' I drove out to a town called Chatsworth on a day that tested the resilience of flesh to apocalyptic heat. One hundred eleven degrees Fahrenheit, and so smoggy it looked like a giant fog bank had descended upon the entire San Fernando Valley. It was like being trapped in a toxic Tupperware container with industrial waste, car fumes, and random bits of pre-owned oxygen. I pulled into a non-descript warehouse district. I found the address on my card displayed on a large metal door at the side entrance of one of the gray block shaped buildings. It read Rapidly Rising Productions.

I knocked and waited. Not wanting to suck down what passed for breathable air outside, I pushed open the door and walked inside. A blast of life giving, cold oxygen hit me in the face. I bathed in the relief until my focus returned and the layer of sweat encapsulating my body dried up. That's when I heard the moans. As my perception sharpened, I noticed a group of people standing around a klieg-lit set. I crept closer. Three naked women surrounding one beast of a man all plumbed together by a collection of devices including one ridiculously sized male organ, two plutonium sized tiger striped dildos, and an assortment of mouths and occupied orifices."

"Aaahh," exclaimed Carmen. "You had no idea!"

"Oh, it gets better. I'm standing there like a statue when I hear, 'Cut, set it up again. We go in twenty.' The shouts came from a small woman in her mid fifties. The 'actors' immediately detached and scattered about the sound stage, toweling off, grabbing coffees, sandwiches, all except the beast master, who plopped back down on the couch next to a half-eaten box of Chinese eggrolls."

'Ginger, the kids here for the interview.' I had been spotted by a walkie-talkie wearing assistant. He radioed over to the director while waving me over to a small table with a box of picked-over doughnuts and some empty Styrofoam cups scattered on top of it.

"UCLA, right?"

I nodded and handed him my resume.

"Grab something to eat if you want, I'll get Ginger," with that he turned and walked away.

I picked up the only untouched donut, and took a quick bite.

"Hey kid. You've got a jizz moustache right here." She motioned to her upper lip. "I'm Ginger."

"I'm Hart. So, fact checker for a rising production company?"

"Listen kid," she held my resume in her hand, "we have liabilities just like anyone else—even more. We need to make sure any names, places, or references we use don't leave our ass hanging in the wind anymore than necessary."

"This is porn, though. Is that really your biggest concern? Besides I'm not a lawyer." I wasn't sure I really wanted the job.

"We just need someone to research what we use and turn it in. The lawyer looks at the list and decides later. It's a chance to get into the film business and meet interesting people…like me!"

"Are you offering me the job?" I asked.

"Why not? You seem like a smart kid, and we gotta get this film wrapped by the end of the week. It pays $500 for the week and includes the powdered sugar donut, starting right now. Are you in?"

I needed the money, and it was too hot to go back outside. "I'm in."

"Great. There's a laptop on the desk over there next to the dressing room. The script is on disk in Microsoft Word. Go through it and check out every name and place using whatever resource you can figure out. Make a list and get back to me when you're done." Ginger darted off.

Taking the rest of my donut, I wandered over to what passed as a dressing room. Four tables with globe lit vanity mirrors lined up in a row, each fronted by a wooden stool.

"Damn, my ass is cold. Couldn't they at least put a cushion on these shitty little Kmart stools?" A dirty blonde haired gal with a Southern accent in her mid-twenties and stark naked was applying make up to her eyes. She glanced over in my direction as I sat down at the table and flipped open the laptop.

"Hey honey, what's your name?"

"Hart. I'm the fact checker."

"Why are you looking at my tits, Hart?"

Hart sheepishly looked at Carmen, embarrassed but truthful, "I actually had made a point of not looking at her breasts, figuring, you know, I'd scan them when she wasn't looking. At least that was my plan. Her breasts looked more like guided missiles peaking out of a silo and targeted at my head. I came back at her the best I could. "Well, you're naked on the set of a porn movie, so I guess I just figured you couldn't possibly mind."

"It's an adult film, not porn. And I don't mind. I'm Jill."

"Nice to meet you, Jill." I went back to my work, occasionally glancing up to see if her breasts were still there and staring back at me.

I lasted the week. Well, almost the week. I lasted right up until the Beast master got a nasty case of dysentery on the second to last day of filming. He ate a toxic Shrimp burrito from Casa Vallarta. Jill asked me to fill in with her and the rest of the girls. They literally rubbed up against me like some group lap dance, hoping to intoxicate me. It nearly worked until Ginger came over and tried the same thing.

"How's that feel, soldier? We need you on the team, Hart. Could be a great experience for you."

She must have noticed my blank look before tactfully adding, "AND there's money too. Don't think I don't have a fat bonus in mind."

"You didn't think about it? For a second at least?"

"Maybe if Ginger hadn't rubbed up against me, but no, not really. I got scared."

"Afraid of disease? Lovemaking on camera?" Carmen pressed him.

"I think it's safe to say in porn they just say fucking. I have a fear of public intercourse. Being in my own reality show presented a whole different opportunity for self-loathing than even my healthy ego could bear."

Carmen smirked. "You had the performance anxiety?"

"Very funny. Your English is fantastic, too fantastic. What if I was one shot and done before the camera dollied to its CLOSE UP SHAFT PENETRATION shot? Sorry, is this embarrassing you? Too familiar? We don't even know each other." Hart noticed Carmen scoot her chair back from the table to get some space.

She smiled, and he felt a connection materialize between them.

He continued, "Anyway, I couldn't fathom the concept of multiple takes. I'm sure Ginger would've suitably castrated me on set and I'd be relegated back to the laptop. I could never work at a place where the prevailing opinion of me would become," Hart searched for the right word, "incomplete? Constant scenes of humiliation ran a tape loop forwards and backwards in my mind. That pretty much iced my choice. I told them I needed to go breathe some poisonous air and think about it. I haven't been back to the San Fernando Valley since."

"That's quite a tale. You don't wonder what it would've been like?" Carmen asked.

"Well. It wasn't that long ago, so I'm not ready to say opportunity missed just yet, but someday maybe."

"You can consider it as an adventure you chose not to take. In Portuguese, we say 'perseguir a coisa que faz você se perguntar.'"

"Follow your questions?" Hart knew Portuguese, but not close to Carmen's idiomatic knowledge of English.

"Pursue that thing which makes you wonder. Follow the yellow brick road, might be another way to say it. Yes?"

"You sound like my pal Simon."

"And that's a good thing?"

Hart thought about Simon's constant pestering of him to stretch out, loosen up, and get laid. He didn't think of Carmen in that light. Well, yes, he did, but he was not about to act on that impulse. Then he recalled Simon asking him to come with him to Brazil and ran smack into another 'No' in his life.

"I wonder what Siddhartha would do?" he blurted out.

"Is that a friend of yours?"

"Siddhartha? No it's from a book I read years ago. I ask myself that question sometimes when I get hung up on options."

"Would he be in an adult film? That's the question you ask?"

"I think he might have. Which proves I'm certainly no Buddha!"

"Well," Carmen summarized and concluded the conversation. She turned her card to RED placing her napkin on the plate.

"Good lunch." Hart reached for his wallet.

"No, no, it's on the company." Carmen signed something on the bill and rose to leave.

"I hope we can have another meal where I learn some deep dark secret about you. What part of the city do you live in?"

"I live in a very difficult part of Sao Paulo called Heliopolis." Carmen felt embarrassed about living in the favela.

"I'm curious about all of Sao Paulo. Would you take me there at some point?"

Carmen pondered the request, then coyly she said, "We will see."

Back outside on the street they quickly made their way to the Maytag office building, headed through the double glass lobby doors directly into the ubiquitous Otis brand elevator. At the fifth floor the elevator opened directly in front of two large, double dark, mahogany wood doors emblazoned with the distinctive deep blue Maytag logo. The reassuring Maytag slogan, Depend on Us sat just below the logo translated into Portuguese "Dependa de Nós." Carmen slid her key into the lock and opened the door. She side stepped to the right and flicked on the lights as Hart followed her inside.

The first item Hart noticed was the iconic, framed image of the lonely Maytag Repairman placed on the entry wall to his left. Jesus, that's really goofy, he heard himself say silently. The internal comment awoke his inner arrogant pig. The pig smirked and mocked him mercilessly for bailing out of his dreams by taking a pointless job at a typically greedy US corporation. Hart recognized the singular flaw in that taunt: no clue to his dreams in the first place. He had simply been practicing the ancient art of placing one foot in front of the other and taking the next step. He swallowed hard, keeping the interior anxiety to himself by paying more attention to the new surroundings. He and Carmen stood together looking at the post deco, wood paneled space, reminiscent of a 1940's law office.

There were six offices lining the outside walls, each with a window to the world, or what remained of it. Unfortunately each pane held a light-blocking view of nothing but the sand-colored, perpetually rippling, architectural classic known as the Copan building.

Carmen offered up, "You get used to it. Don't worry."

The middle open space of the office had four equal size desks placed in an exact diamond pattern. The walls were veneered with a beautiful blonde maple wood, and combined with clear glass internal doors and windows. The place afforded absolutely no privacy. The fluorescent lighting, blonde wood, and sand colored outside views muted the entire environment down to an unexpected Southern California Sunday afternoon mellow. Hart contemplated a James Taylor soundtrack and a wine cooler. His brain flashed into a mild panic. 'I guess I could get used to living in the shadows and toiling away in obscurity,' he started spinning up. 'Man oh man,' figured Hart, 'I have truly derailed my life in epic fashion.'

"I like it," he lied, "which desk is mine?"

"You have an office."

The surprise of Carmen's announcement lifted his spirits.

"Go right down the hall." She pointed around the corner, as Hart began trolling, "Past the first office; that's for Mr. LeVitta. You get the one next to it. You received a package a couple days ago. I'll bring it down for you in a minute."

He kept drifting down the hall until he found an office with a single rectangular window. "Single window?"

"That's the one," yelled Carmen down the hall.

"Got it!"

What kind of package could he have received? Hart figured it was probably some Maytag corporate crap. Carmen walked in holding a small cardboard box and placed it down on his desktop. Hart counted four letters and a Tupperware container.

"Thanks. The folks, my parents," he explained sheepishly. Nothing beats emasculation. Thanks Mom. Carmen shuttled back out to her desk.

The note taped to the top of the Tupperware read, "A little taste of home. Good luck M&D." Hart gripped the frosty white plastic container and tepidly popped open a corner of the lid to peak inside. He was met by a puff of skanky, mold, infested air. The mutant offspring produced when fermenting a batch of Betty Crocker brownies with a Dole banana on an extended overland UPS journey to South America. He quickly snapped the lid shut. He scanned the letters, two from his folks, and shockingly two from his brother, which he assumed his mother had written. Some distance away, he heard the phone ring.

Carmen picked up the receiver from her desk and punched a button. "Good morning, Maytag. He's right here, one moment please," she pressed the hold button, pressed another button. Hart heard the intercom on his phone come to life, "it's Mr. LeVitta for you. Press the blinking light."

Hart, slightly uncomfortable in his executive swivel chair, picked up the phone. "Hello?"

"What's going on down there Ace?" LeVitta thundered in his best Texas football coach demeanor. Even from several thousand miles away his voice boomed with energy. "Rita briefed you on the layout?"

"You mean Carmen? Yes, she did."

LeVitta hesitated for a moment, "Uh, Rita, Carmen, whatever, you got the damn lay of the land right?"

Could the big boss not figure out that it was a weekend? Plus the high likelihood that Hart might be jet lagged as well? "Well it's only Sunday, and I just got here. There was a bomb blast right near the hotel, so.."

"A bomb huh, sounds exciting." All business, Bruce couldn't give two shits about anything save his own agenda. "Listen Ace, I don't give a sniper's bullet that it's Sunday, or if some jackoff went Nagasaki down the block. There's lots of god damn Sundays. I took a chance on you, so the sooner you get down to it, the sooner this hen is gonna lay some eggs. Get me?"

However convoluted and disturbing the metaphor milkshake, Hart got the point. Coach LeVitta had no plans to coddle his new hire. The attitude grabbed Hart by the neck and shook his inner Caesar! A disembodied egoless voice auto-answered on his behalf, "Absolutely."

"There's a man size list of gray market bastards selling Maytag gold without our damn permission. They're stealing our eggs Son. I need you to get on the phone with each and everyone of those horse thieves and bring them to justice."

"You got it Sir," he said. "I won't let you down. I'll give you a call tomorrow and let you know how things are going." Then he tossed in a kiss-ass compliment for good measure. "Nice offices."

"They are pretty god damn nice. I'm not trying to crawl up your ass on day one, partner; I'm just anxious for you to get started. See you in a couple days."

"Yes sir," Hart gave the auditory equivalent of a military salute and briskly hung up.

"Mother fucker!" he lost volume control on his inside voice.

Catching Carmen's stare curtailed his tirade. Bolo had also just walked into the office and stood frozen at the doorway. Hart realized his face must have been locked in a frustrated grimace. He relaxed it, smiled, and dragged himself over to check out his singular outside window. Curling his neck down, he could barely catch a corner glimpse of Avenida Paulista. Actually, he could see the corner of the Olympic banner they had passed on the street earlier. What a shit view, he wanked to himself. He plunked down at his desk and slid open the drawer where he found a dog-eared Sao Paulo tourist book. He thumbed it open.

Carmen popped her head into his office for a friendly check. "Okay?"

"Maybe not such a good strategic move, but I'll smooth it over when he gets here." Carmen smiled politely and went back to her desk. Hart split his attention between the dog-eared book and the pie-slice outside view while pondering his immediate future.

Hart had passed some of the endless airplane hours by reading the Maytag Corporate history—Clean to Green. Founded in 1893 by F.L. Maytag, in Newton Iowa, as a farm implement company, Maytag virtually invented the entire concept of clean. Prior to Mr. Maytag bringing it their attention, America never realized how truly disgusting its national dress standards had been. People routinely wore the same clothing for weeks at a time without the slightest thought given to appearance, and remarkably, odor. Our clothing reeked. We may have taken to the once a week bath for our bodies, but somehow we never made the same consistent connection between soap and clothing. At least not until F.L. and the boys created the first washing machine back in 1907. F.L., a promoter out of the PT Barnum school, coined the phrase, "Cleanliness is next to godliness, but you can't get there from here without a Maytag." Americans could take all the baths and showers in the world but putting on the same skanky, sweat-drenched clothing sizably diminished a body's true sense of hygienic purity. It just plain didn't feel good. Maytag salesmen were known to pack the New Testament on their sales calls. Even though the famous quote does not appear in any bible, Old or New, most folks figured the words came straight from the Lord Almighty. A salesman would utter the cleanliness quote, while holding the bible in plain sight. F.L. called the technique the 'assumed close.' The strategy proved to be golden.

Maytag called his first machine the "Pastime." It lasted two years until they upgraded it to the more politically offensive "Hired Girl" in 1909. The Hired Girl ran on power from tractor engines, hedge trimmers, and other random farm machines the new company cannibalized. By 1924, Americans had fully embraced the concept of industrial-driven cleanliness. The great rush to cleanliness had raised the Maytag Company into a dirt fighting, bible inspired, juggernaut behemoth. Three out of every five washers in America came from Maytag. Farm equipment moved to the backseat, and pretty soon found its way off the bus entirely. Today's Maytag makes over four billion dollars each fortuitously dirt filled year. French may be the language that turns dirt into romance, but Maytag is the alchemist that turns dirt into a more useable substance—cash money—Clean to Green.

Hart realized that his job description may not have included new business, but nevertheless, he had been struck by what he predicted to be a winning idea.

"Carmen!" He burst out of his office with a rush of enthusiasm, "Can I talk to someone at the Brazil Olympic Committee? Do people work on Sundays here, ever?"

"I can try. At worst you can leave a message for Monday. What are you thinking? We're supposed to be getting the office ready for Mr. LeVitta on Tuesday."

"Listen in if you like." He jogged back into his office and confidently leaned back in his Aeron chair, scooping up the tattered old Sao Paulo guidebook to peruse while waiting on his call.

"Miss Nunes, yes please hold one moment." Carmen slid down the hallway appearing in Hart's window. She held up two fingers on her left hand. And after Hart picked up the phone, she quietly slid into his office.

"Please call me Hart, Miss Nunes. Okay, Clara. Thank you. Surprising to find you in on a Sunday but I guess that's hopefully good fortune for both of us."

Clara Nunes had recently joined the Rio 2016 Olympic Committee, voluntarily taking a leave of absence from her position as Director of Marketing for one of Brazil's largest banks, Brazilian Savings & Loan. Her strengths lay in fiscal ingenuity coupled with an understanding of targeted demographics. She knew how to get customers and stay within budget.

"Well, we have relocated into new offices. I'm here setting up my new space. You know hanging some art, sorting through papers," she explained.

"Funny, I'm fresh off the airplane from the US this morning and doing the very same thing over here. May I get right to my purpose?"

"Certainly," Clara thought of herself as someone who cut to the chase, so she appreciated Hart's directness.

"I do hope you're the right person for this. Are you familiar with the Maytag Company?" Hart figured everyone had heard of Maytag.

"You are an American company, yes? What products do you make?"

"We are a home appliance company. We make washing machines. You know, for clothes."

"Ah, of course, you are like Brastemp."

Hart's face went blank as he looked at Carmen for help. She returned his glare, hunching her shoulders as if to say 'what?'

Hart repeated what he just heard aloud so Carmen could react. "Like Braaaastemmmmp you say…" he drew out the company name.

Carmen knew them as the largest appliance company in Brazil—a definite competitor, the actual Gorilla in the marketplace. She nodded her head YES repeatedly, and spread her arms apart, pantomiming their size as huge. Hart got the message.

"Yes, Clara, exactly right. But, I've got an offer for Brazil from Maytag that might be too good to pass up."

"I'm listening."

"By my count, you are going to be hosting over ten thousand athletes in twenty six sports at the upcoming games. Correct?"

"A large number for certain."

"They will be working out, competing, and living here for at least one month during the games."

"Still listening."

"That's a lot of dirty clothes to deal with. What would the Brazilian Olympic Committee say if Maytag offered to wash them. All of them!"

Clara Nunes recognized a good thing when she heard one, plus she understood the many hidden costs associated with an event of this magnitude. She had been standing, but once she heard the offer coming across the line she promptly took a comfortable seat at her desk, "At your cost?"

"Wouldn't be much of an offer if we charged for it, would it Clara? Are you the correct contact for this sort of thing?"

"You have my attention, which means you have presented an opportunity worth exploring. I'm assuming you would do this in return for a level of permissible advertising for your brand?"

"Common sense. Don't you think? So what do we need to do now?"

A wide smile materialized on Carmen's face to match the one on Hart's. She mouthed the word "wow!" and sat down.

"Put that offer on your letterhead and send it over to me. I'll be in touch next, um, this week. Tell me Hart, what is your title?"

"I'm the Senior Country Manager?" Although he didn't mean to answer with a question, it fell out of his brain that way.

Clara Nunes took minor notice of his brief confidence slip. She felt too enthusiastic about the deal possibilities for it to matter. "Are you sure? You sound so young. No matter, speak to you next week. Enjoy the rest of your Sunday."

"Same to you." With that, Hart hung up the call, pumping his fist.

Feeling triumphant, Hart ran several laps around his desk, spinning forward and backward as he went.

"Is that some kind of American ritual?" Carmen asked, bemused.

"Oh yeah, baby! That's the victory dance. Join me. It feels good," Hart grabbed Carmen's hand and towed her reluctant body around with him for a couple laps.

He turned to face her, raised his left hand. "Up high now, come on!"

"No." She shook her head. " I don't high five."

He lowered his arm, made a fist and pointed it at her, waist-high, "Fist bump?"

She shook her head. "Sorry, no adolescent behavior for me."

"Chest bumps are out for sure then." A smiling Hart extended his open hand.

"Absolutely—great job, but…" Carmen met his hand.

"No buts, absolutely no buts, yet. Enjoy the moment." Hart shook her hand.

"I don't know what made me think of it. I was so pissed off."

"It is truly a wonderful idea, but don't you need permission?"

"From LeVitta?" A dose of reality hit home as he plunked down at his desk. "How can he argue against global publicity for Maytag? He has to love it. He'll love it."

"I don't know him, but I'm sure you're right. Even if it will cost the company a lot of money."

"Carmen really, could you have waited ten minutes before crashing my high? Now I need to write up the proposal."

"I have the Olympic Committee information. I will do it for you and fax it over right away. I'm sorry."

Hart sat back at his desk holding a virtual balloon with some of the air leaking out. He picked up the Sao Paulo guidebook and sank down.

The phone rang again.

"Good afternoon Maytag. Yes sir, just a moment." Carmen looked over at Hart and mouthed 'LeVitta.'

Holy shit, he thought. Do I tell him this now, or wait until I see him Tuesday? He assessed a face-to-face conversation had to be better than a disembodied phone call. He'd wait.

"Yes sir?" he answered the phone swiveling his chair to face the window.

"Wanted to give you my arrival info for Tuesday. Are you ready to copy?"

Ready to copy? Did LeVitta think he was an air traffic controller reading a clearance to a commercial pilot? This guy was already exhausting, and they hadn't even started working together. Hart's half-hearted response dribbled out. "Yes, I'm ready."

Carmen clicked on the glass window of his office once again. Looking panicked, nervous, or just excited. Not knowing her beyond half of one day, he could not accurately interpret Carmen's emotional library. Maybe, he thought, she felt bad about not fist bumping after the Olympic phone call.

"Sorry sir, I'm going to call you back." Without waiting for a response he cradled the phone and looked up at Carmen, "What's up? Damn, I think I got LeVitta pissed off at me on the first day. Not even the first day."

"Someone's here to see you." Completely ignoring his brief misery soliloquy, Carmen motioned back behind her to the door of the suite.

Hart looked perplexed, "No one knows I'm here. Are we interviewing new staff? Wouldn't I know that? Should I stay in my office? Check that, I'm definitely staying in my office. I have an office so I'm staying put." Hart then assumed his best guess at executive demeanor and posture, "Carmen," he gathered in another deep relaxation yoga breath, "Get their name and send them in."

Still holding the guidebook, he read "That which you are seeking is always seeking you." Then he swiveled his chair to face the sand colored, opaque view of the Copan building. Mid ponder he heard his door open, and a rustling commotion out in the hall.

"Hey buddy, what's up?"

Hart instantly recognized the ironic tone of voice and the psycho cynical smile that went with it. He was alert just long enough to record a tattoo covered, dark skinned man appear behind Simon, pointing a gun. The man shoved Simon against the office wall, and pulled the trigger. Hart felt an instantaneous needle sharp impact on the right side of his neck. In his one remaining conscious moment, as he observed his head dropping on a collision course with his simulated marble desktop, Hart wondered if his best friend had just killed him.

Chapter 14. | Tutu a miniera

By the time Jao and Singh followed each other back into the flat, Carlos had finished planning their late-night activities.

"Dot's gone." Singh, the last one in the room, broke the bad news to the other two.

Carlos registered neither disappointment or surprise. "Means we're one short."

Jao's response signaled a slightly more stressful sentiment. "Dot's gone? That's not good. Right?" He swiveled between Carlos and Singh, searching for agreement. "Is she coming back? Do we wait for her to come back?"

"She got pissed off and left. I went by to get her, but she was gone. Her shit was gone. Move on." Singh finalized what Shade already knew.

"Like I said a second ago, we're down one. Suggestions?"

"We're not worried about this?" Jao ping-ponged his angst between Singh and Carlos. He paused to intuit their answer. "Fine, I know someone, but we'll have to pick him up."

They headed out to pick up the new recruit. Jao drove. He always drove. His day job as a water delivery truck driver taught him every street in the city. The new recruit in question had recently been paroled to the Jesuit halfway house located a few kilometers outside of Heliopolis. They pulled up to the two-story, faded white clapboard house as the sun headed on its downward journey. A priest in a black cassock stood outside the turquoise blue front door directing three men holding cans of paint. Each man had a different color paint dangling from his brush; one orange, one turquoise, and one red. The priest appeared to be assessing his trim design and discussing the matter with his assistants.

Carlos got out of the car, and leaned on the hood to wait while Jao inquired on the whereabouts of the newly paroled potential recruit. The priest directed Jao into the house. As the priest turned back to continue his color scheme conference, Carlos chuckled to himself and approached him casually. "Life is a circle," he summarized years of separation and assumption in a millisecond of conversation.

Lazarus turned at the instant recognition of an old voice. He walked to Carlos broke through any hesitation and hugged his estranged half-brother.

"Carlozinho, you are not dead!" Lazarus' voice expressed no anger or judgment; only a keen sense of relief.

"Not yet," came the response.

"So?" Lazarus uttered only the one word. He certainly didn't need to say anything. Each man knew an explanation was due.

"I got angry," Carlos answered plainly.

Lazarus took a step back from Carlos taking in the sum total of him with a full glance.

"You will stay for dinner?"

"I'm not praying or doing any religious crap," Carlos replied.

"It's dinner, not a conversion ceremony. Settle down."

Jao emerged from the house with a kid, Phillipe, who could not have been more than nineteen. Carlos thought that placed him about the same age as he was before serving his first prison term. Lazarus eyeballed Carlos with a look he recalled from their childhood. Carlos motioned to Jao, who walked over for clarification.

"Leave the kid and come back in two hours. I'm staying for dinner." No more discussion was required.

"Okay Shade," Jao whispered, then got back in the car with Singh and drove away.

Lazarus' ears perked up when he caught the name Jao uttered before leaving.

Carlos turned back, "Lead on brother, or Father?"

They walked into the house. Only one year apart in age, each man physically reflected the vast chasm of differing choices made in their lives. Carlos, compact in his broad and muscled physique, entered the house.

He shielded his fears by carrying an air of intimidation and confrontation. He warily scoped out the house as he followed Lazarus into the kitchen. Lazarus, tall, lean, gentle and studious, comfortably nodded to the few residents preparing dinner.

"We have a simple meal of Tutu a Mineira. I hope that is okay with you," offered Lazarus.

They sat down at the plain wooden dining room table. Mashed beans served with roasted pork loin, cabbage, and rice was a typical Sao Paulo meal. It may not have sounded so good, but once it was all mashed together no one cared.

"I can't say that's just the way Mom used to make it, since I don't remember what she used to make. Or your mother either, for that matter." Carlos scooped a good-sized portion from the common bowl and placed it on his plate.

"My mother never cooked much. Did she?" Lazarus helped himself to a smaller portion.

"I'm sorry about Sabrina. Did I ever say that to you?"

Lazarus showed a gentle smile. "You never said much to me about anything, but thank you."

"A beer would be great. Do you have any Ambev?" Carlos asked.

"Carlos, this is a halfway house. We don't serve alcohol here." Lazarus smiled again.

Carlos shrugged his shoulders.

"Don't you think that's a strange name for Brazilian beer?" Lazarus pondered his own question, knowing he'd get around to answering it.

"No. It's a fucking beer." Carlos had lost interest in the beer, but not in the meal.

Lazarus forged ahead, "Ambev? It's short for American Beverage. Don't you find that the least bit insulting? This is Brazil, not America. We should have our own beer."

Carlos watched as Lazarus fretted over a beverage he didn't even have in the house. What was the point of that? "Lazarus, you know this place is an absolute waste of time, don't you?" He summarized while scooping another heaping serving of Mineira onto his plate.

"Carlozinho." Lazarus felt the despair draping his half brother's heart.

Adding the trailing suffix of 'inho' to a name changes the sentiment to one of familiarity and affection. It's like changing Bob to Bobby, John to Johnny, or Pook to Pooky.

Carlos recoiled upon hearing Lazarus conjugate his name into what he perceived as a surface sentiment. He bristled, but decided to let it pass. He's a damn priest, he thought to himself. Let him do what he needs to do. None of it mattered anyway, and the dinner would soon be over.

"I heard one of your Sunday sermons, and I've seen your signs—Lazarus Knows." Then Carlos challenged him, "Where are these people going to go after you transition their asses back to society?"

"They will have an opportunity to make new decisions, with God's help."

"I'll tell you where they're going, brother. Back to the favelas, scrounging for money, or hooking up with the PCC, or worse. Your God doesn't buy food or housing, and he certainly doesn't have any paying jobs." Carlos spit out the contemptuous words with the conviction of experience.

"You know I'm not here to check out your new paint job," he added.

"I know why you're here." Lazarus realized the dead-end that most of his borders faced.

"He's young and willing to work. Unless you think he wants to be a doctor or a lawyer?"

A mocking Carlos emptied his bottle of Brazilian Spring water, then reached into his pocket and pulled out a Valhrona 70% chocolate bar. He began to unwrap the bar, and with a gesture, offered a piece to Lazarus, who declined.

"Valhrona makes a great chocolate. Good way to close the stomach."

Looking over to the kitchen, Lazarus now noticed the shocked expression on the faces of his residents. Their voices were hushed; it was like Zorro being unmasked in the town square. Now he too realized that The Shade was having dinner in his halfway house. Philippe headed out of the kitchen with two more bottles of Brazilian Spring water in one hand and a pitcher of passion fruit juice in the other.

"Would you care for some more water, or perhaps some juice?" asked a kowtowing Philippe.

Lazarus knowingly observed his tenants humility around Carlos.

"Water works fine." Carlos watched his brother's changing expression.

As Philippe turned to head back into the kitchen, Lazarus noticed that his own water glass remained empty. "Excuse me, Philippe, may I have a bottle, please?"

"Of course Father. I am sorry to have forgotten you."

"They are nervous around you Carlozinho. Now, I recall I've seen your signs too."

"Perhaps you don't get many guests for dinner, brother?" Carlos gave Lazarus a half smile enjoying the moment.

"It seems we have more to talk about." Lazarus sat back in his chair.

Another half-smile angled across Carlos' face. "I hope you don't mind my calling you brother, since I can't imagine calling you Father."

The sound of a car pulling up to the house stopped both men. Carlos rose to leave.

"I hope you will come back next week for another dinner." Lazarus offered.

Surprising himself, Carlos answered, "Perhaps I will."

"You know where I live. I'll ask one thing of you."

"And what is that?" said Carlos.

"Leave the residents alone." Lazarus put his hands together in the prayer shape and nodded his head.

"It won't matter." Carlos walked away, munching on his Valhrona.

The Shade slid out the front door, skipped down the three steps, past the paint cans and the ratty lawn. He slid into his waiting pink car. Jao, Singh, and he drove off escorted by the omnipresent breeze of the Sao Paulo night. Jao drove the car straight back to the favela.

"Well?" Jao voiced the question for the group.

"Well nothing. We're done for the night." Carlos ended all discussion.

"That was Lazarus," Singh announced to no one in particular.

"Yeah," Carlos said flatly.

"Shade, 'THE' Lazarus! His shit's everywhere. He's the savior guy," Jao chimed in.

"It's noise. More crap that doesn't do anything real for anybody." Carlos said the words, but he realized some doubt had crept inside them. "Now shut the hell up the both of you. We're done."

By now, both Jao and Singh recognized when Carlos's mood turned dark. Silence clamped down on them. Jao dropped Carlos on a corner in Heliopolis as the crew dissolved back into their separate lives for the week.

The following Sunday, Carlos again showed up for dinner with his brother.

"Won't matter." The Shade dropped a non sequitur on the dinner table.

"Carlozinho, why so hopeless?"

"Another drop of water in a bucket of overflowing vomit. I'm the Shade." Carlos wormed around in his chair.

"So I've been told."

"Is your father alive?" Carlos spit out still rustling in his chair.

"No. Your mother is," came Lazarus' reply. He hoped that by bringing up Carlos' mother, perhaps he'd see a trace of emotion.

"Yep," was Carlos' expressionless return.

They sat staring at each other, each one observing the other's differences. Someone brought food, and Carlos scooped a small helping. They ate mostly in silence. Carlos spent the meal holding down his gurgling well of emotion. His stomach began an Olympic scaled gymnastic routine, flipping over itself trying to hold down his dinner. Twisting with frustration and desperation, he realized he had to tell somebody. Why not his brother—even if they weren't truly blood, or, at most, half-blood? When it finally bubbled out, he thought it would take his brother by surprise.

He leaned back from the table, pushing his plate away. "I'm fucked. I have gotten myself tangled up in so many ways I can't find my way out."

"I know why you left home." Lazarus said.

"You mean your home."

Lazarus acknowledged, "You are not alone in that feeling of despair."

"That's the wise advice you have for me; all your education, all your wisdom, Lazarus Knows? Knows shit. I can't call Daddy or Mommy, to help me run away and hide. I'm fucking trapped." Carlos sat back in frustration.

"You're angry because I'm not offering you a magic pill? Your state of mind is your own making."

Lazarus looked unflinchingly at his half brother. "The world is broken in so many places. It's hard to find the loose ends and even begin to put anything back together again. All we can do is pick up one piece at a time. There is no deliverance except through our own force of will."

Facetiously Carlos muttered, "Much better sermon," meaning he felt no better at all. He couldn't give two shits about the world or anyone else unless they wandered onto his path. "What the fuck do I do with that?"

"Work with me. Together we will change everything."

"You and me? Together?"

"Of course, Carlozihno. We are brothers."

"To change everything?" Carlos had to repeat the request out loud to verify that it had truly been offered.

"Time slides away from us each day." The priest then folded his arms and hands together resting them on the dinner table.

The infamous Shade pondered his brother, the famous Jesuit, from two perspectives. He viewed himself as a reluctant, even the accidental populist militant. He had wandered into a role he never sought, but he understood and accepted that violence was the way to provoke the powerful into action. True, simply provoking accomplished very little other than attention and, a steep and certain demise. Carlos rarely encountered a glimpse of his higher self, but hoped it was still there buried beneath the years of rubble he'd created. Maybe, he thought, Lazarus truly had presented a feasible offer for survival.

True to form, the rose-tinted thought lasted a split millisecond, then vanished, overtaken by his own survival instincts. They were brothers by proximity and nothing else. Carlos' overriding needs trumped absolutely everything in view. He needed help extracting himself from the collapsing box he had built over the past two years. Wearing his 'brother' hat, Carlos now stared at Lazarus, convinced that this priest did not understand whom he had invited to the party. Carlos hesitated long enough to project a sympathetic air for Lazarus to latch onto. Of course, if Lazarus Knows… then maybe he truly did know. Carlos knew his options narrowed everyday. There was always a bigger bomb blast, another injustice, another "Dot" appearing to jab and goad him places he was sick of going. Here, across the table from him, emerged a perfectly viable option to disappear for self-preservation. Stuck and conflicted in his mind, he paused for a flash awaiting his spinning moral compass to find true north. Lacking the magnetic center he could never grasp, he found himself nodding.

"We don't make changes the same way." Carlos offered one final out for his brother.

"We will," countered the hopeful Jesuit. "It can all work out."

"Everything works out eventually. A hurricane dies down, an earthquake stops, and bombs blow things the fuck up. Cleanup is the thing,"

Carlos said. He only had a thimble of faith in Lazarus, but lacking a better option he asked, "What do I need to do?"

"I will continue to do what I am doing, and you will stop doing what you are doing. When you do, come back."

"Up to me. I get it." Carlos eyed the door.

"Oh Carlozinho, one small detail. Come back, but not this week. I'm heading out of town."

"It would never be this week, brother. What's out of town?"

"Tennis with an old friend in Botucatu."

"Hah! You? Sports?" Carlos knew Lazarus hated athletics of any kind.

"This is more about friendship."

Carlos smiled, stood, and walked out.

"He needs time," thought Father Lazarus Greve. "He'll screw you without blinking," the pragmatic voice of his father rose up from the depths of memory.

Shade marched out of the house into the waiting car. Jao sat behind the wheel. Carlos' first thought urged him to forget the whole thing. A clean exit from his life was fantasy bullshit. He flashed back to the last words from the Shadow, 'life is unpredictable, be aware." His inner slide show displayed an Imax image of his lifeless mentor lying in a pool of blood, neck filleted ear-to-ear. He recalled the Shadow's first lesson, 'Fuck the fuckers that fuck you before they fuck you again!' He grew angry with himself for the careless moment of wishful optimism.

Jao's anxious, impatient stare brought him back to reality. "So?" Jao prompted.

Carlos organically retreated to form. "We've got some things to work on. Drop me off and come back at eight tomorrow."

Carlos spent the following day sleeping since he planned on a late night ahead. Jao and Singh showed up at eight, as requested. They spent the next four hours building two bombs—one for Embratel, the dominant Brazilian telephone carrier, and one for the behemoth power company Paulista Electric. Over the past two years, Carlos had become quite the master of homemade bombs. A healthy fear of death by accidental explosion kept both Jao and Singh from developing the same level of craft Carlos prided himself on.

Despite their obvious lack of zeal, Carlos still spent much of his time teaching his techniques to the reticent ham-handed members of his group.

Tonight's special included two of his favorites: the Painter's Delight, and the Nurse's Aid. His penchant for nicknaming his creations somehow separated him from the violent consequences of their use. Carlos truly enjoyed his explosions. It relieved his frustrations, ventilated his anger, and reinforced his mantra to pay back those forces responsible for so much social misery. In his opinion, he and his brother were not that different. After the rush of adrenaline that accompanied each explosion, Carlos found himself engulfed by a strange serenity of accomplishment. It remained the only time he enjoyed feeling heroic and at peace. But that ended right after the flash died down. He had never caused personal harm, only property damage.

The men quietly opened the trunk of the Mary Kay Mercedes and pulled out the makings for the Painter's Delight. Jao and Singh planned to place the bomb at the front door of the Embratel building. A Painter's Delight required a fairly decent amount of time to build. Combo bombs usually took a bit longer than straight-ahead explosives. The group easily acquired the needed supplies from the local hardware store, any pharmacy or, in this case, family and friends.

Shade took a grape jelly sized glass jar and filled it with paint remover. Carlos had seen and snagged a bottle of it off the porch of Lazarus' halfway house where it sat next to the cans of paint. The next step called for dropping a CO_2 cartridge into the jar. Jao was not the most fastidious craftsman. He fumbled about, spilling one ingredient onto another in a haphazard lackadaisical fashion, trying Carlos' patience.

"God damn it Jao, you dumb ass! How many times do I need to tell you the same thing? Put your gloves on when you do that shit." Carlos religiously donned his Dr Jekyll white lab coat, a pair of gloves and goggles, when constructing his bombs.

Jao looked up, spilling some gunpowder on his t-shirt in the process. He brushed it off casually, shrugged his shoulders, and continued working. He tamped down some gunpowder like a Starbuck's barista preparing a double shot of espresso.

"Here's the fuse." Carlos handed Jao a thick piece of duct tape.

Jao jammed the whole thing together wrapping it with still more duct tape until it looked like a Jumbo hot dog on a stick.

"Here you go." Jao handed the whole mess back to Carlos.

While depositing the lethal packet into the Grape Jelly bottle, Carlos' mind pondered his encounter with Lazarus. What a hopeless waste of effort. Changing everything without relying on action seemed bleak and ultimately futile to him. Lazarus spent his time dwelling on small hopeless people caught in the jaws of an inevitable future. His own self-reflection didn't travel very far. The salient fact that Carlos spent his time blowing up corporate lobbies and glamorous designer storefronts rated, in his own mind, as the more evolved choice.

Carlos suddenly scratched his head and paused. A giant question mark materialized in his mind. He countered his own self-contempt by citing his own headlines—'Shade Protects!' Graffiti never lied. Somewhere welling up from years ago, the small kid who threw the rock at the priests' windshield knew the uncertainty was authentic. His road was truly coming to an end. The end, as Carlos resolutely defined it, would arrive on his own terms, at a time of his choosing.

Carefully checking its seal, Carlos gently secured the volatile capsule inside the Grape Jelly bottle leaving just enough fuse dangling over the rim to light and run. He sealed the whole mess with still more duct tape.

"Done," he proclaimed. "Jao, be very careful with this shit. Pack it in the trunk and get your ass back here."

They spent the next hour and a half building the Nurse's Aid. Sao Paulo was virtually carpeted by discarded two liter plastic bottles, since Coke remained the go-to drink of choice for most Paulistas. Carlos didn't need to warehouse much, since anytime he wanted to create a Nurse's Aid the starting materials were left lying on the roadside at every turn.

A bottle of hydrogen peroxide, a battery, a hammer, and a one-penny nail would do the trick for the Nurse's Aid. After another hour of assembly, the flash bomb was ready. Carlos withheld some of the additional materials and wrapped them in aluminum foil.

Handing the coke bottle over to Jao, he said, "Put the bottle in the trunk. I'll hold onto this stuff." Carlos put the foil contents in the front pocket of his work pants.

"Why are you holding onto that?" Jao asked.

"Because if I pour this shit into the bottle right now and hand it to you, in about 15 seconds, your hands will blow off." Jao took the bottle at arms length and nodded. Carlos began cleaning up the workspace and getting ready to leave.

"Grab Singh and meet me at the car."

He got to the car where Singh and Jao had finished loading the equipment, which also included a gas can, Vaseline, and the ubiquitous duct tape stacked in the trunk. A third man helped them load: Phillipe. Singh caught the death stare from Carlos and backed away.

"The fuck's he doing here?" Carlos barked at Jao.

"Like you said, we were short one. He just left the house Shade. He called, and we picked him up. What's the difference?"

"Get away from the car and get the fuck outta here." Carlos stalked towards Phillipe as Singh gathered some rarely seen backbone and moved into his path.

"Shade, we need two-man teams. Dot's gone. Come on, he's a good kid and he's got an arm."

Carlos did not mention Lazarus' request, but he told himself he'd send the kid back in the morning. He glared at the young man. "Get in, shut up, and do what you're told."

Phillipe slid silently into the backseat of the car next to Singh.

They drove into the city. By three in the morning, Shade, Jao, Singh, and Phillipe pulled over on Avenida Santo Amaro; three blocks away from the office of Embratel, the State-owned Telephone Company in Vila Olimpia. Around the corner from Embratel on Avenida Estados Unido sat the brand new Paulista Electronica store. The place sat filled to the gills with the latest electronic games and Japanese televisions from Sony, Panasonic and Mitsubishi—a geek's paradise.

The streets were deserted and silent. A faint breeze with a hint of ocean curled around the four men. The Shade whispered his instructions.

"Singh, you're with me." His gaze shifted to Jao. "Take the kid and the Painter's delight to the Embratel building. At exactly 3:20 break the front window, light the fuse, and get the hell out of there. Get the car and meet us in front of Paulista by 3:30. You got it?"

"No problem, Shade."

"Repeat it back to me." Carlos glared at the nonchalant Jao.

"Come on Shade, Paulista by 3:30. We'll be there."

Jao waved Phillipe out of the car and moved to the trunk. Carlos and

Singh grabbed the Nurse's Aid and walked silently away towards the electronics store. Jao pulled a brick out from beneath the spare tire and placed it on the curb.

"Kid, take that Vaseline and rub it all over this jar." Jao handed the grape jelly bottle to Phillipe. Phillipe filled his hand and smeared a healthy quantity of it all around the outside of the jar.

"Like this?" Phillipe whispered, holding the bottle up.

"Perfect, now hold it out over the curb for a second." Jao took out the five gallon gas can opened the lid and poured a healthy amount of gasoline over the bottle, dousing both the bottle and Phillipe's hands in the process.

"Dry off your hands and let's go." Jao put the can back into the trunk, then shut the lid.

He picked up the brick. Phillipe handed the bomb to Jao, drying his hands off on the back of his faded Bob Marley T-shirt as they both headed around the corner to the Embratel building. It was now 3:18 am. Two minutes to go. Still no one on the street, they approached the darkened building.

"Listen kid, this needs to go like lightening. I'll break the window, you light that fuse, and throw it through." Jao assumed the mantle of resident expert.

"No worries, I'll make sure it goes in." Phillipe pulled a small white Bic lighter out of his pocket and got set to light the duct tape fuse leaning out of the bottle. His hands settled deep into the thick layer of gasoline covered Vaseline as he tried to get a good throwing grip.

"Hey," Jao grinned as he spoke, yet still delivered a dead serious piece of advice, "move your ass like you just broke out of jail, 'cause when this thing blows it's mother-fucking Mardi Gras times 10,000!" Jao grabbed his brick and took one look over his shoulder, "Light it!"

Phillipe flicked his Bic lighter and lit the fuse while Jao wound up and threw the brick from ten feet away straight into the eight by eight plate glass window. He winced in anticipation of the shattering glass. The brick flew towards the pane with a slight tumbling rotation like a split fingered fastball. It hit the window making a perfect hole the size of, well the size of a brick. No more, and definitely no less. Seconds ticked away.

Phillipe had a lit fuse and an about to explode grape jelly jar ready to rock with no place to throw it.

"Holy shit!" screamed Jao.

Phillipe was frozen.

"Chuck it!" he screamed at Phillipe.

"Where?" Phillipe ran up to the hole in the glass and tried to stuff the bomb through the small sized hole.

"It doesn't fit!" He panicked trying to force the jar through the uneven cracked glass hole.

The Vaseline created a highly undesirable suction affect on his hand as he scraped it against the cut glass in an increasingly desperate effort to free himself and run like hell. The sharp edge of the glass compounded his problems by slicing a thin layer of skin off his palm, adding a gush of blood to the now consumed in flame Grape Jelly container. He kicked a larger hole in the glass and dropped the bomb in. Jao was already tearing ass away from the escalating nightmare.

Phillipe's Vaseline covered, bloody hand now blew up in white-hot flame as the gasoline covering the jar ignited on his hand as well. Finally freed from the jar, he began to bolt away from the window, wiping his hands on his shirt to put out the flame. He forgot that his shirt had been pre-soaked in gasoline from preparing the bomb. Now it too exploded into blue flame. Phillipe was a human torch, screaming in agony and only ten feet from the window. On cue the whole thing exploded in a dazzling mushrooming fireball. The explosion blew straight out of the Embratel office carrying deadly shards of glass, micro-missile cross pen desk sets, pieces of furniture and touch-tone telephone parts hurling directly towards poor flaming Phillipe. Mercifully, he was gone in a split second consumed by the mass of destruction.

Jao had run far enough away to turn, watch and weep. The nineteen-year-old boy lay dead and burning. Falling glass shards peppered his stilled body lying a short fifteen feet from the now burning Embratel office suite. Jao sprinted for the car, hearing alarms and approaching sirens sounding in the distance.

Carlos and Singh heard the blast and saw the flash. They picked up their walking pace and soon stood silently alone in front of Paulista Electronics. Confidently, they assumed that all had gone well. Carlos looked at his watch, 3:21 am. Close enough. They had nine minutes to do their jobs and meet Jao with the car. As the sirens sounded in the distance, Carlos reached into his front pocket and pulled out the aluminum foil wrapped package. The Nurse's Aid was just about ready.

"Singh," Carlos commanded, "open the top of the bottle and get ready to hand me the cap."

Singh carefully unscrewed the cap from the two-liter plastic Coke bottle. He placed it down on the sidewalk between them. As Carlos began pouring powder into the bottle, Jao wheeled around the corner, slamming to a stop and simultaneously opening the rear drivers' side door.

"Get in. Now!" His eyes were wide and his skin was white.

Carlos immediately stopped what he was doing, poured out the contents of the bottle and calmly walked to the driver's side door of the car.

"Move over and take a breath. Singh, get in the other side." Carlos kept his cool, noticing Phillipe was not in the car. He drove off slowly and began weaving his way back towards Heliopolis.

"He's dead?" Shade was dry and emotionless.

Jao, was taking rapid breaths, but trying to contain himself by gathering his words.

"The god damn window. It's my fault." He struck the dashboard with the palm of his hand.

"You're probably right. Now tell me what happened. Everything you can remember." Carlos needed to form a Plan B, his least favorite exercise.

Jao unraveled the death of Phillipe over the course of the next half hour. Both Singh and Carlos remained quiet. Carlos listened, but also flipped over the options in his head. In the meantime he changed course. They headed north following the ocean breeze far out of the city.

"Where are we going?" asked a nervous Jao.

"North," answered Carlos.

Carlos kept his cool, figuring the unfortunate death would take its place in the long line of unsolved Sao Paulo crimes. The overwhelmed, understaffed police force would mark this down as an act of vandalism gone horribly wrong and perpetrated by a recent parolee. Carlos could easily envision the neatly typed report making its way down institutional green hallways for the various signatures, investigators, on-scene officer, coroner, Chief of the Watch. It would then finally come to rest on a crowded basement shelf in the euphemistic dustbin that passes for the records department. Most likely it would merit a single line in the local paper. But, it might not. It might bring the inevitable much, much, closer to the Shade. Lacking other options, he drove east on Sao Paulo Highway 280 towards Botucatu.

What deeply troubled Carlos certainly had little to do with the Sao Paulo Police force. Not even close. Lazarus troubled Carlos. His decision now made, he'd have to make it work at least for a while. First things first, Lazarus would have to be told about Phillipe. He had not exactly given his word; still, the kid had died, so he owed an explanation. After years without family, Carlos felt a certain comfort in reconnecting with the brother that he was never close to, resented, yet also admired. Lazarus remained the only link to the innocence of his childhood. He told himself that it would all be sorted when he got there.

After an hour of driving, he pulled into a PetroBRas station for gas. He walked over to the payphone dropped, some coins in, and waited. The early morning phone jarred Lazarus awake.

"Yes?" Greve answered in a groggy voice.

"Lazarus, it's me." Strange that after so many years apart an affinity still existed between them. Too tenuous to be a traditional bond between brothers, still something held onto each of them.

"Carlohino," His spirits perked up at the sound of Carlos' voice. "It's very early."

"I know, sorry about that."

"Will I see you this week?"

"I'm not sure."

Lazarus detected something. "What's going on?"

No sense in putting off the news. "Phillipe's dead. I'm sorry. It was an accident."

Lazarus sat up in his bed. He bowed his head, saying a silent prayer for Phillipe, "I asked you to leave him be, Carlohino."

Like a cornered cat, the hackles on the back of his neck rose up, "I never gave you my word on that. People make their own decisions in this life. They do what gets them through. I've been trying to tell you that."

"It's true, you never did give me your word." He paused in silence, holding the phone. "He was so young."

Carlos' anger emerged. His feelings of neglect welling up and reaching terminal velocity then reigniting like one of his flash bombs. "So was I! So are an entire shitload of us who need other choices besides the ones we've got!"

Lazarus heard the desperation in his tone. An emotion that repeated itself in virtually all of the residents inhabiting his small colorfully painted rest stop perched on the cliff of the Heliopolis abyss.

"I'm so tired of hearing the same things over and over. None of this serves the Greater Glory of God. Carlohino, I am failing."

"Forgive me Lazarus, but that's hilarious coming from you. You're a priest. You've given your life to God. I'm a larcenous, thieving militant who just got a teenager killed for no good reason," Carlos countered, surprising himself with the declaration.

"Carlohino, where are you?"

"On my way to Botucatu."

"You know I am headed there today too. There's a place—the Iguaçu Café. Wait there."

"Lazarus, I think I can help you."

Carlos laid the phone back on its hook, paid the station attendant for the gas, and headed back to the car. He reached into his front pocket and pulled out a wad of money as he opened the passenger side doors front and back. Leaning down, he addressed both Singh and Jao succinctly and tersely. "Here." He handed them the wad of bills. "Now get the hell out. Life is changing."

Two deer stuck in the headlights of consequences.

Jao became furious. "Fuck you Shade!"

"No Jao, I get it." Singh's simplicity helped him understand the way of things.

"This is bullshit!" Jao's temper rose.

Carlos dove towards Jao, who shrank back, fearing he was about to be throttled by the merciless Shade. Instead, Carlos reached past Jao, pulling the keys from the ignition and dangling them in front of the two men. "Take the car then, and I'll take back the money."

"Deal." Jao handed the bills over and Carlos tossed the keys to Singh as his final insult.

"Yes! I am driving." Singh appeared content with the parting arrangements and hopped around to the drivers' side. He sat down, immediately adjusting the seat to his measurements.

"We're good." Not a question, but a definitive statement of dissolution by the Shade.

"Gone." Jao rolled up his window and shut the passenger door.

The Shade began to walk away from the vehicle when a final thought occurred to him. He turned back to the car and knocked on Jao's window. Jao rolled it down as Shade stuck his head in, spoke briefly, then took the wad of cash in his pocket back out. He peeled a few bills off the roll, crunched them back in his pants, and handed the rest to Jao. The car pulled out of the PetroBRas heading back to Sao Paulo. Shade stood and watched.

Not long before Simon touched down in Rio de Janiero, Carlos dos Reis, following a new strategy of duck and cover, locked in with the Jesuit priest. He had declared his independence from all that came before. Sort of...

Chapter 15. | Doris Day parking

Monday morning, eight thirty sharp, Bruce LeVitta arrived at the Maytag headquarters in downtown Sao Paulo. He was fired up and ready to coach his raw recruit on the Maytag value train to success. Coach LeVitta opened the double doors expecting to find his protégé eagerly awaiting day one. Striding through the door, chin held high, shoulders back, chest out, the first thing he noticed, a millisecond after realizing he was in the process of falling, was the Aeron chair placed directly in front of the door jamb. LeVitta, the former mediocre left tackle from Texas A&M, hit the plush carpet with a bounce.

Damn, he silently scolded himself. I should have seen that. Rolling onto his knees, he looked to see if anyone saw the embarrassing fall. "Hello? Hello?" He scanned around the offices from his kneeling position, "Bom dia?" Silence. The office looked unkempt. Not bad, but certainly not what he expected. He scribbled on his mental notepad to have a conversation with Rita or Carmen—whatever the hell her name was—about this condition; clearly unacceptable for Maytag. A few chairs were knocked over, some blinds hanging out of kilter. Walking towards the back wall of offices, he ran across Bolo laying on the floor with two darts lodged an inch deep in each side of his neck.

"Bolo! Get up, man." He grabbed a hold, not gently, of Bolo's shoulders and tried to shake him awake. "Bolo!"

Bolo's eyes slowly opened to see LeVitta inches from his face.

"itta ta?" said Bolo in his unique speech. Of course this meant 'Mister LeVitta.'

"Holy shit, Bolo, what happened here? Wait. Never mind. Don't speak. I never know what the hell you're saying anyway." He lifted Bolo up and scooted him over to a nearby desk. Then he grabbed a piece of paper and scrounged up a pen. "Write down what happened on this paper."

"K," slurred Bolo holding his head. He felt for the wobbling darts still resident in his neck.

An impatient and unsympathetic nurse, LeVitta hastily plucked the darts out and tossed them across the room. He pointed to the piece of paper, "Write, god damn it!" he commanded. "I'm calling the police."

"Ink O," came the nodding reply.

"I said I'm calling the police." LeVitta dismissed Bolo and headed towards the closest phone. He began dialing, then hung up just as quickly. He had no clue what to tell the police, so there was no point in calling. Bolo began writing in Portuguese while LeVitta impatiently paced next to him. Each pace brought LeVitta hovering over Bolo's shoulder waiting for him to finish.

"Portuguese?" LeVitta moaned, "Damn, why can't you write in English?"

Finally Bolo put the pen down. LeVitta tore the paper off the desktop. He began to read the scribbling, "What! What? What!? Now I'm calling the police."

He picked up the phone and re-dialed. Within an hour, the office had a fastidious coterie of Sao Paulo's finest snooping about. The lead detective, Jorge Rosado, a tall, fair complexioned guy with a pronounced Roman nose, looked mildly interested in the disappearance. He had larger issues on his plate.

As the officers methodically gathered evidence and took photos, LeVitta, sat impatiently in an office chair, his hypertension on the rise. "Whatever the hell happened here, and how soon can you get to the bottom of it? I sure as shit don't know what the hell has happened to Brazil, but this will not stand. My staff is in mortal danger. How many men will you be putting on this?"

Rosado remained calm and sterile. "Sir, I understand the concern. Sadly, we have many grave problems today. Did you see the bombing only a few blocks from here? We are plagued by bombings. Your American is only missing at this point, not dead. We have the Olympics coming."

It was the word 'concern' that triggered him. The subtle, diminutive, descriptor that Rosado employed lit LeVitta's fuse. He rose up from the chair, extending to his full six foot two height, placing him eye to eye with Rosado. "Detective, I don't give a dogs breakfast about your bombing, and I don't care about your Olympics. I don't care about your caseload. Not even a little. My man's been kidnapped! Kidnapped by one of your countrymen. I am an American; he is an American. WE, America, expect your best effort on finding this employee, starting right NOW."

Rosado winced at the display of arrogance, but kept his outer calm. He was not intimidated, "Because you are American you expect the Brazilian authorities to treat you differently? You say 'we' to represent your entire country? Sadly, this condescension does not surprise."

He may have been red faced and angry, but he also had the ability to size up a situation when it turned south. Realizing intimidation would not work in this case; LeVitta shifted his strategy to cooperation. He retrenched his position with a forced smile. "Have we just antagonized each other Detective?"

"I believe we have," half-smiled Rosado. "I understand you are upset. We will do our best for you. Do you have any suggestions as to who may have done this?"

"Yes. Did you read the report from my employee? Yesterday was his first day here, and it was a Sunday, for Christ's sake."

"Your employees work on Sunday. That is commendable, is it not?" Rosado's tone signaled his cynicism.

LeVitta may have been a hard ass, but he wasn't a dumb ass. "You're right. My fault he was in here on a Sunday, but that's not really relevant, is it?"

"Sadly, kidnappings are a regular occurrence in Sao Paulo regardless of day of the week. Looking around, there does not appear to have been excessive struggle. A few chairs knocked over, no signs of real violence. The doors were not forced open. Whoever came in was let in voluntarily. Often people simply want money. As you say, he is American, and you are an American company. Most likely someone will telephone a demand to your office. I suggest staying by the phone."

"Sergeant, I may have been born at night, but not last night. That's the action you are proposing? What about an investigation, what about a manhunt? You need to start a manhunt. Take some damn initiative, Sergeant." To LeVitta, waiting by the phone felt pointless and futile.

Mostly, he felt like a pussy. To a prideful ex-football player there could be no greater insult than feeling like a helpless girl.

Rosado, who was a Lieutenant, had trouble tracking LeVitta's liberal use of colloquialisms, so he mostly ignored them, "Mr. LeVitta, I am happy to have a manhunt if you tell me the man we are hunting? We will try to find some witnesses, and figure out where to go after we have gathered all of the evidence. Again, generally no harm comes in these cases, whether Brazilian or American. Your chances are probably better than if it was a Brazilian National they had taken." He smiled while circling his troops to leave.

LeVitta felt completely impotent. "What about your card? Don't I get a card with your number? Call me if you hear anything, that sort of thing?"

"Of course you are right." He turned, asking one of the junior investigators for his card. "Paolo, give me your card."

LeVitta fumed. "I want YOUR card. I don't want to call Paolo. Does Paolo even speak English?" He glared. "Paolo do you speak English?"

A friendly smile appeared on Paolo's nodding, dark Mestizo face. He was 5'3" and round, with a friendly face framed by large cheeks.

"Sadly, I do not have any of my cards left. I gave them out at the bombing we investigated yesterday over at Brazilian Telecom. What a mess that was. Paolo knows how to reach me. Simply call and ask for me. He understands that." Rosado shook LeVitta's hand and promptly walked out of the office doors.

"Paolo," LeVitta called his name. The officer stopped to look back at him. "Rosado?"

Paolo smiled, "Sure, why not," then he pointed to the vacant space once occupied by the now-departed Detective Rosado and signaled back to LeVitta with a thumbs up sign.

"Fantastic, really great. Thanks." LeVitta waved him off and sat back down in his chair with a blank look. He remained that way for quite a while, sifting through various scenarios in his brain. Bullshit, he thought. This cannot be happening. Not to me. The kid's dead. No, they want money. That's the way these things go, according to detective lame ass. I'll wait for the invariable phone call, then tear them a new asshole and get him back myself. These thugs don't know who the hell they are messing with.

"Didea," said Bolo who had walked up with a new completed statement in Portuguese.

"Huh? What's that supposed to mean?" LeVitta's nerves were frayed.

"Haga dea." Bolo shook his head from side to side.

He was trying to tell Bruce what a terrible idea it would be to screw with whomever took Hart. Bruce snatched the paper from Bolo's hands.

"I already read this. You got shot in the neck and don't remember seeing anything or anyone. Huge help. Didn't really need a rewrite."

Bolo motioned for him to read it again. LeVitta shrugged, grabbed the one sheet of paper to make another futile scan. He pulled out his pocket Portuguese-to-English dictionary a couple times for the first sentence alone. "Does that really say Willie Nelson?" Bolo nodded.

The phone rang. Bolo bounced over to the nearest desk phone and picked up.

"Ag?" That's all Bruce needed to hear. He leaped up grabbing the phone away from him.

"Bom Dia, this is Clara Nunes from the Brazilian Olympic Committee. May I speak with Hart please?"

"This is Bruce LeVitta. I'm the Country Manager. How can I help you?"

"Well, we received your written proposal for laundry services at the upcoming games and would like to discuss the matter in greater depth with a mind towards securing an agreement. Would this Thursday be convenient?"

Of course having zero knowledge Hart's bid LeVitta improvised, "Absolutely, we can make that work. Would you like to come to our offices, or shall we come to you?"

"I am happy to come to you. Our offices are in the Copan building and I see that you are virtually next-door. Would ten am work?"

"Perfect. Ten o'clock Thursday morning. I'll be there."

"You and the young man I spoke with yesterday?"

"You mean Hart. Absolutely. We'll be there, here, ready to go."

"Terrific. Bom dia."

With that, she hung up the phone. The call launched LeVitta's brain into a full barrel roll: me and the young man? In his mind he felt like a long-tail cat in a room full of rocking chairs. What else could happen? What did Hart get himself into in only twenty-four damn hours? Christ, he thought, I've got to find this kid. LeVitta dug into his pocket and pulled out the card for Paolo Girardo. Then he dialed the phone.

"Hallo?" answered the female voice.

"Rosado," demanded LeVitta.

The phone went silent.

"Rosado! Rosado!" impatiently yelled LeVitta.

"No," answered the monotone voice.

"What do you mean no? I say Rosado and you say okay, not no! That was the deal."

"Por que está tão rude?"

"Paolo? You're not Paolo? God Damnit! I need to speak with Paolo, not you."

A long sentence in Portuguese directed at LeVitta followed, "Eu só atender o telefone, Eu tapa que você deve. Empurrão!" Then, "Paolo, alguns DICK é sobre o telefone para você!"

"I know what that means! I know what that means. Who is this?" yelled a tirading LeVitta.

The loose translation, which LeVitta clearly understood, meant 'Paolo, some dick is on the phone for you!'

Paolo had left his phone on the counter of his favorite lunch stand Arabia's. Jasmine, the blonde haired, hook nosed chef, waitress, and proprietress had answered the phone as a courtesy for one of her regulars. Arabia's, one of many delectable lunch stands that dot the Sao Paulo landscape, occupied an exceptionally high traffic location. Jasmine Shehab had cannily planted herself next door to the executive headquarters of AES Eletropaulo. Plenty of people, with plenty of money, worked within footsteps of her food stand. Eletropaulo sat comfortably perched atop the energy industry mountain as the largest supplier in all of Latin America. More than sixteen million Paulistas paid them gazillions of Reals for doling out electricity to over five and half million homes, shacks or facsimiles thereof. If you've got an outlet in Sao Paulo, and want to charge your iPod, watch TV, turn on a light bulb, grab a cold one from your fridge, or talk on the phone, Eletropaulo's hand sat right next to your wallet.

Paolo had walked back to his squad car, gathering the loose change off the dashboard to pay for his falafel. As usual, the Arabia stools were filled with regulars—three suits, Rita the Eletropaulo receptionist, one new customer—a pale freckle-faced girl with spiked red hair. She hadn't ordered anything yet, and was just sitting, pondering the menu.

From Jasmine's description, Paolo knew exactly who waited on the other end of the phone. He shook his head, took a breath, and casually said, "Allo?"

"Paolo?" asked LeVitta.

"Si," as in, of course jerkoff you called my phone whom were you expecting.

"Ro-sa-do!" Syllabically punctuated an increasingly frustrated LeVitta.

"Sure why not," responded Paolo while grabbing his falafel off the counter and waving goodbye to Jasmine.

He folded his phone back into his jacket pocket without saying goodbye and walked back to his squad car. Paolo had lucked out and found Doris Day parking directly in front of Eletropaulo's double wide tinted glass doors. He hungrily raised the tahini sauce-dripping falafel up for that first mouth-watering bite. Sadly the sudden explosion sent both of Eletropaulo's steel framed glass doors bursting off their hinges directly into poor Paolo, his falafel, and his squad car. Paolo was instantly buried by the follow-on avalanche consisting of most of the contents of Eletropaulo's richly appointed entrance foyer. Paolo, the three people in the lobby paying their bills, and Rita, the fifty-year-old receptionist just back from lunch, were all gone in an instant. Arabia's survived the concussive blast without a scratch. The customers sitting on their stools, save one, had crammed themselves below the overhanging bar for cover. All except the new customer whom Jasmine observed casually walking away towards an incongruous luxury car with a conspicuously painted pink trunk.

When Detective Rosado showed up at the scene, he learned from a weepy Jasmine about the last phone call Paolo had received. He called Brazilian Telecom to have the number identified. He promptly phoned LeVitta back at the Maytag offices.

"About damn time you called me back," barked an irritated LeVitta.

"Why did you call Paolo?" Deadpanned Rosado.

"What kind of a stupid question is that? To get a hold of YOU! That's exactly what you told me to do." LeVitta, already on a short fuse, was burning down to his nub.

"Paolo is dead. A bomb."

With a barely discernable inflection of empathy LeVitta replied, "That's terrible and I am sorry, but what in Hades do I have to do with that? I've got some info for you on my man's kidnapping."

"I'll get back to you." Rosado, now moving on to bomb squad investigation, folded his phone back into his pocket and left LeVitta hanging.

LeVitta froze motionless for a second in disbelief. "Rosado? What the? That bastard hung up on me?"

Rosado walked back the few meters to the Arabia to get his bearings. Only then did he notice that the singed yet remaining side of the Eletropaulo building now sported a new piece of graffiti—LAZARUS SAVES.

LeVitta slammed down his phone and glared at Bolo. "Shit," he said to himself out loud. "Bolo, we're going to have to figure this out for ourselves."

Chapter 16. | Ten degrees

Hart woke up with a splitting headache and a titanium hard-on. He was in a full sweat, with a bursting bladder, and blurred vision as he hazily emerged from the tranquilizer.

He flashed on a lesson from Professor Segalove: "Remind yourself that all sentient beings have at one time been your mother." Imagine this and generate appreciation and goodwill for all sentient beings, whether they cut you off in traffic, compliment your smile, or shoot you in the neck with a tranquilizing dart for no sane reason that comes to mind.' Fortunately, this thought bubbled up into Hart's conscious mind right when he felt ready to clock someone. He struggled to prepare himself for the certain, upcoming confrontation. Remaining calm with a full bladder has its challenges.

Carmen burst into the room at the very moment he reached down to rearrange himself for comfort. "Hart, I'm so sorry about all this. He said he just wanted to talk to you. I didn't see the other guy at all."

"My bladder's about to explode," Hart prioritized: first things first.

"Okay," she said flatly, noticing his predicament.

She pointed over to a door in the high-ceilinged hangar-like structure they were sitting in. "Go through that door. Can I get you something to drink? Are you hurt?"

He tried to maintain his best Buddhist-inspired calm while remembering that Carmen or Simon could have been his mother at some point in time.

"Yes, I'm hurt, and yes, you can get me some goddamn water. It's a thousand degrees in here."

As Hart dizzily staggered over to what he hoped was a reasonable facsimile of a bathroom, Simon strolled in.

"Hey buddy! You look like shit. Sorry about all this," He said the words, but it sure didn't feel like an apology.

"My best friend Simon." A sarcastic Hart kept walking to the bathroom.

"Gotta take a piss, huh? Normal reaction I hear."

"I'm not laughing, Simon." Hart figured Simon was being smugly disingenuous.

"You only wanted to talk to him." Carmen veered herself over to Simon, who answered sheepishly, "I did. You don't know him. He's impulsive."

"Why shoot him?"

"That wasn't my idea at all. But now we're stuck."

Hart, still shaking off the affects of the tranquilizer, staggered to the bathroom door. A skanky brown stained toilet was anemically attached to the floor at a Tower of Pisa tilt. He helped himself while noticing a window in the room located over his left shoulder. Fortunately, Hart had a seemingly endless supply of urine, and a bit of his hard on left which allowed him to back away from the bowl, maintain a steady stream, and pry open the window—quite the acrobatic feat. Running from his best friend felt surreal, wrong, and absurdly unnecessary, yet, there he was contemplating the act.

Simon shouted from the main room. "It's all that unnatural sleep from the toxin. Bodily function ceases; urine builds up in the bladder. Makes you wanna piss like a racehorse."

"Shut the hell up Simon!" Hart yelled, stalling for time.

His hastily devised plan had him leaping out the window cued by the sound of the toilet flush. He got set, gripped the ledge, sucked in a charge of air hard to manage through his splitting headache, then kicked the lever down with his left leg. The water released, FLUSH! Channeling Jason Bourne, he ducked his head preparing to leap through the open window. At the exact moment when Hart realized his scheme was a cinema infused fantasy, and thoroughly pointless, Simon opened the bathroom door.

"Like I don't know how your mind works?" Simon stood perfectly still leaning, against the doorjamb.

"Really? Like I was going to overpower the guards and Vin Diesel my way out of this? That's ridiculous," he lied.

"Simon, that's incredibly rude!" Carmen watched in shock.

"Zip up dude. You're embarrassing the lady!" Not a hitch in his voice Simon smugly glanced at Carmen. The unflappable Simon standing there calm as can be with Carmen holding an eco friendly bottle of Brazilian Spring water.

Rationally, Hart knew there was no real threat of danger from his best friend, still he felt both powerless and enraged. "You know that right now what I truly want to do is rip out your left kidney. Not both, because I love you. But one down will screw up your dietary needs forever, and that works for me."

"There's no guards pal. Just us," Simon answered.

Carmen handed Hart the water bottle as he finally turned to zip up, "There's no place to go anyway. Whoa, that is a very nasty bruise on your forehead." She looked disapprovingly at Simon. "He needs to put something on that."

"Ice. Around the side." Simon pointed no doubt to some MASH unit he had on the other side of the hangar. Hart hadn't noticed the bruise, but that explained his headache and blurred vision.

"Oh yeah, I guess that must be from my desk catching my fall after you SHOT ME in the god-damn neck!"

"You've got a nasty welt right there too." He touched the side of Hart's neck sending him into a pain spasm.

"God damn it, that hurts." Hart winced. "Don't do that again." He shoved Simon away.

"It'll be fine in a couple days. Just don't touch it." Simon recognized the anger in Hart's eyes, "Buddy I can explain this."

"Where are we?" Hart demanded.

"Drink your water. It's important to stay hydrated in the tropics."

Hart unscrewed the top and slugged down half the bottle. At least Simon scored a point for seeming to care about his well-being.

"Funny thing about Brazilian Spring water," Simon begins his tale.

"The Idea for Brazilian Springs was conceived by a retired American living just a bit east of Sao Paulo in the town of Botucatu. His ex-wife was born in a town south of Sao Paulo called Curitaba. Curitaba was built on the bones of a huge Atlantic rain forest. It's all gone now. Wrecked by satellite dishes, furniture designers and Colonel Sanders. The same thing is on track to happen in the Amazon where, over the last fifty years, twenty percent of that forest has been vaporized. All of this destruction has drastically accelerated over the past five years."

"Tragic," Hart mocked. "And you are telling me this tale of woe because?" Hart could not figure out why Simon suddenly launched into a Save the Rainforest history lesson.

Simon ignored him. "Can we blame the average Jorge, Pao, or Gilberto for this? Not a chance. They are completely preoccupied with their own daily survival; whatever that takes. No different than the early years of the US. We can lay the responsibility for this on the greedy progress hounds who totally disregard the law and steamroll over this country like so many others. Strictly for profit."

"I don't work for the Discovery Channel, pal. I work at Maytag. Please promise me this leads somewhere I am going to care about."

Simon continued unfettered by the complaint, "This particular American business man felt hopeless about the situation. What could one man do about helping to save these rain forests? He and his wife moved back to Curitaba. Not only was he now living within the shadow of the rainforest, but he spent his days walking around on its cemetery: a foul predicament indeed. He sat down and came up with a serious plan to help protect and restore the 'lungs of the planet' to good health. His company donates at least 10% of their gross profit to this cause and certain others every year."

Hart is dumbfounded, "Wow, truly a great story of corporate generosity. Why don't I take some of that back to the folks at Maytag and see what we can do about gray water here in Brazil?"

"You're missing my point, Hart. I'm not talking about ecology."

"Is this about the Nazis? I knew it. They're behind this aren't they? Weren't you supposed to be down here tracking your Dad and NAZIS?"

Simon started walking towards the other side of the hangar. He motioned to his two guests with his arm as he walked away, "We have to go. I'm already running behind. I'm sorry, but I'll explain the rest on the way."

Taking in the surroundings, Hart now saw they were in a rural area next to a dirt landing strip. They could be anywhere in the proximate outskirts of Sao Paulo.

"I'm confused. How do you know Carmen?" Hart swiveled his head between the two. "Carmen, do you know Simon? What's going on?"

Carmen and Hart followed Simon around the side of the building revealing a small high wing airplane sitting alone on the packed dirt surrounding the hangar. It looked old, and frail, with chipped paint, and balding tires. Hart noticed some of the rivets were popped, rusted, and even missing.

"Is this safe?" Carmen looked at Simon, then at Hart.

Hart's eyes darted back and forth, "You do know him!"

"It's complicated, but yes, I know Simon is your friend. Believe me, I had no idea about the rest of this, and especially not the other guy."

"What other guy?" Hart was in the dark about what seemed like an infinite amount of things. He desperately wanted to start peeling the onion.

"You've met him," Simon tossed out, "you just don't remember. We'll sort that out later. We're really running behind." Simon began walking around the airplane. He opened the pilot side door, reached in and flipped a switch. A humming sound started. Then the flaps of the airplane descended along the inside of each wing.

"This thing's a piece of shit." Hart followed Simon walking around the plane, scanning the hull and landing gear.

"It's not safe then?" Carmen looked fearful.

"Hell no, it's not airworthy! Simon, tell me you know how to fly a plane now?" Hart said this with some historic authority.

"You're not the only one experiencing big changes. Climb in."

"No way. Why do you need me?" Hart pleaded with his friend in disbelief.

"In all seriousness, Hart, buddy, you're in no danger. I promise. Now get in. This isn't about you, it's about bigger things."

Simon opened the creaking passenger side door revealing a yellowing, ripped fabric interior and four seats. Hart recognized the airplane as a Cessna 182—the classic flying station wagon. He got his pilot's license before his driver's license. That's what a former Air Force flight instructor father will do for you, but Hart hadn't flown in years. Teaching tennis never provided a wealth of disposable income to pay for such luxuries. He had learned to fly in a smaller version of this plane, a Cessna 172. Carmen climbed into the back seat, as Hart folded himself into the co-pilot's seat and buckled up.

"I needed to talk to you." Simon said in a serious tone while fastening himself into the left seat.

"About spring water?" replied an exasperated Hart.

Simon tuned Hart out while busily attending to the airplane's checklist. He quickly flipped through a series of plastic enclosed pages.

"Telephone, post card, email, appointment? Are you opposed to traditional forms of communication? I wrote to you."

Simon smiled at Hart. "I got your letters. You didn't sound so good. It was a good idea for both of us that you came down here."

Simon now voiced the checklist aloud, "Circuit breakers in, master on, fuel pump, mixture rich, ignition switch, turn."

The plane choked, rumbled, backfired, and spit itself to life. Once the engine actually kicked over, it sounded smooth and powerful, contrary to its external appearance. Simon checked the oil pressure as the sparse but basic instruments spun to life. The compass tracked to their facing direction—southwest at two hundred twenty compass degrees. Hart made a mental note of the direction hoping for a clue to their position relative to Sao Paulo. They had no headsets so the deafening noise level stunted virtually all conversation.

Simon swung the plane around began a taxi over to a dirt strip running east to west. Hart scanned the gauges, noticing the fuel read roughly half full for each wing tank. He figured at that level they couldn't be going too far. Certainly no more than two hours. The weather was hot and blue with a few scattered clouds drifting about the sky. Simon positioned the airplane on the runway facing east. A small windsock fluttered with a breeze from the same direction.

"Where are we going?" Hart screamed over the engine roar.

Simon smiled, and shouted back, "We're going to meet a couple friends of mine. You'll like them."

Hart watched his oldest friend at the controls. Here they both were together as if no time has passed. If only for a split second, Hart felt like they were both back on the tennis court, knowing Simon was about to rip a huge American Twist serve, pulling the opposition off the court. The guy would be lucky just to stab at the ball leaving, Hart with a sitting duck put away at the net. The ball one-bouncing its way to the back fence, he'd turn around to see Simon smiling; that same smile.

The plane easily lifts off the ground. After a slight bank to the right they head southwest. Ten minutes later, they pass by a couple Stay Puft marshmallow clouds to reach a cruise altitude of thirty five hundred feet. Hart turns his head to check the back seats. Carmen leans against the pilot's side window; feeling his glance she turns with wide eyes and raised eyebrows. She looks frightened and uncertain. Check that; she might be angry and frustrated. What the hell, thought Hart, she might be out-of-her-mind ecstatic. He realized he hadn't clue one to the mystery box of Carmen's emotional library. He made a snap decision that Carmen felt as violated and pissed off about the whole cascade of events as he did. Another moment passed and Hart knew he had conjured up a weak fantasy simply to soothe his fears. Yielding to reality, he finally settled on the one absolute truth: he didn't know shit about shit. He returned his gaze to straight ahead and remained silent watching Simon focus on flying the plane.

After an hour plus a few minutes they begin a slow descent for a suddenly materializing mountain top runway. Simon dropped a notch of flaps. The airplane slowed as they began a descent for landing. Simon banked the plane left, as they turned straight towards the runway. They slowly, gently, drifted down towards the packed dirt strip. Simon focused his gaze on keeping them pointed straight ahead for landing. It was all very green and lush, with a small town coming into view off the right wing. The plane glided over the runway threshold. Simon turned to Hart as he suddenly took his hands off the yoke and the smile appeared again.

"You got it from here, pal." He folded his hands on his lap completely relaxed.

Hart flashed into immediate panic, "Shit." He grabbed the yoke and ping-ponged his head from Simon to the runway. "What the hell are you doing? I haven't flown for years."

"It's like riding a bike, dude. You'll remember."

Hart clutched the throttle and pulled back the power. Reaching back in his memory he then began to pull back the yoke to flare the airplane and get it on the ground. He pulled too hard. They ballooned up in the air, which shook Carmen who began an immediate internal review of her life on earth. Her eyebrows rose up traveling past her forehead in the shock of seeing Hart at the controls.

"What's going on? Are you crazy?" Carmen blurted out to Simon.

"Relax, he knows what he's doing. Don't you Hart?"

The plane continues merrily floating down the runway, which, as in all things, has a serious endpoint in the form of a sheer cliff.

Hart does not answer. Internally, Harts sensory recall frantically scans through his parking garage for a useable pilots handbook. All the while, the runway beneath the plane continued to diminish. Gaining his wits, Hart managed to stabilize the float. Pulling gently on the yoke he re-flared the airplane holding it off, off, off the runway until it firmly, and mercifully, plopped down on the dirt, with just enough braking room left to stop twenty feet short of Gods final end zone.

"Nothing like an adrenaline rush to find your focus," Simon smirked.

Still clutching the yoke, now in relief, Hart puffed, "Hilarious. At least I know you've still got your warped sense of humor." Simon taxied the idling plane over to an empty field next to the runway, and shut down the engine. A waiting jeep driven by an older, eightyish man, rolled up to meet them beside the plane.

"Hart, I'd like you to meet a friend of mine." Simon hopped out of the plane, and walked over to the jeep helping his friend out of the driver's seat. Hart followed.

"Meet former German Army medic, Humanities professor, and tennis player Raymond Gil. Gil, meet my oldest and best pal, Hart. You guys have very little in common other than me."

"Nice of you to come," offered a very prim and proper Gil.

"I'm not here voluntarily, so I'm not sure how nice it is to meet you right now." Hart replied skeptically.

Gil demonstrated not an ounce of surprise at the sarcastic greeting, "I completely understand your attitude, young man. I might add, I too, am surprised to see you."

"Can I get out?" Carmen started to fold herself out of the back seat.

"Stay put!" shouted Simon.

Turning to Simon and within complete earshot of Gil, Hart let loose, "I thought you were here to hunt down characters like this, not hire them as limo drivers."

"Not a real Nazi," Simon answered, before turning back to Gil, "That went well." He ushered Gil into the back seat next to Carmen.

"Simon, I've got a job down here I barely started. When are you going to tell me what this is all about?" Hart said.

"Come on man, isn't it enough to spend some quality time with me? Besides, work is not what you're down here for. I'm doing you a favor."

Everyone folded back into the plane. Simon raced through the checklist again, fired up the engine then taxied back out to the strip for takeoff. Every time Hart turned around to check on Carmen, Raymond Gil offered him what he believed to be a supercilious smile. Hart's inner cynic wondered, "What are you smiling about Nazi?" He stopped looking behind him after one more glance netted him yet another creeper smile. His nerves bubbled out as anger and frustration. After another thirty minutes in the air Simon let go of the yoke again and motioned for Hart to maintain the course and fly the plane. Hart flipped him off, and folded his arms in protest. Carmen and Gil went silent in the back seat.

Hart looked over at his buddy. "Cut all the shit and tell me what's up?"

"It's not about telling you anything. It's about showing you," Simon shouted back over the engine noise.

Both of them go silent. Ten minutes later things changed. Again.

The Lycoming O-470 225 horsepower engine let loose a brief stutter. Hart believed only he heard the misstep since both Gil and Carmen were asleep. The reduced level of oxygen at high altitude makes most people drowsy. For a brief moment, Hart questioned his hearing, thinking perhaps he simply imagined the sound, until it happened again. This time more pronounced.

"Shit!" Simon blurted, as he immediately shifted his scan from horizon to ground.

Hart instinctively began a rapid scroll through his internal Pilot's Guidebook under 'Holy Shit' Emergency procedures. Grabbing hold of his wits before they bailed out and parachuted to safety, he quickly toggled the switch to change fuel tanks from the left wing to right wing. Both gauges read exactly the same as when they took off—half-full. Not expected, and definitely not good. Simon flicked both the left and right fuel gauges with his index finger. Waking from their nap, the gauges came to their senses sliding all the way to the left, like a well choreographed dance team exiting stage left—Empty and Empty. The engine sputtered again, and then, as both best pals knew it would, went dead silent. They both paused to ponder the options accompanied by the whisking sound of the powerless propeller.

"Old plane." Simon sheepishly offered, while continuing to scan the ground for a landing zone.

"Your plane." Simon gave Hart the yoke.

"Keep it. I trust you," Hart fired back surprising himself with the reflexive answer. The words blurted out too fast. They were based on an out of date thought from a joint history, which had taken an unforeseen, dramatic left turn.

"I got the prop." Hart called out, trying to reclaim some sense of control. He pulled on a blue Vernier adjustment knob sitting between two similar black and red knobs. This action feathered the propeller, which in theory, gave them a few more moments of flight.

Shockingly, Carmen was still sleeping, maybe from stress, lack of oxygen, panic shutdown, or how the hell should Hart know once again. Simon and Hart stuffed their panic, remaining outwardly calm, determined to rescue the situation. Josef Mengele, the sequel, appeared fast asleep too. Hart decided at that moment, when death rang his goddamn doorbell he sure as shit would not be sleeping. "Carmen," Hart twisted, and reached back shaking her, "Carmen! You've got to wake up! We need your eyes."

She groggily came to and noticed the quiet.

"Are we landing?" She glanced out her window, saw they were over jungle, realized the engine had gone silent, then did the math, "Merda! What do you need me to do?"

"Look for a place to land. Make it quick." Hart returned to his outside scan. They were descending from two thousand feet above ground level, and sinking at six hundred feet per minute. That amounted to roughly three minutes until Newton's inevitable consequence.

"Hart please take the plane for a minute." Like a Werewolf on his deathbed, changing back to human form, Hart's old friend Simon emerged. He grabbed the yoke.

"Over there, two o'clock, a river bank," Simon spotted it and pointed.

"That's hardly a river," Hart said looking at the projected landing spot. "More like a stream."

"You feel like debating body of water size right now?" Simon quipped.

Hart banked the plane directly towards the stream on a downwind. That is the opposite direction they needed to land. Simon went for the flaps.

"Don't even think about putting those down until we're on final."

Hart yelled, "God damn it Simon. Is this what you needed me for?"

"Uh, who should be flying this thing?" Carmen questioned Simon's decision for Hart to fly. Hart was thinking the same thing to himself.

"He's got more time than me." Simon glanced forward then turned around again to look at her now rigid, anxiety filled face. "Strap in tight and get ready to jump out quick when we're down."

The treetops got closer as they turned a slow base leg, descending at a faster rate. "Put the flaps down now," Hart commanded. "We might get some more lift."

Simon dropped the flaps and the plane perked up its nose. As it skimmed just above the tree line, a branch banged against the landing gear. Again, Hart pulled back on the yoke quickly giving them a momentary lift. He banked the plane, heading it straight down the gap between the trees and directly over the stream. Distance and elevation conspired to blur the line of perception. The closer they got to the ground revealed the true nature of the speed they were traveling. That speed, which seemed surrealistically slow and leisurely in the air, suddenly felt reckless and uncontrollable. Skirting down the streambed at seventy miles an hour, they drop out of the sky as aerodynamic as a Steinway grand piano falling from a ten-story building. Hart watched the terrain blur beneath them. He scanned ahead, and had a late realization that the stream looked deeper than he first thought. While he pondered the benefit of that realization, the airplanes fate slid further and further from his control.

They were committed to landing on whatever was down there. The muddy bank now passed by the windows of the little 182 in a distorted haze. Simon and Hart exchanged looks, not too different from the tennis court. Hart at the net, Simon serving, they both knew they needed a big serve at this point in the game to squash the opposition's momentum.

"So what do you think of Carmen?" asked Simon nonchalantly.

"Now? Kind of busy," answered Hart.

"We'll be fine," said a strangely calm Simon, "Bank or river?"

"River," Hart said, adding, "We need an ace here brother."

Simon got the message and smiled, "Turn up the burner."

"Santa mãe foda!" yelled Carmen as the Cessna drifted twenty feet off the water.

Both Simon and Hart pulled back on the yoke, holding it off as long as possible. Everyone heard the stall horn trigger, signaling the plane was about to abandon the air and slap down in the water. Would they flip, roll, skip, smash, live or die? It was all up for discussion in a silent pause.

The stall horn wails "beeeeep beeeeep beeeeep." The wheels hit the water and hydroplane for an instant. Hart relaxed for a micro moment. He felt an immediate sense of relief wash over him as they made it down to earth, and began rolling roughly over a shallow stream. He heard himself sigh "we made it," and exhaled a healthy portion of fear. Suddenly, the left side main gear caught a giant boulder and ripped clean off the plane. As the plane dipped into a spin the right wing hooked into an overhanging tree branch. The branch, operating like a Ginzu steak knife, cleanly sliced the wing loose from the fuselage. The wounded airplane careened into a swirling dervish, like a nauseating carnival ride, at forty miles an hour. Somehow, the plane avoided flipping, preferring the spin to the twirl.

The universally branded adjective for fear, hysteria, and general emotional upset, echoed through the plane like some Dolby surround sound IMAX experience. First hitting Hart's right ear—"SHIT!" then his left—"SHIT!" then his right again—"SHIT!" Like eye surgery, Hart felt his seat for the experience vastly exceeded his personal thrill seeking curiosity. The collective group scream created a panic inspired motet of profanity. Hart held down a rising vomit bubble, and remained strapped tight in his rattling seat. Seatbelts saved all of them from becoming rag dolls. The plane moaned and groaned as the chaotic, frenzied insanity slowly began to wind down. The now half dead plane, rose up on its one remaining main right-side gear, like a Hobie catamaran tenuously balancing on one pontoon threatening to tip over. At the peak of the lean, teetering between a tragic angry death, or a peaceful retreat, the plane chose salvation. It came crashing back down to rest on the amputated stump of its left-side landing gear.

All stop.

Silence.

Only the sound of rushing water, gasping breath and heartbeats thumping. Hart turned to see how everyone had fared. Simon sat panting for breath noticing a small cut on his left leg where it banged into the circuit breakers. Carmen was hyperventilating and weeping. Gil was silent and still, his head slumped forward. Not a good sign for Gil.

"We made it? Jesus, god, we made it!" Simon says with surprise not taking the same inventory Hart did.

Simon forced open his somewhat dented door and stepped out into the stream. He slipped instantly and pratfell onto his ass. "Damn it," he yelled.

Hart opened his door and took greater care before stepping down into the rushing water. "Carmen wait there for a second and I'll help you out," he gallantly offered.

One step good, next step not so excellent. His foot found some slick, fresh water algae draped over a smooth stone sending him down hard on his ass, "Damn it!"

"Right?" Simon commiserated, rubbing his tailbone.

Realizing Simon had not seen Gil yet, Hart broke the news. "I'm sorry Simon."

His friend peered into the back seat taking in the slumped over Raymond Gil. He hung his head.

Simon offered a hand to Carmen. "You need help getting out?"

She is angry. "I don't need help from either one of you. Leave me be."

Carmen sat calmly in the back assembling herself for an exit. "I gather we're not about to blow up?"

"You'd need to have gas in the plane for that, so I doubt it's going to burst into flames anytime soon." Hart stated the obvious, "Wouldn't you agree Captain?"

"I can still help you out over here Carmen." Simon motioned for her to come out his door.

She wanted no part of that exit route given it required her to crawl over a recently dead Raymond Gil. "I'm going out the other door."

Hart picked up his soaking wet self, but inelegantly slipped back into the water soaking his shirt. He crawled over to help Carmen, who took her shoes off, and stepped down into the Brazilian slip and slide. She stood effortless in the stream with perfect balance. The water, affirming her grace, obligingly found a new path around her. A small smile slid quickly across her face then dissolved in the reality of their nightmare situation.

She walked towards the closest bank, twenty yards from the Pilot's side door. "If you take off your shoes it's easier."

Simon and Hart removed their shoes, then found a tenuous balance on the slick rocks. Stepping back into the plane Hart hopped out again on Simon's side tilting the pilot's seat forward. Simon leaned in wiping tears from his eyes. The two unbuckle Gil's seatbelt and ponder how to get the body out of the plane.

"Who is this guy?" Hart asked.

"I told you, Raymond Gil. I found a Nazi in Brazil. He was just living there—teaching!" Simon shook his head.

"I'm sorry because I guess he was a friend of yours, but…Is it really that big of a tragedy that he's dead? Kind of karma, right?" The words previewed perfectly in Hart's head, but definitely didn't sound so great coming out of his mouth.

"That's a despicable thing to say. He's a human being." Carmen yelled from the bank.

"Is that supposed to make me feel better?" Simon looked pretty disgusted. He reached towards Harts neck and retaliated by pressing on his dart welt.

"Bastard! Stop doing that." Hart rubbed the spot.

Simon started entering the plane reaching for Gil, "Just help me get him out of the plane please."

"He reeks; dead guy smell." Hart held his nose.

"You're all heart. So predictable." Simon needled.

"Hah, hah. So clever." Hart shot back.

"Don't be a moron, they don't smell until hours later." Simon unbuckled Gils seatbelt.

Reluctant but embarrassed, Hart pitched in.

Carmen called from the far bank. "Do you guys need my help?"

"I don't know whose help we need, but you can stay there." Hart yelled back.

Both struggled to pull the dead body of the former Raymond Gil out of the mortally wounded airplane. Neither had ever moved a dead body before. For being such a slight guy he felt heavier than they expected. They bent, folded, then stretched him out through the tight doorway. They finally got him down and out, virtually tumbling him into the stream, the water running over his legs.

"That's sick. Get him out of the water." Simon struggled to move him alone.

"It's not like he's going to catch a cold," Hart stood back watching

Simon struggle. Raymond Gil had no signs of trauma on him from the crash. Thinking about it he looked the same for almost the entire flight, minus the smile of course.

Hart conjectured, "Maybe he had a heart attack or something before the crash? Towards the end there I thought he was sleeping, but probably not."

Simon didn't seem to care about Hart's hypothesis, "He's dead all the same."

Simon looked as sad as Hart had ever seen him.

"Yep, but he does smell a little. How long does it take for rigor mortis to set in? Does anybody know?" Hart asked.

"I'm guessing we're about twenty miles from Botucatu?" said Carmen, from the bank, ignoring the question.

"I hope we're that close. Otherwise, we could be in deep shit." Simon answered. Bending down, he picked up the body, slung it over his shoulder, and slowly made his way over to the left bank. Hardly the Rive Gauche of Paris—brown, packed river sand, and smooth stones pockmarked the way up into a thick growth of forest.

"Buddy," Hart shot out to Simon, "you've got to take his pants off and clean him up in the water."

Carmen walked away the smell overpowering her. "He's right," she said.

Both guys struggled to straighten out his slightly bent legs before yanking off Gil's pants.

"Let's use the radio and call in our position." Hart suggested tugging off a pant leg.

"Maybe you hadn't noticed I never used the radio. This is Brazil. We are way outside of normal commercial traffic zones." Simon walked back to the plane.

"Where are you going?" Hart yelled, "I'm not stripping this guy by myself! He's your friend."

Simon reached into the airplane and tossed Hart a well-worn radio. "Try on 121.5 and see if someone hears us. Why not, right?"

"I'll give it a shot." Making his way back over to Gil's body, Simon picked up the leg Hart dropped and pulled the pant leg off.

Hart took the radio and headed over to Carmen standing on the bank away from Raymond Gils' former corporeal headquarters.

"Carmen, on top of the host of questions I have about this whole episode, who the hell was this guy?"

"Ask your friend, not me," she answered.

That pissed Hart off. "Can't you speak about anything? What's the mystery?" He ranted on, mocking her, "Hey Carmen—Jesuits?" Looking at her he answers his own questions. "Oh nothing! Carmen, who's Gil? Don't know! Is 'Welcome to Brazil' your only complete sentence?"

"Take it easy. She doesn't know anything about this." Simon rode to Carmen's rescue. He looked over at her, "I promise, he's really a terrific guy once you get to know him."

"Uh huh.." Carmen disregarded Simon.

Feeling mocked, Hart stalked off to his own corner and tried to work the radio.

"No one's answering," Hart said out loud now shaking the radio. "I transmitted an approximation of our position based on Carmen's take of twenty miles from Botucatu. Wherever the hell that is. I checked the battery in our emergency locator transmitter—it's dead." Still fuming he walked over towards the airplane. His first foot in the water slipped on an algae covered rock. The radio hurled out of his hand flying and then colliding with a river rock where it exploded into a million pieces of electronic debris. The End.

"Shit."

"An understatement." Carmen tossed over.

"Nice work pal." Simon looked at the pieces not even bothering to try and recover anything.

Reminded of his near death experience in San Blas so many years ago Hart suggested, "We better pick a direction, gather what we can and head out to somewhere. Right?"

Nothing seemed desperate at the moment, but the three of them all realized it could head that direction in the blink of an eye. Simon paid no attention, locked in on stripping Gil's body.

"Help me dip him in the river." The request was aimed at no one in particular.

"Foul." Hart winced.

He looked up at both Carmen and Hart then shook his head side to side. Simon started to tug on the body straining to drag it into the river. Holding his breath, Hart reluctantly grabbed Gil's legs and helped ease it into the flow of the water. They let Gil stay there for a couple minutes watching the current flow over and around the corpse.

"You have to bury him Simon." Carmen urged.

"No," he muled back. "He deserves a decent funeral."

Simon, with Harts unenthusiastic assistance, pulled Gil out of the water. He grabbed Gil's button down LaCoste sweater and placed it over his genitals. Hart's internal Emily Post appreciated the move. Frozen, shriveled up, old man testicles are hardly a drawing card in the best of times. Simon sat down next to the body. Carmen sat down too. The smell was gone. Hart stood and waited a couple minutes of respectful silence.

"What are you proposing we do with him?" Hart asked with the barest tinge of compassion.

Simon answered, "We'll take him with us."

Hart recoiled, "He's dead. He's naked and dead! The dead don't travel well."

Carmen backed up her first suggestion, "In Brazil, our custom says to bury the body within twenty four hours. Taking him with us seems, politely, not very practical."

Composing his answer with a pregnant pause, Simon responded. "First of all he's German not Brazilian so that custom doesn't apply. Even if it did, that means we've got at least one whole day to bury him properly. We're not that far away."

An exasperated Hart said, "Come on man. That's not right. Have some decency."

"We'll carry him," Simon answered.

"We won't." Hart sat down on a nearby stump.

"Fine, I'll carry him," he said.

Simon got up and trudged out to the airplanes remains. He scrounged through the baggage compartment, and appeared again with a large rolled up tarp. Making his way back to the bank, holding the tarp above his head like a Channel Islands surfboard, Simon proclaimed his elegant solution, "we'll wrap him up in this."

Wagging his finger, Hart declined. "Wrapped or unwrapped I'm not carrying a dead body through the god damn jungle."

"I already said that I'd be responsible." Simon plopped the tarp down on the riverbank next to Gil's body.

"We don't have to carry anything. We can float down the river," Carmen had already thought two steps ahead.

Hart looked around to try and get on the same page Carmen had turned to.

"The wing! It will float all of us," she said pointing at the already detached spare part.

"I've walked out of the jungle before. Trust me, it's a better bet," dismissed Simon.

Hart agreed with Simon. However, given all that had transpired, and regardless of how the sanity of a jungle walk far outweighed the daft notion of building a raft for a float to freedom, he voted for tempting fate on the water. He actually voted for flouting Simon and royally pissing him off, but it came out as endorsing Carmen's idea.

"Flight of the Phoenix baby! Let's use the wing." Hart generated his best false hope and fell in line with Carmen.

Simon had no faith in the idea. He ignored both of them.

Hart inspected the discarded wing. "We'll have to seal up the open end, but great idea Carmen."

He walked over to an unsuspecting Carmen and gave her a full body embrace. It certainly did not come to him as a romantic embrace, but he did notice a subtle sense of relief hugging her. He guessed the last man on earth syndrome fueled it; like some bleak Sergio Leone spaghetti western. Darwinian instinct declares that someone must win the woman and kill the rival. Even though Hart realized it was more likely for Carmen to survive, than either him or Simon, he clung to his cinematic fantasy. Hart determined during the spontaneous embrace that he actually wanted the girl because, like some nineteen forties Clark Gable movie, someone had to want the girl. Didn't they? That brought up a series of pondering questions. Did Simon want the girl? Did Hart only want the girl because Simon wanted the girl? Would he still want the girl if Simon didn't want the girl? Did Carmen care about any of this crap?

Simon's voice jarred Hart out of his head. "I said fine. I'll help. Are you deaf?!"

"Give me some help with this please." Carmen, gripping one end of the wing, gave Hart an order.

Carmen and Simon stood knee deep in the flow trying to negotiate the wing to the bank. They needed to figure out a way to seal up the open end. Hart waded over making an immediate impact by lifting the wingtip end out from its pinned position between two river rocks. It felt lighter than he imagined. The trio stumbled their way over to the bank and laid the wing down on the sand. They all went back to the plane to scavenge anything else that might help get them the hell out of Dodge. Everything ended up on the bank. They took stock of their empire of jetsam: three pairs of shoes, one tarp, one broken radio, one life jacket, Carmen's purse, four cushions stripped off the plane seats, carpet mats, one five foot extending metal tow bar, and a collapsible metal step stool used for checking the gas caps on the wing. Oh yeah, and one Nazi corpse.

Hart admonished Simon for failing to use the step stool to visually check the fuel tanks before they left the ground. Simon returned fire for dropping the one working hand-held radio into the river.

"That was an accident!" Hart rebutted.

Hart determined not to spend any more time trying to occupy the moral high ground on his kidnapping. A simple middle finger dissipated his anger for the moment.

"How do you propose we seal this hole?" Simon waggled his hand inside the wing knocking on the walls.

"Seat cushions," Carmen had a pragmatic non-emotional solution. She picked up a cushion and started to rip it up into pieces to fit in the hole.

They set to work first shredding then stuffing the seat cushions into the openings in the wing root where it had formerly joined the fuselage.

Simon looked up at Hart, "You want to ask about Gil?"

"No idiot. I want to ask what the hell I'm doing here."

"I'm part of a group to change things around." Simon began ripping up a cushion.

"You mean you and the dead Nazi are a group?"

"I'll tell you about Gil, and then you'll get it."

Hart wandered away to relieve himself in the jungle.

While shredding seats and out of Hart's earshot, Carmen said to Simon, "This became way more complicated than it should have."

Simon's shoulders drooped. "I know," he answered flatly while continuing to stuff foam pieces into the wing.

Chapter 17. | Tico Tico

A steady breeze blew through the jungle keeping things a marmite cooler than they might have been. A Paulista breeze moves languidly on its journey from the warm currents of the Atlantic Ocean before tracing a cooling path up the valleys, over the streams, and through the verdant green hills to Botucatu. Poetic breeze be damned, Hart simply felt thankful for anything that diminished his unending, drenching, festival of sweat. No matter what tune he sang to distract himself, or how lyrical he tried to imagine his circumstances; he was suffocating, and deliriously, hot.

"I can't breathe. I'm going to have an asthma attack any second and wheeze myself to death," Hart announced.

Carmen, unphased by the conditions looked concerned, "You have asthma? That can be really dangerous."

Simon took a hard look in Hart's direction, "Get back to work and stop being such a Sheila. He had bronchitis once when we were twelve. He doesn't have 'asthma'."

"What is a Sheila?" asked Carmen.

"It's a sexist insult based on the premise that women are inferior," smirked Hart.

"Am I a Sheila? I'm a girl." Carmen glared at Simon.

"No, you can't be a Sheila. Hart is a Sheila because, Nevermind. I apologize. He's right. It's a sexist comment." Simon was embarrassed. "If explain what happened to me when I got to Brazil. Will you knock off your wanking?"

"Finally!" Hart reluctantly went back to work, holding a satisfied smirk on his face. Simon launched into the tale of his journey to Brazil.

Simon got off the plane in Rio to no greeting whatsoever. After a brief visit to the Tourist Information desk at the airport he grabbed a taxi into the city. The agent at the desk had booked him a room at the once prestigious Flamengo Palace Hotel. Now it was an over rated two-star with a marketing slogan that promised "The Flamengo, a few steps from everywhere."

The hotel had very few amenities, but it did sport a convenient ATM in the lobby. Simon slept off his flight for one full day. He then walked out the front door of the hotel to a juice bar five doors down from the Palace. He got a maracuja smoothie along with, a globally available, ham sandwich to take back up to his room. He watched Brazilian TV for another full day. At only forty-five dollars a day, he could afford a few days of peaceful mental vegetation.

Before leaving LA, Simon had stopped at the Simon Wiesenthal Center in Beverly Hills to have a conversation with their chief Nazi Tracker, Ida Zucoff.

Hart laughed incredulously, "You really did that? Like they'd tell you anything anyway?"

"See," Simon said, "I told this would take your mind off sweating."

Undaunted, he pushed on. In point of fact, Ida gave Simon the phone number of her contact in Rio, Rabbi Morris Luzzato. On his first day before collapsing from jet lag, Simon had left a message for the Rabbi. On day two, while watching a Portuguese dubbed episode of a vintage seventies show, The Six Million Dollar Man, his phone rang.

"This is Simon."

"Good afternoon, this is Rabbi Luzzato returning your call."

Simon fumbled with the remote looking for the mute button as Lee Majors raced a locomotive engine to the nearest crossing. Train whistle blaring, he finally managed to turn down the sound.

"Mr. Jovenda, are you there?"

"Yes, Rabbi, uh thank you. I'm wondering if it's possible for me to come and see you today?"

"Ida sent you." He sounded chagrined, as if Simon was number four hundred and thirty two in a long line of pointless referrals.

"Sure did. Is that a bad thing?"

The Rabbi let loose an exhausted exhale, "No, no, I just don't know what to tell you. You are, of course, welcome to come over to the Temple. We are at Rue Tenente Possolo 8."

"I'm at the Flamengo Palace Hotel." There was a slight pause. Simon thought he heard the Rabbi snicker, but he filled in the space with a question, "How long will it take by taxi?"

"About twenty to thirty minutes depending on traffic, and there's always traffic. I like to walk places instead, but a taxi is probably a better idea for you. I could tell you how to get here on foot if you prefer."

A simple answer would've sufficed for Simon, but evidently the Rabbi felt like chatting.

"Taxi for me," Simon interjected in the small space between the Rabbi's thoughts.

"Most of these guys understand enough English if you don't speak Portuguese. Tell the driver you are going to Templo Israelita. He will know where we are. By the way have you been to the Museum?"

"Which one?" Simon asked.

"The Carmen Miranda museum, of course. Your hotel is only a few blocks away."

"Nope. Well, I'll see you in a bit," Simon wanted to hang up and move along.

"I promise you it is a not-miss. I suggest a visit. Perhaps one hour from now would be a good time, it's not very crowded in the afternoon. Most Cariocas take a long nap this time of day."

"I have no idea who Carmen Miranda was. Plus, I'd really like to come down there and see you now."

"I'm not going anywhere. Take my advice son, enjoy yourself a little bit."

The Rabbi sounded strangely insistent on the visit.

"Okay Rabbi, if you say so. I guess I'll plan on coming by the Temple late this afternoon then?"

"Fine, fine, let's not worry about that right now." Click! Rabbi Luzzato hung up the phone.

Simon sat around for another half hour replaying the conversation in his mind. Was Carmen Miranda Jewish? A Nazi? Maybe she ran some warped Brazilian version of Harriet Tubman's underground railroad, smuggling deserving Nazis from Germany to Rio. Could there be such a thing as a deserving Nazi? No matter how many times he rolled it around, it still wound up as bizarre. He finally tabled his thoughts. He stood up and got dressed; shorts, a Bob Marley T-shirt, a pair of well-worn sandals, and his backpack. Skipping stairs, he made it down to the lobby and secured directions from the smiling desk clerk who assured him the museum was, as advertised, only a few steps away. He headed out the side door of the Flamengo Palace onto the main drag and took the fifteen-minute walk down the street to Avenue Rui Barbosa.

A faded, rectangular sheet metal sign featuring a pointing image of the 1940's bombshell, signaled the museum's modest entrance. He paid the equivalent of a five-dollar entrance fee. The sleepy-looking elderly woman, dressed in a flaming red polo shirt with Carmen Miranda's likeness stenciled over her right breast, took the money and slid him a ticket. As Simon walked in, she depressed a button behind the counter. It triggered a scratchy recording of Ms. Miranda singing the classic "Tico-Tico no Fubá." Her voice sambaed out of the PA system filling the museum. As Rabbi Luzzato had predicted, he had the place entirely to himself.

The sparse exhibits made him wonder about the need for a museum in the first place. He wondered how large a mark in life someone must make to rate a museum. What if you get a museum and no one ever visited? Did someone seriously overestimate Carmen's impact on the universe? He drifted past the assorted pineapple and banana headdresses and an umbrella hat, thinking her significance was as transient as a basket of ripe fruit. The thought occurred to Simon that his own impact on life might be just as fleeting. He drifted along until he came across the movie posters. Passing That Night in Rio, then Four Jill's in a Jeep, he saw a man standing in front of a poster of the 1953 Dean Martin & Jerry Lewis film, Scared Stiff.

"I'm a HUGE Martin & Lewis fan. Are you?" The man's voice had a familiar sound. Then it hit him. Wearing a khaki suit, with a peach colored shirt, and a well-groomed goatee, he looked more like a maître' d than a Rabbi. He spoke quietly as if surrounded by a crowd of people.

Simon realized the gentleman was speaking to him. "Rabbi? What are you doing here?" a mystified Simon asked.

The Rabbi continued to rhapsodize. "They had exquisite timing—just a perfect rhythm. Dean Martin was the master straight man. Sure, Lewis was a comic genius, and I loved the Errand Boy, pure genius, but he lost something magical without Martin. They were pals."

"Looks like the telethon guy?" Simon replied.

"You're telling me you never heard of Jerry Lewis or Dean Martin?" He said threw his hands in the air.

"No, no, I'm sure that's the Muscular Dystrophy guy. I know him. He's dead though."

"He's not dead. He's old."

"Alright." Simon had no inkling what his correct response should be.

"I love Carmen Miranda. Did you know her Dad was a Portuguese barber? Pure working class; simple folk. Carmen represents the signature Carioca cultural icon. The world holds a picture of Brazil as thong wearing, amber skinned beauties, samba music, and those fruit packed head dresses you walked by a minute ago."

"I'm looking for Nazis, Rabbi."

"No son, you are not. You are looking for retribution for a past that's been avenged."

Simon looked crestfallen and puzzled, "You're a Jew. You're not angry?"

"I am sad about that past, and vigilant," he answered, "but I am trying to talk to you about today." He waved a hand pointing to a bench behind them, "Sit."

They sat between a giant poster of Miranda and Groucho Marx from the film Copacabana. Next to that hung a larger than life stunning black and white close up photo of the radiantly beautiful Carmen. She appeared focused on something off screen and far, far away. Her dark arching eyebrows fixed over a piercing determined gaze. The normally wry smile vanquished by a firm tight-lipped poise. The trademark headpiece, perfectly perched on her head, seemed out of step with her stoic, purposeful gaze.

"That's an uncharacteristic photo, don't you think?" the Rabbi asked.

Simon hadn't the first clue about Carmen Miranda or her brief history on the planet. Still, he made an effort to be polite.

"Can't say since I've never seen her before. From the other shots of her, I figured she played the party girl most times." Simon looked around the room to see all of the images of Carmen in gleeful abandon, laughing, singing, witty, and cleverly coy, while always exuding a steamy sensuality.

"This one's my favorite." The Rabbi stared at the photo once again.

"I like the privacy. She sees something we don't. To me it represents a determined hope for modern Brazil. That's what you are looking for, Simon. Not Nazis."

Simon gave the Rabbi a sideways glance. "Have I been followed or something? Why the cloak and dagger routine?"

"Jews are in danger everywhere at every time. It's a strange fact of the world since the fall of Babylon. However, there are larger problems on earth than decaying Nazis. And yes, the temple is always being watched. It's better if no one knows about you. Better for you. For me, it's all the same. I'm just giving you an opportunity to help in a different way."

"I've made a commitment to myself about this Rabbi. If you can't help me, is there someone else I can talk to?"

"Simon, the Nazis are all dead or a whisper away. It's the new millennium."

"There must be some left somewhere." Frustrated, Simon got up to leave, "Thank you for your time."

He shook the man's hand. Hesitantly, the Rabbi held on and spoke quietly.

"Get yourself up to Botucatu near Sao Paulo. There's a man teaching humanities at the University there. He's got a past. Dr. Raymond Gil—see what you can find out. I will make a phone call for you. Stay at the Chaillot Plaza Hotel."

Before he left the museum, the Rabbi bought Simon a copy of his favorite photo of Carmen.

"Here," he said, "My gift to you."

Simon thanked him and tucked it into his backpack.

"That's when I got the postcard from you," Hart remembered. "The Nazis are all dead, Simon. You got the last one! It was a dumb-ass idea anyway,"

"I wish you would've come with me. That was definitely my low point." Simon paused to gather his thoughts.

Returning to the Flamengo Palace Hotel, Simon had packed his bags and caught a cab to the Rio de Janeiro-Galeão Airport. He paid the ninety-real one-way fare for Sao Paulo. He arrived in time to rent a car and start the three-hour drive to Botucatu before sunset. Unfortunately, the traffic had snarled in all directions leaving the airport. It seems someone had bombed the Brazilian Telecom Showroom at the brand new Sao Paulo Airport Mall about an hour before Simon's plane arrived. The whole airport zone was yellow taped and crawling with police.

After slowly escaping the airport area, Simon followed the signs as the road wound its way up and into the mountains surrounding Sao Paulo. He arrived in the small city of Botucatu by ten o'clock that night. He found the Chaillot Hotel, paid the one hundred Reals for a room and promptly fell asleep. The University was only a few minutes' drive from the hotel. Simon awoke in the morning to a ringing phone.

"Hello?" he hesitated wondering who was calling.

"Mr. Jovenda?"

The voice was unfamiliar to him.

"Can I help you? Who's this?" Simon couldn't help being grumpy. He had just awakened in a strange city; the Rabbi's cloak and dagger behavior had made him overly paranoid. Sure he was on the trail of a Nazi, but the guy must've been well into his eighties. He wasn't going to be chasing the fugitive through the jungles in a Hummer. How difficult could this be?

"Actually, if I might correct you, it is 'May I help you, not Can I."

Simon's irritation boiled over, "Who the hell is this?"

"I apologize, Mr. Jovenda," said the voice, "appropriate grammar is a pet peeve of mine. My name is Raymond Gil. I believe you have come to see me."

All of the air in Simon's lungs spontaneously vaporized. He sucked in an audible gasping breath as if the phone receiver had suddenly morphed into a scuba regulator.

"Pardon me, Mr. Jovenda? Are you still there?" asked a concerned Gil.

Simon took a lengthy pause for thought. The Rabbi said he'd make a phone call, but he never considered the call would be to the damn Nazi!

Gil continued, "I think it best if we could meet for lunch this afternoon."

The man sounded polite and non-threatening. Simon now had to suppress all of his "most wanted villain" stereotypes and create a new mental picture to deal with the current turn of events. Renting the Hummer, sneaking through the jungle in camouflage fatigues, a chloroform kidnapping, followed by helicopter airlift to The Hague for a hastily-convened world tribunal would have to wait; at least until after lunch.

He pushed out a stumbling response, "Yeah, okay."

"I will pick you up at two pm in your lobby." With that, Mr. Raymond Gil hung up the phone.

Simon paced his modestly appointed room, recovering from the change of events. Simon had an innate knowledge for surviving a universe that couldn't give two shits about anyone on a day-to-day basis. No father slashing a path ahead does that for you. Tennis does that for you. One minute Hart and Simon could be sailing through a set, annihilating their doubles opponent. The next, they would lose three games in a row, momentum subtly shifting to the other team as they whiffed a hint of a comeback. Simon loved those moments. He would huddle with Hart on the baseline, his long body draping Hart in its artificial shade. Then he'd give a demonic smile and simply say, "Burners up, baby."

Simon sat back on his bed and thought about his upcoming civilized, lunch with Raymond Gil. Nazis could evoke a bizarre unexpected sense of sympathy from the modern world. Their able lawyers portraying them as reluctant warriors either seduced by Satan, or forcibly conscripted to do the devil's bidding. Simon felt dramatically different. He believed in accountability at full retail value; no melting away allowed.

Two o'clock rolled around fast enough. His phone rang twice. Simon picked up and curtly said, "I'll be down."

"Fine, I am at the front desk." Simon had clicked off before Gil finished talking.

He walked the two flights of stairs down to the vacant lobby. He found a slight, well-tanned elderly man of 84 years awaiting him. Raymond Gil wore a pair of khaki pants, a neatly pressed white shirt covered by a yellow, three-button LaCoste sweater, and beige topsiders. His remaining white hair appeared orderly and strategically placed around the fringes of his mostly bald pate.

He stood politely to greet Simon. "Thank you for seeing me, Mr. Jovenda."

"Okay," Simon replied.

"There is a small café right around the block that I thought would be suitable for us. Nothing fancy, but excellent food."

"Fine." Simon remained steely-eyed and cool.

They walked out the lobby door onto the small town square. Both men pensively hunted for the right words around the gigantic elephant lumbering along between them.

Gil began, "Moe, pardon me, Rabbi Luzzato and I have known each other for some time."

"Your friends? With the Rabbi?" In a flash Simon felt confused and ambushed.

"Acquaintances mostly. We meet on occasion," continued Gil.

"You mean at the annual Nazi Wine & Cheese Festival? What the hell does that mean?"

Gil decided to take a different tack and address the issue head on, "I was a corporal; a medic in the army."

Simon attacked, "Hitler's army." He emphasized the name.

"Of course, that is correct Hitler's army," Gil was disarmingly plaintive in his declaration.

"Am I supposed to feel sorry for you at this point?" Simon asked.

"You may call me Raymond if you like. I presume, nothing sir. I expect nothing."

"You're a Nazi. I can't call a Nazi by his first name. It would mean I was accepting you as part of the same human race as me." Simon's vitriol rose with each word.

Raymond nodded his head in understanding and pursed his lips, pondering his next remark.

Simon spit out a damning inquiry. "How many people did you kill?"

"I did not kill anyone. As I stated, I served as a medic. My job saved lives." Gil remained calm.

"The wrong lives," Simon accused.

"Perhaps that is true, but they were lives all the same. I have been a teacher for over fifty years now."

"So what?" Simon dismissed the remark.

Even though he regretted the conversation's direction, Simon felt unable to alter its course. He now embraced the role of a Nuremburg Judge defending humanity. Infuriatingly, Gil assumed no role at all. Perhaps he had decided to lie down in front of the oncoming train and absorb the impact. He seemed content to let Simon take pot-shots at him like Ali versus Foreman.

"Nazi," Simon said.

"Raymond, please," Gil interrupted.

Simon blew him off, "Nazi are you trying to use the Rope-a-Dope strategy on me? You think that sooner or later I'll just get tired of pumping shots at you and lay down?"

Gil laughed. "I remember that fight—The Rumble in the Jungle. Ali's strategy proved highly effective. That man had an innate genius, didn't he?"

To his surprise, Simon nodded and popped a slight smile. They rounded a corner, landing at the screen door to the Iguaçu Café.

"Here we are. Would you still consider lunch with me?"

"Yes, Nazi." Surprising himself, Simon actually joked with him.

Gil ordered for the both of them. Acaraje: Fried shrimp pie for himself, and Feijoada: a stew of black beans and a variety of meats, served with rice and kale for Simon. They sat in uncomfortable silence. Though his demeanor appeared calm and patient, Simon felt a sinister undertone nagging at his sub conscience. Nazis—weren't they all kings of duplicity? Surely his ulterior motive would rear its viperous head at any moment. Simon remained on guard.

"The local beer is quite good. Would you like to try one?" A seemingly guileless offer.

"I knew it," snapped Simon.

"You have already tried the beer then?" Gil looked puzzled.

"Why didn't you stay in Germany and face the music? If you were just a medic, as you say."

Gil nodded his head. "It is even worse than that, Mr. Jovenda. I deserted my post."

"You deserted? So you're both a Nazi and a coward?"

"Please grant me some time." An old man asking only for time, Simon detected the dreaded sympathy card flip over. He watched the card fall, but felt unable to respond. He sat and listened to Raymond Gil relay the story of his journey to Brazil.

"I was twenty-two, Germany was in ruins, and my family was dead. I was alone. There was no opportunity, and would be none for years to come. Shame and humiliation are powerful foes and even worse neighbors, Mr. Jovenda. Living with them and among them became too large an obstacle for me."

Staring at the old man sitting across the table a sliver of empathy welled up inside him; a crack in the solid wall around his heart. The man was virtually the same age as Simon was now. He rolled it over in his brain, "No family and no prospects for hope trapped in a disintegrating, violent...wait a minute...NAZI, NAZI, NAZI!" His psyche fought back, but somehow, amidst the internal screeching, a sliver of sympathy had grabbed on. It shocked him.

"I left my post one late afternoon and made my way to Hamburg. I trolled the docks and found a Brazilian freighter bound for the port city of Santos, seventy kilometers from Sao Paulo. It was six months before the war ended. I finished my college education, and got a doctorate in Humanities over the course of the next fifteen years. I supported myself by teaching tennis until I earned my PhD."

Simon listened. He felt his heart wedge open a sliver more; maybe enough for a small ray of light to enter knocking his precise personal balance off its axis. "Holy shit," Simon thought to himself, "did he just say TENNIS? God damn it! How could that possibly be?" He had something in common with this virulent life form sitting across the table from him.

"And then I began teaching here at the University." Gil's voice faded back into Simon's awareness.

"You ran away from your accountability." Simon countered dismissively.

"I ran away from an horrible nightmare life from which there was no escape except the one I took."

"Of course you knew nothing about the atrocities," Nuremburg Judge Simon Jovenda spit the words at Gil facetiously.

"No. I knew. I also knew I was powerless to stop it and —"

Simon cut him off. "Too cowardly to call attention to it?"

"That is certain. You may condemn me for being a coward." Gil held his perfect posture.

"Fine. I'm judge and jury. Consider yourself condemned," Simon said.

Gil absorbed the blow. "Most certainly, but what does that change today?"

"How do you live with that?" Simon rustled in his uncomfortable wooden chair.

"With that, we have arrived at the essential question." Gil actually seemed relieved.

"Maybe my real question is how do we let you live with that?" countered Simon.

"I try to make a difference now. I try to reclaim some sense of contribution today."

Simon spat out, "You absolutely cannot be forgiven. I won't forgive you."

"I agree with you. It is a tall order. I do not ask for your forgiveness."

"Don't try any of that Jedi mind shit on me. It won't matter."

"How long will you be here?" Gil asked.

Simon pondered the question. How long would he be here? Where else did he have to go? Why was he here now anyway? He thought about shooting Raymond Gil right between the eyes. He'd get up, walk to the bathroom; get the gun taped above the crusty old toilet, like Michael Corleone in the Godfather. Then he'd walk back to their table, and against the gentle Brazilian breeze, pull out the gun, and blow old Raymond Gil right through the front window into the next life. He'd put the gun down and walk out of the restaurant, back to the 2nd floor of the Chaillot Hotel, pack his things and drive out of town. He'd hop the next flight from Sao Paulo to Los Angeles, call Hart, meet for a game of tennis and resume his life. Simon got as far as crabbing up in his chair. Right after his vision ended, he felt the thoughts slowly ebbing away.

"I don't know how long I'm here. I'm just here," He admitted.

"May I introduce you to someone?" Gil asked tentatively.

"Another pathetic Nazi pal? I'm full up," Simon answered.

"Certainly not. I suspect one Nazi per day should be more than sufficient." A small smile scooted across Gil's face. "Things are always larger than they seem is all I was thinking."

"I think I'm mostly done meeting folks right now, unless it's the Dali Lama or someone of equal value." Simon stretched back in his chair in a fit of frustrated exasperation. He had concluded that shooting Raymond Gil between the eyes could wait, or even be completely dismissed as pointless.

"Hmm. I think I understand. Perhaps you are short on sustaining funds?" Gil seemed to have an offer in waiting.

Simon held his breath for a moment, then let out a deep sigh, "Sustaining funds means money? Why not simply say money?"

"Too vulgar." Gil straightened up his posture and adjusted his sweater buttons.

"Yep, some money would be great. But more than that, since I'm not going to be shooting you, arresting you, or turning you into disinterested authorities, I guess I'm in-between thoughts on what to do."

"Certainly a dilemma I can appreciate. What skill sets do you possess?"

"Not many. I can teach tennis, quote Voltaire, and read and write Hebrew."

"All fine skills. However, I am quite sure you have more that have simply not yet awakened." Gil smiled.

Simon replied, "You are a bizarre old dude Nazi. How do you know this isn't the whole deal?"

"Rarely is. You are a tennis teacher. That is most fortuitous, Mr. Jovenda. As I mentioned, in my youth I used to be quite the tennis player. I believe you can secure gainful employment at the Botucatu Country Club, where I am a longstanding member. We will see about it this very day."

True to his word, Gil got Simon his first and only real job in Brazil teaching tennis to the socialites at the Botucatu Marine Tennis Club. Why they called it the Marine Tennis Club when there was no actual boating or ocean within two hundred miles remained a mystery to even the eldest members. Nevertheless, an American tennis instructor brought the club a heretofore-unrivaled measure of cache. Women clamored for lessons from a reluctantly grateful Simon Jovenda.

Quietly, Simon settled into a simple life in Botucatu. Botucatu, a Mestizo word that means "good air," was located a little over one hundred fifty miles southwest of Sao Paulo. It lies near the Pardo River in the Serra de Botucatu at 2,549 feet above sea level a critical fifty-six feet higher in elevation than Sao Paulo. That was just enough difference to feel the cooling ocean breezes passing over the Sao Paulo plateau. Enough merciful, heavenly breeze to make Paulistas happy they came, and Botucatu homies guard their small city against any invading, pollution breathing, metro-dwellers.

Simon taught tennis to a variety of club members, old to young, every morning from eight am through noon. He ate his lunch at the snack bar off the tennis courts. He was not ecstatically happy, but he was not rudderless either. He realized he had fallen into a reasonably good gig. Raymond Gil, whether he was truly a former Nazi or not, had done something for him. The two spent considerable time with each other; mostly late afternoons when Gil would come out to the courts for an hour of rallying. They would then proceed into town for tea at the Iguaçu Café. Occasionally, Simon attended Raymond's university classes in Humanities, quietly perching on a desk in the back of the room. His picture of Gil gradually shifted as he watched him open the eyes of his students. Gil probed them with questions spun from the literature they studied which he applied to their own lives. One day, when the class discussed Siddhartha, he heard Gil ask a question he had heard before. "Would you rather be an ox driver or a Buddha?" Simon left the room.

Gil posed many of his questions to Simon, "How do you empty yourself Simon?" Simon pushed back on these seemingly ridiculous thought masturbations.

"I take a leak, and then I'm empty."

"Never mind." Gil smiled.

On a rare rainy day in Botucatu Gil, pushed further. "Simon, we are now friends, are we not?"

Simon knew that they had in truth become friends, even a little more in a short period of time. Still he couldn't resist, "How could I be friends with a Nazi?"

Gil had learned to ignore Simon at appropriate times, "Good. Can I ask you a question from one friend to another?"

"No."

"Why do you hold so much anger inside of you?"

"Stop asking me questions I have to think about old man."

"Would you like to?" Gil clasped his hands around a cup of ginger tea.

"I'll tell you Gil, I'm tired of thinking. I like thinking about nothing. Nothing feels exactly right to me. That, by the way, is the answer to your other lame-ass question. I'm already empty." Simon took a slurp of tea.

Gil dismissed the cynical retort and pressed forward. "If I told you to go outside and sit in the rain, would you do it?"

"I'd get bit to shit by the mosquitoes."

Gil smiled. Simon felt challenged.

"You want me to get bit to shit, Ray?" Simon thought about it, saw Gil's face, and reasoned the answer. "You bastard. You want me to get eaten alive. I should've turned your ass in when I didn't know you."

"You might get a few bites, but you might get more. It is up to you," Gil sipped his tea.

Simon got up from the table, "If I die from Yellow fever, Dengue fever, or some other disfiguring blight do not tell my mother how it happened. She'll be deeply disappointed in me."

Rain in the tropics falls like no other place on earth. Simon went outside the Iguaçu, crossed the street into the park in the square and sat on a bench. It began to rain harder. When the rain came to Botucatu, it came with time to spare: no particular place to be or time to be there. It routinely rained for three days at a time.

Simon let the water douse his body. It soaked his hair, ran over his shoulders, drenched his clothing, ran down his hips and legs, into his Nike air soled tennis shoes and his matching Botucatu Marine Tennis Club socks. It overflowed into his body, flooding his skin and organs; spilling over then refilling in endless cycles. Even though the rain that washed over and around him fell warm from the sky, he felt the cold. Still he lingered inside the rain. He stayed until he felt nothing. No difference between water and skin, skin and air, air and water, water and soul. He forgot about the rain. He forgot the reason he sat alone. He became part of the downpour. He drifted, weightless, in a blur, quiet, contained in a somati tank of white noise and water. He could have been asleep or awake. He could no longer distinguish the difference. The droning sound of rain filled all voids. His eyes opened and closed disconnected from his thoughts, unrelated to him. His legs began to tingle: first the right, then the left. Tingling, but why? He thought to himself, am I on fire? Am I frozen solid? He could not tell where one sensation faded and another began. They appeared one after another, transmuting into one infinite blur. Numbness overtook him. Suddenly he felt as if he were lifting off the bench, levitating up into the clouds, above the weather, into the clear, sun-drenched sky. Weightless in body, he imagined a flock of hawks soaring high in the sky, batting their wings along side him. Then his balance seemed to falter. He was falling. Falling back to Earth, back to a small, quiet, hardwood bench in the rain. He shook with fear.

"Jovenda! Jovenda! What the hell are you doing?"

A woman was shaking the living shit out of him. She had him by both shoulders, jostling him back and forth.

"Jovenda! Are you on drugs? Get out of the damn rain, you fool! What's the matter with you?" Dia Gaspar had a tight grip on him and was not about to let go until he answered her.

Dia, a fiery Italian-Spanish hybrid loved her weekly tennis lessons from Simon. She had a wicked forehand and a scurry around backhand. Small but powerful in body and spirit, she would not be denied anything she had set her mind on attaining. She was a wealthy widow whose husband had founded the Botucatu Marine Tennis Club. Right now Dia had a death grip on Simon's shoulders, and was shaking him with the force of a magnitude twenty-seven earthquake.

"Dia," Simon groggily came to lifting her arms off his shoulders. "I must have dozed off."

"You looked comatose, my friend." Holding her umbrella, she backed off and looked him coolly in the eyes. "Is everything okay?"

Simon appeared drenched but energized. "What time is it?"

"You have a watch on your wrist." Dia said puzzled.

"Holy shit, that bastard left me out here for five hours? Amazing!" Simon darted off on the hunt for Raymond Gil.

Botucatu was mostly a college town. It had its dividing line between the classes, but not as pronounced as the large metropolitan areas like Rio and Sao Paulo. Simon stuck his head back into the Iguaçu looking for Gil. He walked through the rain and found Gil in his office at the University, a tight space crowded with shelves of books and papers stacked in neat piles surrounding his institutional metal desk.

"You need a towel." Gil handed Simon a dry towel and invited him to sit down on a chair opposite his desk.

"You left me out there for hours." Simon feigned anger.

"I did no such thing. I left you to your own designs. You surprised me." Gil leaned back in his chair, absent mindedly re-buttoning his sweater.

"I know; strange experience. Felt like an acid trip. What am I supposed to take away from this?" He knew it was a question Gil could not answer.

"How should I know? Take nothing. Notice nothing. Go take a shower, dry off, have a passion fruit mojito, look for beautiful women." Perfectly guileless in his advice, Gil offered nothing more.

Simon stood, confused, empty in answers but full in an experience he had no ability to classify. He took Gil's advice that night. He went over to the Marina Club bar, found a suitable partner and vaporized the night away. All the while absent and present to his experience in the rain. So it went. Months went by in the blink of an eye for Simon. Gil continued giving him one suggested experience after the next. Simon, go into the mountains, find a great heron and follow it into the sky. Simon, fast for two days, go to the countryside and help Jao Romero harvest his corn crop. Simon, get drunk and play cards.

"I'm doing what you ask, but I don't know exactly why," he asked Gil one day while cringing from a mojito hangover.

"I told you things could be larger than they seem at first blush. I am only trying to help you find your answers." Gil said.

"Get drunk?" Simon questioned rhetorically. "Some of these are tougher than others."

"Which ones?" Gil inquired.

Simon confessed, "Find a heron? I sat up there for three hours looking for a damn heron. All I could find was a falcon. I substituted it for the heron, and convinced myself you didn't need to know about the switch. Only then I got myself racked with guilt for lying to you. Another couple hours vaporized with me and the damn falcon locked in a cage match stare down. By the time the bird had enough of me and flew off, I had about a thousand fire ant bites on both ankles with swelling welts the size of Brazilian walnuts. So I came back to town, drank mojitos until I got dizzy, went home, and puked."

"What is the point of these meditations? Is that your question?" Gil chuckled.

"Sure, why not," Simon scratched at his ankles.

"Give someone a step ladder if you can."

Gil sat down behind his desk, hands folded together.

"and...there's more right?" Simon waited.

"My friend, I cannot run away fast enough or far enough to escape my own reality. I can go numb, but I know the thoughts and memories are always there with me. I have to hold onto them, atone, and survive them each day." Gil stared straight into Simon's bloodshot eyes to ask, "How can I ever feel peace with that?"

"I don't have the faintest idea how you finally wrestle that beast to the ground, Ray. You teach, I guess." Compassion welled up in Simon as he felt Gil's circling sadness around his lifetime burden.

"Neither do I," chagrined Gil, "I pass on what I have learned. I get up each day and go again."

"At least you're not a fully fermented drunk," Simon added brightly.

"A drunk gets numb, which is not a bad thing. He might find the briefest flight and insight from his despair, but at the end of the night, aside from some additional calories, he ascends no levels and retains no lessons." Gil spoke with the certainty of having detoured down that path.

"So how long do I keep this up?" Simon inhaled deeply knowing the probable answer.

Gil responded with a question, "Do you want to be an ox driver or a Buddha?"

"That can't be the only choice," Simon said.

Simon saw as the look of recognition and ringing endorsement appeared on Hart's face. "Why is that damn question trailing my ass all over the world? Do I have some kind of Buddha face? I'm sick of it."

"Cause it's a great one to ask, and answer," Hart said thinking that episode seemed like many years ago instead of months.

"Well, I didn't, so quit asking." Simon returned to his story.

Glazing over looking at Gil, Simon wondered if he had stumbled onto the yellow brick road, or was just meandering around some third world Disneyland. Distracted by fantastic rides and perfect pathways lined with neatly trimmed topiaries, but in the end still trapped in a series of well-disguised dead ends with an adventure pass. Then one afternoon while at tea with Raymond Gil the Dalai Lama came up in conversation.

"Simon, you mentioned at our first encounter how you would like to meet the Dalai Lama."

"Or someone of equal value," Simon recalled.

"Ah yes, of equal value." Gil remembered.

"You've got just the fellow, is that it?" Simon smugly sat back in his tennis shorts and Botucatu Marine Tennis Club T-shirt.

"I have a friend coming up to visit. My step ladder."

"Are you trying to convert me to something?" Simon joked

"That is for you to do, not me."

"Sure I'll meet him. When?"

"You will have to mind your language," warned Gil.

"Why, is he the damn Pope?" Simon smugly asked.

"He is sitting at the table next to us." Gil stood up to make an introduction, "Simon Jovenda, this is my good friend Father Lazarus Greve."

Greve stood up matching Simon's height. Wearing his black Jesuit robes, Greve reached down to Simon's chair with an extended hand. Caught off-guard Simon clumsily pushed his chair out and grabbed onto Greve's hand, which both lifted him up and greeted him with one clean captive motion.

"Pleased to meet you, Father," said Simon.

Gil pulled Greve's chair over to their table grabbing the priest's maracuja smoothie and placing it in front of him.

Greve looked into Simon's eyes and before beginning what would become a long conversation he commented, "So you are Gil's new project. We have something in common."

Simon's eyes wandered about the café as he considered Greve's insight. He noticed a man sitting at a table across the room staring at them. He was covered in tattoos.

Chapter 18. | Fascinating Rhythm

"Gil the Guru?" Hart's sarcasm pinched a nerve.

"I never had anyone watching out for me."

"Leice? Your mother?" countered Hart, appalled that Simon had discounted her existence in his life.

"My mother took care of me, but she never offered any sort of path."

"Fathers don't choose your path. Maybe they leave some breadcrumbs, but maybe not," Hart countered.

"I never got any breadcrumbs. Never. Period."

Hart clammed up. He stayed silent for a moment while reaching inside himself trying to feel empathy for his friend. He pondered how suddenly fortunate Simon must have felt to find someone that took a genuine and deep interest in him. Hart decided he should apologize for his jerk moment. Sadly he waited a beat too long to come to that conclusion.

"Don't you worry you're fucking it all up?" Simon asked.

Hart's anger re-emerged, "Me? You've been off planet for a year, and can hardly wag a finger at me given the circumstances! I've had an amazing year, with tons of personal growth, and other cool stuff you know nothing about."

Smelling Hart's lie, Simon tried to reframe and apologize. "I know this has all gone horribly wrong, but I am trying to share something important with you."

Hart went cone of silence swearing off all conversation. His focus shifted entirely away from Simon, concentrating all of his anger driven energy getting their pathetic aluminum raft ready. Simon and Carmen went mute, as well. They finished stuffing the open end of the wing with seat cushion foam, covering the unruly mess with banana leaves and tying it all up with multiple layers of thick hemp jungle vines. It ended up looking like some Bob Marley inspired Rastafarian robot.

Using a screwdriver from the tool kit Hart poked three holes in the top side of the wing and jammed the three-legged metal step stool into them. Next he took the airplane tow bar and strapped two stray aluminum pieces from the planes elevator to it. This created a makeshift rudder for steering the raft. Hart's plan had him sitting on the stool at the back of the wing and using the rudder to manage their course down the river.

A scarlet macaw perched high up in a nearby cacao tree appeared to track their progress with bemused interest. Hart felt its stare. He took to glaring back at it whenever he felt it peering down. Carmen had spotted both the bird and the tree.

"It doesn't care about you," she advised Hart.

Hart glared up at the bird again yelling, "Stop judging me!"

The macaw tilted its head to return Hart's stare as Carmen chuckled, "It's a bird. Their brains don't have the capacity for judgment."

"Maybe. I don't like the idea of nature's representative condemning my presence." He bayed at the moon, "It's not my fault I'm here Pepe!"

Barefoot, Carmen nimbly climbed a lower branch of the cacao tree. She grabbed a yellowish red pod about the size of a small pineapple dangling down from a smaller branch. Hopping back down to the ground she cracked it open with a river rock. She reached inside, plucked out one of the slimy white seeds then popped the seed in her mouth. She started sucking on it like a kids jawbreaker candy.

"Kind of foul, but it still tastes like chocolate and I'm hungry. Try it?" She offered another seed to Hart.

Hart grabbed the seed but it slimed out of his hand plopping down in the dirt. "Gross. The thing is covered in snot! I'd rather eat the damn macaw."

"I'll take one, Carmen." Simon reached into the pod and grabbed a seed.

The macaw remained high up in the tree studying them as if shooting a documentary for National Geographic titled 'The Futility of Man.' He finally glided down off his branch lightly landing on the end of the airplane's wing. The bird flashed another quizzical head tilt then, with what certainly appeared to be a dismissive headshake, took flight downstream. He never looked back. If he could have, Hart would've tucked himself in right behind Pepe all the way back to LA, back to the Pacific Ocean, and back to anything safe.

"The thing is, I got your letter from the American Express office in Rio," Simon calmly let out.

"Which one? I sent a few." Hart answered keeping his eyes fixed on the shrinking ass-end of the departing macaw.

"All of them. I called the Rio office to see if my Mom had written, and they forwarded your letters to me in Botucatu. Excellent service." He smirked.

Hart sat still, before glancing over at Carmen, searching for an explanation. Carmen was working on squeezing a bamboo splinter out of her finger.

"SHIT!" She gnawed at her finger with her perfectly straight white teeth.

"Let me see that." Hart hopped over his workspace then walked over to grab her finger, "That's gotta sting, right?"

Carmen nodded.

"Bamboo's the worst kind of splinter." Hart pinched his fingers together like a pair of manicure tweezers trying to grab hold of the end.

She winced, "Shit, shit, shit! Foda-me that hurts like hell!" she bounced up and down in pain.

"Wow! A Portuguese truck driver! Your command of English is impressive."

"She's full of surprises," chimed in Simon.

"Will you please pull the damn thing out," she moaned.

"Okay, Lenny, relax. It ain't no bullet in the gut." Hart mocked. "Take a breath," he continued tweezing, "I've almost got it." Carmen stopped bouncing and gripped for the coming pain.

Hart had the end out and free, but did not have long enough fingernails to pull it out completely. He gripped her finger and bent down to grab the end with his front teeth. Strangely, it felt romantic. Carmen relaxed her hand in Hart's. He finally grabbed the end and slowly slid out the bamboo. They looked in each other's eyes scanning for something more than pain relief.

"Merda! That hurt," She whispered.

"Very romantic." Simon had witnessed the event from a far.

Hart glared at Simon. He turned back to Carmen to reconnect but by then, embarrassed, she had moved off.

"How sweet," Simon said. "Now help me roll Ray up in the tarp."

Simon had knelt down by Gil and begun pulling his limbs straight in preparation for the corpse burrito they were about to create. Reluctantly Hart came over to assist. They rolled him up together tucking the ends inward and lashing them with more Rastafarian jungle vines. They cleaned up the tools, then they all grabbed hold of the wing lifting and laying it into the water below the airplane remains. The fact that the wing actually floated felt like a miracle. Hart celebrated with a little circle dance. He grabbed Carmen who grudgingly participated. Their liberation from at least the crash site now appeared a certainty. What lay down river remained a dubious mystery. Hart began contemplating how he and Carmen could ditch Simon, and whatever he had in store, and get back to Sao Paulo safely. He truly did not want to call the police, or the army, or even Batman for help. He simply wanted to vaporize as quickly as possible.

"Simon," Hart asked, "if you read my letters and knew I was coming down here, why not just write back, call, or come visit like a normal human being?"

"The dart wasn't my idea. Point of fact, I didn't shoot you in the neck." Simon had started sliding the Gil burrito over to the wing. Carmen grabbed one end and together they slung it onto the wing while Hart held them fast to the bank.

"But," he claimed, "You probably wouldn't have come."

"Something attaches onto the front end of that statement. I wouldn't have come, if what? You told me you wanted to toxin dart me in the neck, crash a plane in the jungle, and hand carry a dead guy back to civilization? You're right; I would have had some hesitations. If you didn't shoot me, then who did?"

Hart's preoccupation with Simon caused him to let the raft wander away from the bank. Carmen looked up and noticed. "Hart! Watch what you're doing!"

He quickly grabbed hold of the raft and towed it back to the bank.

"You believe only your ideas have weight. You know best. You're so American." Simon finished tying Gil to the wing.

Carmen piled on, "I said the exact same thing to him. It's Americans."

"For Christ's sake SIMON is an AMERICAN too!"

Hart looked at Carmen askance. Now Carmen, who he figured ought to be as righteously pissed off as him, suddenly united with Simon.

"It sounds complicated," offered Carmen, "I mean your relationship is complicated. Seems like a lot of luggage between you. The two of you."

"Baggage. It's called baggage." Simon corrected her while cinching down the ropes holding Gil to the wing.

"English has too many words to say the same thing. It is a waste of energy," Carmen said.

"Gil would say the language shows a distinct lack of discipline, but he was a stickler for precision." Simon smiled at his memory.

"Yep, those Germans, sticklers for discipline," Hart mocked.

"Carmen," Hart continued, "you're collateral damage and shouldn't be here either. How can you be defending his actions?"

"That's not what I'm doing at all. His actions are despicable. But, strictly speaking, he is correct. You are judgmental. It seems like that is simply a hard fact of your personality that I didn't know about."

"I don't feel despicable." Simon's feelings were hurt.

"Your behavior is paranormal. Both of you!" Hart stormed.

"And you're normal?" Simon said.

"Sure as shit I'm normal. And, by virtue of the high commission of normal I rule you, and Carmen here, who might be suffering from Stockholm syndrome by the way, as clearly over the boundary lines of even International normal!"

"This is my fault for certain. I wanted you here, but not here." Simon spread his arms surveying their predicament. "But honestly Hart, you have to try to make it over the wall sometimes."

"He's not interested Simon. That's got to be okay too." Carmen suddenly rose to Hart's defense when he was unaware of the true nature of the attack leveled against him.

"I wanted him with me because I love him." Simon explained himself to Carmen before turning back to Hart.

"Can we get on the wing now, or do either of you need to thrash me some more?" Hart had grown weary of the nonstop confrontations.

"Take Carlos into Sao Paulo, take the airplane to pick up Raymond Gil. Bring him to Botucatu. That's it. Simple. I fucked that up beyond belief. It's not your fault at all Hart. It's mine."

"No argument from me," Hart said.

"We were in Sao Paulo by sheer coincidence the day you got here. I wanted to surprise you. You know, 'hey buddy' didn't expect to see me, did you? Carlos offered to go into the airport and see if he spotted you. It was pretty decent of him, considering him. I had talked to Carmen and knew where the Maytag office was, so we headed over."

"I'm missing the part where you call me up, we exchange long lost bro greetings, then plan our reunion."

"You're my save pal." Simon said it shaking his head and smiling,

"Nice job so far." Hart stood by the raft ready to push off.

"Gil said saving someone will change your life."

"Before or after he mesmerized you with his Karate Kid philosophy?"

"We passed all of these police cars and yellow tape. I don't know what shit happened, but Carlos flipped out on me. Some psycho switch went off in him. 'Listen you little shit,' he said, 'I don't have time for this bullshit.' I told him it wouldn't take long and to wait in the car. Carlos stayed put, sulking, while I headed upstairs. Next thing I know he rushes up behind me when I'm about to greet you, elbows me to the wall, and fires the dart into your neck. Oh shit!" Simon's guilty, nervous laughter slipped out.

"It wasn't that funny to me," Hart said.

"Man you were lights out in a heartbeat. BAM! That terrible cracking sound, I thought you might be dead!"

Hart rubbed his neck, "I remember the 'hello' part!"

"Believe me, I had no idea about that damn gun." Simon felt horrible.

"Where the hell is he now? He just shot me and took off?" Hart asked.

"He had other stuff to do in Sao Paulo. He'll find his own way back. You have to know I'm a very small cog in all of this. You're a zero cog, I mean, no one knows about you at all. Surprising you was a spontaneous, stupid, dumb ass personal impulse on my part. Now Gil is dead, and here we are completely in the shit. I'm so, so sorry Hart."

"No offense but what's so special about Gil? What's in Botucatu?" Hart asked.

"Only Greve's best friend from childhood. Not like you and me, but like you and me, only exponentially longer. I killed the guys' best friend. Imagine someone is only supposed to pick you up, then drop you off somewhere, but kills you instead? How would you feel?"

"Don't think it would bother me at that point." Hart corrected Simon knowing the example was ridiculous.

"You'd be completely devastated and PISSED OFF!" Simon answered his own question.

"I'm having second thoughts about this," chimed Carmen while teetering her foot on the makeshift raft floating tenuously in the water.

"But this was all your idea?" Hart countered.

"I realize that, but now I believe we should stay with the plane. Someone will find us based on where we went down. Right? Simon?"

"Carmen, no one saw us go down. No one heard us on the radio. We don't even have a radio anymore, thanks to my pal. Also, I think you are right that we're not far from Botucatu. We can get ourselves out of here. Come on, it's an adventure."

"She doesn't feel safe with either of us. I'd have to say mostly you, since I'm an involuntary prisoner and don't know where in the hell we're headed, or why, in the first place. Am I right Carmen?"

"No. Remember, I'm not the Sheila here! We could find ourselves in more difficulty by moving rather than staying put. You guys can continue to fight your Hundred Year War regardless."

Simon airdropped an announcement on Hart, "You're free to go pal. No harm no foul."

That sudden option took Hart by surprise. Up to that moment he had not contemplated taking back charge of his own destiny. He took an internal breath. Could he simply walk away, leaving both his twisted friend and someone he barely knew alone in the jungle? He was not Indiana Jones. Navigating his way out of the jungle back to civilization on his own was completely out of the question. He sank. A silent chant circled around his brain—Simon was my mother in a previous life, Carmen was my brother, Gil was some holy dead guy from a past life. All of this had to have some infinite meaning he needed to decipher.

Frustrated, Hart said, "Moron, I'm as lost as you are! Can we please get on the good ship 'get me the hell out of here' and leave? Staying put would be the lamest of all our limited options. Our best chance is together, on that raft."

Everyone knew Hart was right. Simon and Carmen jumped on the wing. They used a series of dreadlock looking hemp vines wrapped at intervals around the wing for hand and foot holds. The wing bobbed and dipped, but surprisingly after everyone found a spot it maintained a nice stable flotation. Simon carefully checked the lashing of his mentor one more time as Hart pushed off and stepped onto his Captain's perch: the three-legged stool. They began a gentle float downstream with the easy going current. Holding his makeshift rudder, Hart tested the steering and made a series of small 'S' turns in the river. Provided he didn't try to lean into the turn, which sloshed water over the sides, the craft proved to be a nimble vessel. So far they were not taking on water through the back, and the stronger breeze passing over them felt refreshing and even hopeful.

An hour or so passed without any significant conversation other than an occasional "Holy shit, rock!" Simon kept a lookout perched as far forward as the shaky center of gravity would allow. Hart mostly watched the route ahead, checked the seals for leaks, and contemplated about how to get himself and Carmen the hell away from Simon as soon as practically possible.

"Carlos," Simon turned towards Hart to shout the non sequitur.

"Okay. Carlos. Got it." Hart shrugged his shoulders.

"He shot you in the neck."

"You already told me that."

"I want to make sure you knew his name," added Simon.

"Makes a huge difference. Thanks," Hart said.

"I was as surprised as you were. It was completely fucked, but then he's a real legitimate fucker."

Simon allowed himself to relax knowing he had come clean with a select piece of the truth. Hart glared at Simon as a cloud moved across the sun throwing the trio into shadow.

"You've got no response to that?" Simon expected an attack.

Hart felt a creeping sadness lifting up inside him, "Because I'm not saying anything doesn't mean I don't have a response." He went silent focusing on their course.

A second hour moved by as the sun began rapidly sinking.

When he ignored the circumstances, Hart found himself actually enjoying the peacefulness of the journey. He glanced over at Simon tossing him a long overdue smile. Simon returned the sentiment. Time for both friends blurred back to easier days.

A slight speed change in the current caught everyone's attention. Carmen mentioned she heard the sound of drumming. Hart, preoccupied with the new sound of rushing water, dismissed her observation. The current continued to pick up speed as small white caps appeared next to the raft. A quick flash of recognition all around confirmed to each of them that an unanticipated rapid lay in wait.

"It's most likely not much to worry about." Simon feigned calm.

"Cause you've been right-on about everything up to this point." In his mind Hart imagined a behemoth Niagara Falls spilling into a jagged rock strewn ravine of doom. Their time to prepare grew shorter, since the rapid most likely lay up around a fast approaching bend.

"And you guys don't hear that drumming?" asked an incredulous Carmen with her head cocked sideways.

She slowly threaded her way back to Hart's perch. Hart flinched. Her scent. Her chemical scent had snuck up on him. He felt his dopamine count rising by the millisecond. Strange, that he didn't feel this sensation sooner, over lunch, in the office, in the car. He attributed the delay to the anesthetic from the dart. Carmen jarred him back to awareness.

"Hart! Pay attention. Now I hear music too. Coming from over there." Carmen pointed off to the left riverbank with her right arm. Her left arm resting on Hart's shoulder deepened his chemical rush blurring his concentration.

"Sorry," he composed himself looking Carmen straight in the eyes, "I don't hear anything but —"

"Oh SHIT!" Simon sounded the alarm.

A roiling, turbid rapid emerged as they rounded the bend. The river split into three paths of voluminous flowing waters. The glassy, arching water raced over a ten-foot ledge exploding onto the rocks below, forming a mountain of white water and potential personal destruction. Contrary to Simon's previously carefree assessment, this was definitely something to worry about.

Harts' thought got clipped off mid sentence; a direct result of their floating wing slamming into a well-worn granite river stone. The stone set the raft spinning counter-clockwise against the current. They caught another boulder bash on the back end, which knocked Hart off his perch into a tumbling Carmen. Both of them crashed down onto the wing, slowly sliding off into the swirling current. Hart grabbed hold of one of the dreadlock ropes with his left hand. His right hand latched onto Carmen. He held both of them on the wing; feet skim-dancing on top of the rushing water. The thundering sound of the river rose with each second their raft fought against the inevitable.

The rocks and rushing current glued the aluminum raft in place sideways hugging the ledge. Their vantage point ramped up the fear and dread each of them sifted through in their minds eye. Hart recounted his near death San Blas experience and retreated for a moment. Then, he leapt forward to his elevator experience, only one day in the past.

Simon looked at Hart shouting, "There's no way this is even close to San Blas!"

Surprised at his own reaction, Hart laughed out loud before refocusing on their predicament. The pinned raft sat firmly wedged against two boulders. Rushing water instantly adapted to the rafts presence by spilling over the sides of the wing slowly submerging more and more precious real estate. The longer they stayed wedged in place the shorter their tenure on the wing would become.

"We have to push ourselves off!" Hart yelled at Simon who was gripping a dreadlock while holding onto Gil as well.

"I can't let go of Gil to push off. He'll slide in," Simon verged on frantic.

Carmen and Hart dangled above the water clinging to the wing by the ebbing strength in his left arm. Their dripping wet faces inches away from each other. Hart bore down on her eyes reading her rising panic. Strange moment to feel calm, but he did. He was not being driven by courage or survival, but by the alchemy of physical attraction. He managed to raise both of them from the side of the raft onto the water-sloshed deck. Carmen gave him a Princess Leia cheek kiss. He filed the kiss under the heading 'places I'd like to visit again when my life is not hanging by a jungle vine,' and shifted his attention to Simon.

Hart looked at Carmen and asked, "Can you hold onto Gil?" She nodded.

He kissed her cheek. She climbed off of him crawling her way towards Simon who clutched the wrapped burrito of Raymond Gil. They exchanged places. Carmen now held both the burrito and a dreadlock line slung around him. She signaled to Simon that she had it covered with the thumbs up sign. Simon released his grip.

"Both of us need to push off the rock and let the current spin us straight over the drop." Simon had the plan exactly right.

"Can't thank you enough for this, pal." Hart's adrenaline had overruled his visceral anger and restored his humor.

"Yeah, but you and Carmen are hitting it off, right?" Another ill timed Simon commentary.

Once enough of the forward wing slid back into the river the current would turn them downstream. Hopefully it would all happen before they shot over the falls sideways flipping everyone onto the rocks for a bad date with destiny. The both began to nudge the raft along the rock. Scooting along the rock face, the current began to pick up rushing over the bow in an engulfing wave that threatened to tip the whole raft end over end. "Faster!" They both yelled to each other. Hart felt the stern end lifting off the rock.

"Hang on Carmen!" Hart yelled, but Carmen did not hear him. Simon gave one final shove, almost falling onto the rock before catching a hold of a dreadlock vine and leaning back onto the front of the wing. Hart had time enough to watch Carmen grip Gil, and her own tie down. Then, as hoped and dreaded, the current caught hold.

The whitewater swallowed the raft whole. It made a tight racing turn pivoting around the large boulder that had held them in place. The raft dropped over the falls. At least they had managed that part of the plan as the raft straightened itself out. Everyone lay prone against the wing as a building sized wall of water swept up, covering them completely. The bow emerged first, like a champagne cork blasting out of the bottle. The momentum from the fall off the ledge, and the buoyancy of the wing, created a slingshot affect. Hart looked up from his spot in the back, and watched Raymond Gil launch directly overhead, and off the raft. The ballistic burrito's trajectory rocketed it towards some unknown jungle destination. Waterlogged, Hart searched the wing through the torrent of water for Carmen. A wave of water washed over the three one final time, as they finally bounced back to level floatation. Amazingly, the only loss was Hart's Captain's perch and, of course, Raymond Gil.

"Simon," Carmen wept, "I'm sorry I couldn't hold him. I don't know what happened."

Simon had not realized Gil had not made it through the torrent. Hart, now heard distinct drumming. Glancing over at Carmen, he pantomimed a drummer and gave her an acknowledging look. Simon either didn't hear it, or didn't give a damn.

Resolutely, Simon stood to look up river for any sign of Gil. "We gotta go back for him."

"I'm sorry Simon, but he took off like a stinger missile on a heat trail. Up river, maybe swept down by now. I couldn't tell." Hart shrugged.

"I can put us over to the bank. You're welcome to go hike back up and look for him. I feel bad for you, but I'm not going back." Hart shifted his gaze down river.

Then, undeniably everyone heard the drumming. Faint, at first, then growing progressively louder as the raft continued its recovery drift downstream. Not a simple jungle drumming like some Tarzan B Movie, but a gentle, undulating, syncopated Sergio Mendes Brazil 66 rhythm. They heard a guica: its steady whining, squeaky sound, interlaced between the drumbeats. Then they heard voices weaving around the drums and the guica with a melody line that lifted their mood.

The music floated out onto the river pulling them over to the left bank. There, bare feet in the river, stood a group of coffee colored women wrapped from head to toe in brightly colored scarves. On top of their heads each one wore an indigenous collection of fruit. A tribe of fresh fruit basket wearing, samba singing, native women who were apparently thrilled to have unexpected guests. They sang and moved to the rhythm of the music Carmen had heard. They shouted a greeting and waved them over. When does hello mean hello? All of Hart's Freddie Krueger slasher shadow thoughts meteorically rushed to the front lobby of his brain.

"Don't get off the boat!" Hart admonished to no one in particular.

"You're paranoid of women wearing fruit? Get us over there. We're saved." Simon waved back at them.

Bending the barely surviving makeshift tiller to the right, Hart pointed the wounded wing towards the dancers. Simon was correct. He tossed a vine over to a regal elderly woman with a mango-populated headdress. She tied them off on a well-used stump of wood. No one stopped dancing or singing while the three survivors stepped onto solid ground. Carmen was immediately whisked off by a group of older women while Simon and Hart found themselves surrounded by a gaggle of dancing fruit bowls.

Chapter 19. | Smoothie

Detective Rosado backed away from the blast scene, trying to collect his thoughts. To his constant irritation he had seen the particular graffiti, LAZARUS SAVES, plastered all over various parts of the city ad nausea over the past two years. He took a seat at the bar of the Arabia to take a personal inventory. In between sweeping up shards of broken glass, Jasmine dropped a maracuja smoothie on the counter in front of him. "My complements, Detective," she offered somewhat unsteadily.

Jasmine looked, shaken up by the blast. She managed to hold herself together, focusing instead on cleaning up around her stand—putting pots away, clearing off the grill and saying farewells to her customers for the day. An ambulance crew on the scene along with the Sao Paulo bomb squad was busy trolling for injured victims.

One of the paramedics, a tall, lanky twenty-something, came over to the Arabia on a break. "Anybody hurt over here?"

"Some downed pans and a few broken glasses knocked off the counter," Jasmine answered.

He let out a whoosh of relief, "Whew! What a mess, at least only two people died."

Rosado took a slow sip of his drink and looked up, "Yeah, it's just that one of those two was a friend of mine."

"Sorry, but I guess it could've been much worse than two dead and a couple of car windshields smashed by flying furniture." The paramedic headed back over to the remains of the Eletropaulo building.

"I'm glad to see you're okay. Do you mind?" Rosado opened his notepad reluctantly. He did not expect to hear anything substantial in yet another random Sao Paulo bombing.

Jasmine summed up with a jittery response, "My regular lunchtime crowd. Paolo got his usual, one new stool, and one irritating American asshole called on Paolo's cell phone. Unhappily I answered it."

"I know exactly who the American is, so we can skip that call for now. Who was the new stool? Do you recall what they ordered?" Rosado sipped again at his drink.

"She ordered a maracuja. She took off right after the blast. Can't blame her for that, right?"

Even though Rosado's curiosity was barely peaked he decided to follow the line and keep asking the rote questions, "Do you remember what she looked like, or which direction she headed out?"

"Spiked red hair—hard to miss. She trotted over to her car—kind of a swanky ride with a pink trunk. Didn't see where she drove off to. I was too busy keeping my heart beating to notice that. Sorry."

Rosado gulped down the remains of his smoothie and shot back to his squad car. He kept a somewhat orderly mental file cabinet on most of the bombings which had occurred in the Sao Paulo area over the past couple years. He knew the pink trunk could be found in one of his drawers, but could not find the right one…yet. The pink trunk, the pink trunk, he kept repeating it to himself.

Then it bubbled up. The bomb at the Brazilian Telecom showroom at the Sao Paulo Airport Mall where witnesses reported a Mercedes with a pink trunk driving away; and last year's downtown bombing of the Embratel office in Vila Olimpia, with a dead parole victim. Witnesses had reported seeing a Mercedes with a pink trunk in the vicinity. That bombing had been tagged to either The Shade or the PCC. Normally those bombings had no victims other than office furniture or the occasional luxury car. The suspects always vaporized into Heliopolis. Looking for anyone inside Heliopolis was a complete waste of police manpower. Now, with two victims - one a police officer, Eletropaulo had crossed over. Rosado knew he would have to produce results. He hopped on his radio to put out an all points bulletin for a car with a pink trunk driven by a girl with the description Jasmine had provided.

Rosado made a phone call asking for the Airport suspect to be picked up from Sao Paulo's holding facility. He needed to have a conversation. Rosado wondered what LAZARUS SAVES scrawled on the outside of the building had to do with anything. He had a couple ideas to pursue when his phone rang again.

"I've got your manhunt!" LeVitta was fired up.

"Mr. LeVitta, I need to call you back." Rosado was about finished with LeVitta's insistence.

"Willie Nelson! God Damn it, it's Willie Nelson!"

Rosado barely heard the words Willie Nelson as he folded his phone and slid it back into his pocket leaving, LeVitta in mid-explosion.

Chapter 20. | Start Me Up

Late afternoon and the unmistakable sound of a cappuccino maker frothing milk discordantly echoed across the rolling tree covered hills of Botucatu. Father Greve hunches over as he gently backs his cup of milk away from the steam wand. He pours a measured shot of espresso into the center of his cup. Letting the steam waft around his ample nose, he brings the mixture up for a sip. A hardened man in his mid-fifties wearing a sleeveless faded gray T-shirt with the Rolling Stones signature red tongue logo, walks into the farmhouse kitchen. His muscled arms are covered in tattoos representing various seventies rock bands from the Stones to Led Zeppelin, to Deep Purple and finally Willie Nelson. Willie's visage crinkled around his left elbow appears like some shrunken head from the jungles of East Timor. When his arm bends to shake hands with Father Greve, Willie miraculously rejuvenates for a split second before returning to his pruned existence. The man wears an earpiece wired to a belt-hanging walkie-talkie.

"Brother, they're overdue," he rasps.

Greve looks up holding his mug.

"We think there's been an accident," adds the man.

A grave look came over the priest. "What does that mean?"

"We think the airplane has gone down."

"Where did this happen, Carlozinho?"

"Close, on the river side of Jacarezinho we think, Cachoeira do Laranjal," answered Carlos.

"I know a place there for help looking, but it's too late today. We can go first thing." Greve's concern furrowed his brow.

"You can't. We won't get back in time," countered Carlos.

Greve looks around the sparsely furnished farmhouse finding one of the four mismatched wooden chairs around an old 1960's vintage Formica kitchen table. It has been a long road to Botucatu from Vila Olimpia. He wears a simple black robe belted with rope and a pair of worn Teva sandals. Each sip of coffee finds him gathering more energy.

As the last sip disappears, Greve stands, "There will be time." He grabs the cross hanging around his neck. A few hours later the night slams down on Botucatu. Greve stays awake past his normal bedtime. He thinks about Raymond Gil. He recalled a moment of his childhood listening from the hallway of his home as his father and mother argued in the kitchen.

"God damn it, Sabrina, the kid is going outside. He's going to learn a game. I don't give a damn which game it is." Tired of seeing his son either hidden in a book or watching American TV reruns. Florante Greve raged about the boy to his frail well-meaning wife.

"How about tennis?" She offered.

"It's embarrassing. Something must be done, and done now."

"Tennis, Florante, I said tennis. You're not listening."

"Exactly, tennis! We belong to a damn club, let's use it."

"Since you feel so strongly about this, you can make the arrangements," Sabrina's frustration with her husband's constant tirades bubbled out.

"Don't think I won't."

True to his word, Florante Greve arranged and scheduled a series of tennis lessons for his withdrawn son. He hoped to lure Lazarus into a happier, more traditional childhood experience and remove some of his own personal embarrassment with his peers at GAS. There was only one proverbial fly in the ointment.

"I'm not going," he said, hiding behind his book The Life and Times of Ignatius Loyola.

"Son," Florante patiently began, "you need to engage yourself in a non-intellectual pursuit. Tennis is a fine game to learn."

"Why?" Lazarus had zero interest in learning this sport or any other physical endeavor. He had no interest in the outdoors or, for that matter, interacting with other human beings.

"Let's look at the Greeks; the creators of healthy body—healthy mind. The very word 'gymnasium' is Greek," his father tried appealing to the boys' intellect.

"They're a dead civilization so something went very wrong for them. Don't you think Father?"

"Your brother loves sports. He excels. Don't you think he's happier for it?"

"He's not my brother."

"Fine. But, Lazarus, as your Father I'm making this decision for you. You are going to play tennis. You are going to enjoy it, maybe not today, but eventually. Now that is the end of this conversation."

A gentle Sao Paulo breeze heralded another beautiful spring day at the Vila Olimpia Tennis Club. Despite Lazarus' protestations, there he sat impeccably dressed in his all white tennis togs holding onto a TA Davis Imperial Deluxe wooden racquet imported from America. Led by the hand of his loving nanny, Manuela dos Reis Machado, Lazarus begrudgingly prepared for his first tennis lesson at the exclusive, tony VOTC. The Club had ten perfectly maintained clay courts and one tournament level stadium court. Shaded seating rimmed the small stadium court accompanied by a terrace dotted with a few scattered umbrella covered tables with chairs. Manuela and Lazarus took up station beneath one of the umbrellas awaiting the arrival of the resident tennis pro.

On the precise dot of the scheduled lesson time, two pm, the lanky, deeply tanned, distinguished looking instructor arrived on the court. Looking up, he motioned for Lazarus to join him. The slightest encouraging push from Manuela sent him on his way down the stairs to center court.

"How do you do, young man? I trust you must be Lazarus Greve?" The man had a slight hint of a German accent.

"Yes sir," Greve answered eyes down.

"My name is Mr. Raymond Gil and I will be your instructor. Do you have any questions before we begin?"

"I don't really want to play tennis sir. I don't like sports and the Greeks are a dead civilization." Lazarus displayed no emotional content whatsoever.

Gil nodded in understanding, "Hmmm. No doubt this instruction was your parents' idea?"

"Yes sir. My Fathers."

"I quite understand. I will tell you what Lazarus; I will make a pledge to you. Between the two of us, we will figure out a way to make this experience bearable. And, if it does not work out to your satisfaction, I will assist you in discussing termination of the lessons with your parents. How would that be?"

Lazarus, eyes up, nodded his acceptance.

"Shall we shake on it?" Gil extended his hand, and they shook. "May we get started now?"

"I guess."

Gil thought the boy looked overwhelmed and lost—a jumble of emotions. He determined friendship was his best option for success.

"That racquet feels a little big for you. Is it a bit unwieldy?"

"Yes, sir."

"Why don't you put it down for now. We will not use it for today's lesson." Gil felt a sadness emanating from the boy that strangely reached out and linked to his own.

"Today we will play some catch with a tennis ball. Okay with you?"

They walked around the outside lines of the court together. Gil explained the rules of tennis—singles lines versus doubles lines, service box, baseline, then lastly, and most confusing, the scoring system. There are many discussions on the origin of scoring, but they simply become meaningless chatter since at the end of the day the deranged system remains intact.

After the scoring discussion Gil stood with his bucket of balls at the net. He simply tossed one ball at a time towards his new pupil whom he instructed to catch it with his racquet hand. One toss, one catch, followed by a word of encouragement and repeat. Before Lazarus realized it the time had flown by and the one-hour lesson ended.

"What did you think Lazarus?" asked Gil planting one knee in front of the boy.

"It was okay."

"Better than you thought?"

After some pondering, "Yes."

"A man of few words. I appreciate your honesty Lazarus. Let us make a further agreement to always be completely honest with each other during these lessons, shall we?" Gil extended his hand.

Lazarus extended his hand and, once again, they shook on it.

"See you next week Mr. Greve."

"Yes sir." The stoic little boy walked off the court and back to the open arms of Manuela.

The lessons continued weekly over the next few months. Lazarus did not actually learn to hit the ball with the racquet until the fourth lesson. Even then the task was to stand next to the court boundary fence, one bounce a ball, then cradle his racquet up against the fence trapping the ball between fence and racquet.

"Great job, Lazarus. Good racquet head speed."

The praise from Gil garnered a rare emotional expression from the boy.

"A smile! You must feel accomplished today."

"Yes sir."

"Good for you. Let us do five in a row and call it a day, shall we?"

"Yes sir."

The lesson ended on another success. Lazarus' self esteem and confidence blossomed. Gil could tell the boy did not really like the game, but enjoyed the steady and reliable company.

As the end of summer neared, Lazarus and Manuela arrived for the day's tennis lesson. They patiently waited beneath an umbrella. The habitually punctual Gil was now fifteen minutes late—a highly unusual turn of events. Twenty-five minutes after the appointed lesson time Lazarus spotted Gil down on the court bouncing a ball off his racquet—rather awkwardly. He popped down to the court to find his instructor in an uncharacteristically disheveled state. His un-tucked shirt falling over his shorts; he wore his tennis shoes with no socks. His normally impeccably groomed, slicked back hair absent in favor of a distinctive bed head do, coupled with a full day's growth of beard.

"Hi." Lazarus didn't know what to say to his teacher. He knew something was out of balance, but didn't want to let on to Manuela for fear of causing Gil some harm. The boy reached into the bucket of balls on the court and began bouncing a ball with his racquet mimicking his instructor.

"You don't look so good today. Are you sick?" Lazarus asked.

"I am tired today Lazarus, very tired." Standing next to Gil, Lazarus could smell the scent of alcohol. He recognized it from his father's nightly after work martini.

"My Dad has drinks after work sometimes, but that's at night."

"Uh huh." A foggy headed Gil now realized Lazarus was asking if he had been drinking.

"I am sorry to be late for your lesson Lazarus. We can go longer today if you can stay. I need a minute or two." Gil began to brush his hair back, tuck in his shirt, and take some deep breaths of cleansing air.

"Mr. Gil we have a deal to be completely honest with each other right?"

"That is right, we do."

"Would you prefer not to teach me today?" And then Lazarus threw in the kicker, "are you sad?"

Gil paused to look at the boy, "May we sit down for a second?"

They moved over to the concrete seats on the side of the court.

"You are quite right. I am not feeling myself today. Perhaps, when I truly consider it, you are right twice, and I am sad."

"I get sad too sometimes. Can I help?"

Gil gathered himself, "I had some problems when I was much younger, and sometimes they overwhelm me. I get sad trying to figure them out. You know what I mean?"

Lazarus looked puzzled and remained silent. Gil read the confused expression on his face and felt disingenuous. Gil decided to drop the veil and come clean.

"Lazarus, I had too much to drink last night, the night before last, and also the night before that. It is wrong, but every once in awhile that is what I do. I cannot seem to stop my pattern. You are looking at me after a few nights of over the edge behavior. I am embarrassed."

The boy stayed silent. Bounced his ball and said, "Amen."

Gil stared at the boy, chuckled, and nodded his head, "Perfect. Shall we play some tennis?"

"Yes sir." They never spoke of the incident again.

Lazarus realized from a young age that he was not blessed with great athletic prowess. Although not a gifted tennis player, he could hit the ball over the net with enough frequency to satisfy his need for the occasional sweat. Even after he received his doctorate and eventual teaching position in Botucatu, Raymond Gil continued providing tennis lessons to Greve. He rarely charged him more than the occasional lunch as the two men created an enduring friendship. Greve smiled recalling his memories while holding a place of sadness for what he feared had happened to his friend.

Fitfully, Greve managed to fall asleep only to be awakened well before dawn. "Brother." Despite the early hour, the tattooed man had slipped back into the room. "Lucy called."

Chapter 21. | Ring me

LeVitta, frothing like a junkyard dog on a fraying leash, especially after Detective Rosado had hung up on him for the second time in a row, slammed down the phone. 'God damn it,' he thought to himself, that man doesn't realize I'm about to release the hounds!
"Bolo! Get the keys. It's time to kick some ass, Texas style!"

Bolo had no idea what LeVitta was talking about, but knew they were going somewhere. He rustled around for the keys to the Landcruiser and flashed them to the boss. They gathered themselves and headed out the door, down the elevator, into the parking garage. LeVitta slammed the passenger door. Bolo mimicked him slamming his door as well. Then Bolo sat there with the keys dangling in the ignition.

"Don't look at me like a bucket of rocks son. Start her up!"

"ew ere?" Bolo asked.

"Holy shit, man. I have no time to decipher your tongue. Take me to the closest goddamn police station." Realizing the blank look on Bolo's face meant he did not comprehend; LeVitta rephrased his request in Portuguese with a dash of English, "the God damn Delegacia de la God damn Polícia! Agora!"

Unsure of the exact location of the closest station, Bolo started the car anyway. LeVitta realized he had the address on the business card from Rosado's formerly living deputy Paolo. He handed it over to Bolo and pointed. Address in hand, they headed out, winding their way through the crowded streets of Sao Paulo.

Meanwhile, in front of the Brazilian Savings & Loan branch and the Bimba Capoeira Institute, at the edge of Heliopolis and Sao Paulo proper stood Detective Rosado. Dressed down in jeans, with a faded green and yellow Brazilian National Futbol Team tee shirt, he casually merged into the end of day pedestrian traffic coursing into the favela. The pockmarked streets meandered, curving and merging like a river picking up tributaries on its way downhill to the ocean. Sadly the only ocean connected to Heliopolis was one of the garbage dumps located on the far side of the favela. Rosado did not know exactly what he was searching for; only that he wanted to be closer to the unknown than he would be sitting behind his crappy metal desk downtown.

He walked past a small dusty futbol field in use by a flock of assorted kids from eight to eighteen. That made him smile. Heading deeper in, he caught sight of some graffiti on the crackled brick side of a crumbling old building. He veered over to get a better look and found himself staring up at words written in faded green paint: SHADE SAVES. He continued his slow cruise to find another piece of graffiti—a cross, painted with one word on the horizontal axis and another on the vertical. It read: LAZARUS KNOWS. Right beneath that Rosado read a new phrase. Each letter was painted in a different color cycling from blue to yellow to black to green to red then over again ending on black: FODA OLIMPICOS.

Rosado wearily agreed with the sentiment. Entertaining the world, busy booking airline and hotel reservations for its upcoming summer soiree to Brazil, felt like having his local priest come for dinner but stay for an unexpected two weeks. Brazilians would be expected to act responsibly, politely, and accountably for an upper-crust, double fortnight at least. That translated into a month of formal wear for breakfast, lunch, and dinner. The collective population would feel like it had to drink chardonnay instead of cold beer, and mindfully select the correct metaphorical fork for eating an undemanding plate of lettuce. Nothing could stay festooned and buttoned up that long without blowing. "Yes,' Rosado concurred, 'fuck the damn Olympics!" Still, he had a job to do. He weaved his way deeper into the favela. The cell phone tucked in his front pocket vibrated.

"Rosado, I'm coming to see you or your boss. I don't give a witch's tit which. I'll be there in twenty minutes!" Click! LeVitta did not wait for a response. He only wanted to grab Rosado's attention and shake him up.

The Detective took a deep breath before heading back towards the Brazilian Savings & Loan and his unmarked car. Even if he decided to put the flashing light on top, it would still take over twenty minutes dodging traffic to get downtown. He felt in no rush to greet a steaming hot American pain in the ass like LeVitta. He'd get there when he got there. He spotted a fruit smoothie stand not unlike the Arabia and decided to pick up a drink for the walk back. His phone rang again, but it wasn't LeVitta this time.

Rosado nodded his head after listening for a minute, "Sure go ahead. Let's see what we get."

He sat down at one of two empty stools next to a man sporting a jet black pompadour wearing an 'Elvis is God' tee shirt. Rosado ordered a maracuja smoothie. Elvis soon departed. A small, fair skinned gal bounced in and took the furthest seat away from Rosado. She ordered a maracuja smoothie as well. That wasn't unusual, but her spiked red hair was.

"Here's the thing," Rosado flatly began staring straight at her, "Shade doesn't know and Lazarus doesn't save, does he? So why the confusion?"

Dot didn't bother waiting for her smoothie or anything else. She jumped off her stool and bolted down the street. Rosado gave chase. He realized his wind would not hold up long enough for some extended movie pursuit through the streets of Heliopolis. He spent all his energy on a maximum burst—thrusters on full for as long as they'd last. He caught up to Dot in seconds and passed her as she had simply stopped running. Comically, she watched him race by. He turned his head in surprise, trotting to a halt.

"You got shit, I've got everything. You're on the wrong side of history." Smirk in place, Dot leaned against the wall of a closed used bike shop.

"Where's the car?" Rosado asked.

"What car?" Dot answered nonchalantly.

Night slipped in as Rosado escorted Dot out of the favela past the Brazilian Savings & Loan, heading to his office, and a rendezvous with LeVitta. Thirty minutes later they walked into the Sao Paulo Vila Olimpia Police sub-station. Sitting in the lobby fuming, was Bruce LeVitta and Bolo, along with a uniformed officer holding onto a tall, sallow looking young man.

"Holy shit! Dot? What are you doing here? Where's the car?" Jao appeared genuinely surprised. The air let out of her arrogance-filled balloon, Dot sank.

Recognizing a magic moment when he saw one, Rosado sardonically commented, "You were saying …Dot?"

Chapter 22. | Bananas is my business

A pulsing, gyrating, giggling, and singing collection of women moved Hart and Simon up a carved jungle path towards the source of the music. Night swept over them on the way up the trail. Lit torches appeared along the sides of the dirt and vine covered path, guiding the way through the descending darkness. Nighttime doesn't screw around in the jungle. A black hole, light-smothering darkness submerges every living thing crawling, flying, or walking. A trail without torches is an express road to certain oblivion. Obliging their hosts, Hart and Simon tailgated their way up the trail.

The two exchanged glances, though neither uttered a word. Hart was concerned about Carmen. Would he need to execute some sort of paramilitary extraction rescue? He figured he'd be killed in less than eight seconds, but it was the effort Carmen would remember. Instead, he focused on his certainty there would be a road, or some other type of tether to the outside world attached to the village. He began to formulate a plan. Once they got to the village he would find the chief, the big boss, the supervisor, or whoever formally greeted them. He would then relate the tale of his captivity. He felt confident that his freedom was close at hand, reassured by the reasonable, fruit-centric people leading them down the trail. His mind looped back to Carmen and decided she too would be fine, hopefully.

As they emerged from the path, the music suddenly shifted to an old Les Brown dance tune—"Rock Me To Sleep." It was the absolute real deal, complete with muted trumpets and saxophones. Then he heard the silky smooth voice.

"What in the hell? The jungle has a forties soundtrack?" Hart looked at Simon, astonished.

Simon mirrored the same look, "Twilight zone, man."

There in the middle of a torch-lit village square sat a bandstand filled with musicians playing behind monogrammed pedestal music stands. The words "Lucky Lucy" were emblazoned in late-forties-style white script across the front of each pedestal. Hart counted a full complement of jazz band members: four saxophones, five trumpets, two trombones, two clarinets, a standup bass, a guitar, the drummer, and one flugelhorn. The whole assemblage was fronted by a Doris Day-type, grey haired gal, gliding through the vocals in perfect rhythm.

Hart mouthed a 'what the hell?' as he stood in disbelief. Simon had a far away look. His body stood next to Hart, but his mind had wandered off downstream.

"He'll turn up," Hart whispered with a feint hint of compassion.

Simon countered, "He won't. I've got to find him."

Hart shot back the obvious. "Simon, for Christ's sake, he's room temperature. What else could possibly happen to him tonight?"

"His body could get eaten. It's not right. We've got to go get him." Simon started to slide back towards the path.

"You're right. I'm sorry, but he probably splashed and floated way down stream. We can't get him at night regardless."

"Yes we can. I'll borrow a flashlight." Simon scanned the gathering for someone to ask.

"Fine, Bomba. You can do that all by your lonesome since you're Señor Rain Forest now anyway. Good luck."

"You're all heart," Simon replied, emphasizing the word 'heart.' Still he knew that, in this case, Hart had the more rational argument. He had no real desire to stumble through the black hole, and no real shot at finding Gil's body at night with a flashlight, spotlight, or a 150 million candlepower Xenon Arc searchlight and an Apache helicopter.

Hart grabbed Simon's arm and held him in place, "You're not going anywhere. As pissed off as I am at you, for galactically justifiable reasons, I am not telling Leice I let you trek off into the jungle alone, at night, with a penlight. I'm what's called a good friend."

Simon hung his head. The band broke into a wailing clarinet heavy Benny Goodman tune as Carmen emerged from a hut swathed in the same scarf-wear as the rest of the village women. She made her way over to her two companions.

"You know where we are?" she asked in an animated voice.

"Club Med?" came Hart's smart-ass answer.

"I've heard about this village for years." She checked in with Simon to see if he knew what she was talking about. He shrugged his shoulders.

"It's Carmen! Carmen!" She said it twice; once to herself in disbelief, then once to Hart and Simon as a certification of fact.

"As in Miranda?" Simon asked.

"Exactly!" She shot back.

"This journey continues to raise the bar on definitions for bizarre," Hart moaned.

"I'm named after Carmen Miranda," Carmen began.

The band ended their set and the gray haired singer headed straight over to the little group.

"Welcome to Carmen. The name's Lucy." Lucy was a most unlikely Brazilian name, but her accent gave it away.

"I told you," Carmen said to no one in particular.

"You're American!" Hart felt a sense of home as he let out a sigh brimming with safety and relief.

"Home of the free, land of the brave: that's me honey. Lucy Ann Polk."

"Finally some good luck!" Hart was effusive.

"Lucky is the word. You might know me as Downbeat's 'Girl Singer of the 50's'? Lucky Lucy?"

"Ah, no that was way before our time," Hart said.

"Don't be so rude." Simon gave Hart a shove to the shoulder. He had never heard of her either, but gave her the benefit of the doubt.

Hart wanted his freedom. "I apologize, Lucy," he said, "but may I please speak with you privately?"

Lucy ignored Hart's request. "Lucy Ann Polk's my full name. My friends call me Lucky Lucy 'cuz, well, 'cuz I'm lucky." She showed them a wide smile and cocked her head for emphasis.

"Lucky at what?" Hart felt restless and tired. It had been a long couple of days.

This time Carmen flashed him a stern rebuke. She knew what he wanted, but also realized they were out of danger at this point.

Simon didn't catch Carmen's glare. "Don't pay attention to him. He has a cynical streak that cycles every sixty seconds."

"It's a fair question." She faced Hart and smiled. "Alright Honey, pick a number between 1 and 100. Share it with him." Lucy thumb pointed at Simon.

"Really? We're doing pick a number? Fine, but I'm telling her." Hart sneered at Simon and whispered to Carmen.

"Twenty two." She answered, looking between Carmen and Hart.

"Right!" Carmen confirmed. Hart was unmoved.

"That's not luck. It's a parlor trick."

"Honey, if you ask too many questions, it spoils the mystery. I'm not strictly about numbers. It spills over into parking spots, boyfriends, vacation weather, health, and dental care. I don't question it anymore."

Simon posed the obvious, "What are you doing way out here?"

"Well darlin', I could ask y'all the very same question, but I know the answer."

Hart saw his opening. "Exactly what I need to talk to you about!"

"Don't snap your cap. We'll get there." Lucy dismissed Hart and launched into her own story.

"I met Carmen at the height of her fame in the forties," she began.

"Carmen Miranda?" Of course Carmen knew the answer, but asked the question anyway.

Lucy nodded. "She had it all; movies, records, concerts, global fame and fortune. I was twenty-one and fronting for Benny at the time. Right when Benny Goodman hired me, the band took off, not that they weren't on the direct path, but you know, like the bandstand says."

"We played all the swanky clubs of the day and, for a couple brief moments, ruled New York City. That's where I first ran into Carmen. Three in the morning at a little place in the village off MacDougal Alley called Figlos. A little hole-in-the-wall bar, but they had 300 different types of giggle juice and a great cup of coffee. I figured Carmen for a rum-and-coke gal, but I missed the mark. She had wrapped her show. I had finished mine. There she sat alone at a table in the back. I walked right over and introduced myself. She offered me a glass of twenty-five-year-old

Macallan, so I sat down.

'I'm as wealthy as anyone in my country, or any country has a right to be,' she told me.

She looked neither ecstatically happy nor distressingly sad when announcing that fact. I figured she'd be a dumb Dora or something, but she was nothing like I expected. Carmen Miranda was the world's current definition of exuberance, joy, and exotic beauty. She sat there soft, calm, with this kind of silence that surprised me. 'You've got it all,' I said to her.

'What does any of that nonsense matter?' Carmen posed the question staring directly into my eyes."

'You get to choose though,' I answered.

'I get to choose which fruit cocktail mixture to wear on my head? I get to choose what songs I sing about bananas?' She kept her eyes pinned on me. 'I don't think it's enough for me anymore. Seems like nothing I do truly matters.'

"Applesauce!" Lucy looked around at Simon, Hart and Carmen staring back at her, "Honey, I hadn't a Chinaman's clue what she was going on about. After all I was a baby. Like all of you kids. From my seat, she looked made! Had her pick on the Great White Way. I would have killed for ten percent of that action. That was before I sat down for the whiskey with her. The only thing I found to say, kind of sheepishly, was, 'Can I help?'

"Yes.' Carmen had perked up. 'Eventually, but let's finish our drinks.' She threw back what was left in her glass, encouraged me to do the same. Then she ordered a couple more, and a couple more. Bombs away with Carmen, we sat together for another hour or so, then exchanged info and went our own separate ways. We kept loosely in touch over the years. I considered us friends. On February 10th 1953, she sent me a plane ticket to Rio with a terse note saying 'Now's the time, before I run out.'

Carmen interjected, "But she had a heart attack dancing to 'Bananas is my business' on the Jimmy Durante show and died. The rest is myth, or, at least that's what everyone thought."

"Not quite right, sweetheart, but close enough." Lucy followed on. "Our little 'save Brazil' oasis began in 1953: all Carmen's vision. She's buried right over there, holding all of this together." Lucy pointed to a semi-circle pedestal of brick surrounding the band equipment.

Hart wondered if the amount of 'crazy' he'd encountered in Brazil was in the drinking water. He thought back to that first 'Welcome to Brazil' sign he spotted at the airport, and vowed never to question his intuition again. Ever.

"Save Brazil, in the fifties? Like, Save The Rain Forests?" Hart asked.

"Don't be so clueless. It's not about the rain forest," Simon chimed in.

Lucy laughed. "The Rain Forests? Honey, first things first."

"Fantastic story, and what a wonderful place you've carved out of the jungle. How lucky we are to have stumbled across you, your tribe, and this rich history of Carmen Miranda. I apologize for my rudeness, but may I ask for a ride back to anywhere with an airport, a bus station, paved road, juice bar, dirt road, any link at all to the outside universe will work."

Lucy inhaled a deep breath and continued. "Slow down child, don't be in such a hot hurry. Look around you. Take it all in. Carmen endowed her fortune to save something even more precious than a rain forest."

Hart turned to Carmen, "Carmen? It's time to go, right?"

"It's night. We're not going anywhere right now. Be smart."

"Where are you running to anyway? Maytag? What the hell do you care about them?" Simon piled on.

Hart answered, "Back to our planet. The one you and I grew up on. You should really consider coming with me this time. And, yes, I do have integrity around my job."

"Hart, all I've been trying to do is save you!" Simon exclaimed.

"I don't need saving. You do."

Simon plopped down on the nearest log. He looked up and shook his head.

"Admittedly this has not turned out like I pictured. I emphatically apologize yet again! I know you didn't ask for any of this, but Jesus man, you weren't always this scared of life."

"No, I've always been this way."

"You had swagger."

"You're my closest friend and can't tell swagger from insecurity?"

"It's my obligation to save someone's life, and yours is it."

"Your moral compass has been calibrated by a Nazi? Come on, man!" Hart figured Simon had taken a deep dive off the wrong cliff.

"After the letter, when I found out you were coming down here, that's when I knew you needed my help." Simon countered.

"That was a 'hi how you doin', guess what' letter, not a cry for help. You can't force me to let you save me when I'm not drowning."

Carmen standing on the side listening, "Hart, even I know you followed him down here."

That brick had already hit Simon in the head weeks ago. "Absolutely," He turned back to his friend, "It's crystal clear to everyone around but YOU. When I met Carmen I thought how perfect the two of you.."

The immediate impact of that last comment landed hard on Hart's head, "How titanically messed up is that? I'm here stuck in the land that time forgot because…because? You're matchmaking? This is all about the world's worst blind date? Seriously?" Hart waited for Simon to finally explain then looked at Carmen, "Carmen?"

"Don't be an ass. It's more than that."

"I'm game. What's the more? Illuminate me." Hart expectantly tapped his foot.

"Yes, this all got away from me…a little bit. It's what Lucy was talking about."

"What the hell happened to Lucy?" Hart eyes darted around searching for their hostess.

Lucy had wandered away during the competitive haranguing between Hart and Simon. She came back followed by a tall, reed-thin mulatto man and a slight little girl.

"It's late. You will all sleep here tonight in the guest cottage. We'll sort you all out in the morning. Besides, tomorrow is Jazz Brunch Wednesday. Things always look better on a Wednesday. This is Licorice Stick and his daughter Giza."

"Licorice Stick? Uh, just a tad racist," Hart mumbled to Simon.

Lucy recognized the misunderstanding and responded in a deliberate voice. "He's our clarinet player. 'Licorice' is the nickname for a clarinet."

Lucy had them follow the clarinetist to a mud brick hut complete with mosquito netting and a ceiling fan running off the village generator. There were three beds with linen and two bamboo nightstands, plus a fully functional indoor bathroom.

Simon, who like all of them, was ravenously hungry asked, "Whatcha got there my man?"

"I a at ice ean sh go," Licorice answered.

Carmen and Hart shared a moment before Hart answered Simon. "He said, rice and beans with some mango slices."

"How in the hell did you get that from what he said?"

Carmen thanked the little girl as she handed them plates of food.

"Practice," said Hart and Carmen in unison.

"Huh? Whatever. At this point, I'd eat bark." Simon

Hart wolfed down his plate without a word.

"Can we all agree this ends tomorrow?" Carmen said.

"LeVitta's probably got a gigantic search for us going on," Hart replied.

Simon laughed, "In Brazil?"

Carmen knew Simon was right, "No one's looking for us, but that doesn't matter anyway. We're in no danger and we're leaving tomorrow."

Each silently picked a bed and collapsed onto it. The background humming of the generator slowed, then ceased as the lights around the village faded out. A few candles on the nightstands provided a low flickering glow. Silence engulfed the room. Mostly silence, until both men serenaded Carmen with a snoring duet.

Chapter 23. | Wake Up

Bolo and LeVitta sat in the Police Station waiting for Detective Rosado to complete his interrogation. Rosado had suggested that LeVitta go back to his hotel with the assurance that he would call him in the morning. Taking the Detective at his word, LeVitta stuck with a neck-aching cat-nap in the hallway metal chairs. Bolo went home.

"Wup!" Bolo gripped LeVitta by the shoulders, shaking him awake. He woke up in the same annoyed state of mind as when he grumbled himself to sleep.

"I'm up, god damn it. What the hell time is it?" LeVitta rocked and rotated his neck from side to side trying to work the kinks out of his cervical spine. He flashed an irritated glare at Bolo, who appeared freshly showered and dressed, then checked his own watch. "Eight thirty! What's going on? Where's Rosado?"

"I told you to go home and I would call." Rosado walked up holding out two cups of burnt coffee. He handed one to LeVitta, offering the other to Bolo, who waved him off.

"No offense Detective," LeVitta grumbled.

"I called Bolo here. Didn't I?" He looked over at Bolo, who nodded. "I know you want to talk about Willie Nelson. So do I. Here's what we know. Both of these kids, and that's pretty much what they are, work for a paroled man calling himself the Shade. His name is Carlos dos Reis Machado," Rosado rubbed his jaw line. "I know him."

"That news don't make a chicken dance the Texas two-step," LeVitta said.

Upon hearing the last name, Bolo sat down on the nearest metal chair. His flinching reaction caught the immediate attention of both Rosado and LeVitta.

"Bolo, what's up? What do you know?" LeVitta asked.

"Aim. Wren as aim aim." Bolo shook his head trying to figure things out.

Rosado flashed a sideways look over at LeVitta. "I know, he's virtually unintelligible, but he is trustworthy, reliable, and writes better than he speaks." LeVitta tried to explain to Rosado, who grabbed for his pad of paper.

"Write that down." Rosado handed his pen and pad to Bolo.

He grabbed the pad and began scribbling. Both men waited impatiently while he wrote. Seconds felt like hours as Bolo worked. Finally satisfied, Bolo handed the paper over to the Detective. LeVitta and Rosado read the information and simultaneously dropped their jaws.

Rosado spoke first, "I believe we have a line on your employee. We think we might find him a couple hours southwest of Sao Paulo in the town of Botucatu. I will organize an effort now. Go back to your hotel and —"

LeVitta cut him off, "Not a Chinaman's chance."

Chapter 24. | Take the next left

While the jungle night collapsed dawn slithered in at a vastly more deliberate pace. It slid gently through the trees, skimmed up the valleys, lifted from the rivers and met the sky at the precise moment an unseen hand removed the previous night's blanket. The triggering sound of water flowing over rocks stirred up a host of nature's most bizarre insects, rodents, birds and mammals. They all punched the clock knowing it was time to begin a new day of hunting, foraging, consuming, and irritating each other up and down the multi-level, jungle food chain.

Hart yawned himself awake lying still enough in his shockingly comfortable bed to recall the surreal circumstance of this unexpected campout. He sat himself up, crept into the bathroom, relieved himself, then splashed cold water on his face. He emerged quietly, and knelt down next to Carmen's bed. He gently tapped her shoulders as she rolled over, staring up at him.

"We gotta go," he whispered holding a finger to his lips.

"I know, I'm coming," She looked beautiful even with sleep in her eyes, a mop of bent hair.

Carmen rose and headed into the bathroom.

"You wouldn't have agreed to listen," Simon said quietly and calmly with his back still turned.

Hart pivoted looking at Simon's back, still speaking in a hushed tone, "There had to be some middle ground between a phone conversation, lunch, and a kidnapping."

"You're right. It's the people I'm hanging out with. My life is all changed around."

"So you figured you'd infect mine as a favor to lost, forlorn, desperate me?"

Simon makes his attempt to level with Hart. "I wanted you to tell me if it was all real. If the things I've been thinking about were right."

Hart listened to his lifelong friend. He felt only a disembodied interest in Simon's doubt surrounding whatever bizarre direction his life had veered onto. He knew that Simon waited on his answer. He realized, rightly or wrongly, that Simon had most always waited on his answer.

"Simon," Hart took a pregnant moment hoping his friend would truly listen, "how in the infinite universe of life's options should I know? Why do I need to know? I'm just putting one foot in front of the other. You were right there next to me, doing the same drill."

Carmen emerged from the bathroom as the terminal argument between the two suddenly went silent. She smiled, "Please. It's not like I didn't hear anything guys." She glared at Simon first, "You are a dick!" Then she turned to face Hart. "And you, are a whining, fearful, pussy!"

"Holy shit man, that's awful," said Simon.

"Why? You're a dick. She's right," puffed Hart.

"I know, but she called you a pussy. That's cold."

Hart pulled on his pants and headed out the door without another word. He observed the village of Carmen in a somewhat cloudy midmorning state. A long table had been set up to the left of the bandstand draped in a bright multi-colored tablecloth. He actually took a second to register some excitement about the brunch setup. After all, he loved a breakfast buffet. The disconnected, incongruous thought of a bountiful display of food lifted his spirits for a merciful microsecond. He turned his head to witness a bit of a commotion at the far end of the village.

Simon and Carmen emerged from the hut as they caught a glimpse of Lucy and Licorice Stick walking away from a four-wheel drive Jeep parked at the edge of the village. Screw the buffet toe tapped Hart my liberation is at hand! Some of the other villagers were busy greeting the passengers of the vehicle as the collection of people headed toward the bandstand. Hart, Simon, and Carmen stood still and watched as two older men in their late fifties emerged from behind the band equipment. One was tall, had a nose that spanned two time zones, a receding but polished hairline, stick straight posture, and wore the black cassock of a Jesuit Priest. The other one following behind the priest stood squat, rugged, and powerful. He was wall-papered in tattoos.

Hart turned to Simon stating the obvious, "That old guy shot me? He's a freak."

Before moving off to greet the two, Simon shot Hart a lightening fast 'beware of dog' glance.

"How did you know we were here?" Simon was happy and perplexed to see the two men. Well, at least one of the two men.

"Lucy called last night," said the older man with a grim expression.

"Hart," said Simon proudly, "this is Father Greve, and the reason I came to get you."

Smart-ass Hart, "You mean one of the reasons; the dead Nazi being the first reason, or the second? I'm confused; who's number one?"

Greve appeared stoic as his eyes scanned for the missing man. "Where's Gil?"

"I'm so sorry, Father. I can't tell you for certain what happened. I really don't know. We crash-landed, but I think he might have been gone before all of that."

"Where is his body?" Greve scanned the area, looking for a corpse.

Hart volunteered the information, "Sorry to say, but we couldn't hang on to him. He shot out of the raft like a—," Hart corralled the words 'stinger missile' before they escaped, and even before he caught the disapproving glare from Simon. "I suppose by now he could've washed up on a bank downstream somewhere. I'm sure all of you can, and certainly should, find him when you look."

Carlos spoke up. "We don't have time for that right now, Father. You have to get back. We can look for him after."

Carmen greeted the priest. "Hello, Father."

Greve looked puzzled, but nodded to Carmen, then approached Hart, extending his hand.

"And you are?"

Simon quickly stepped next to Greve. "This is my best friend. From home."

Greve looked perplexed, "I don't understand. Why exactly is he here?"

"Exactly, Father," answered Hart, "I should not be here. Carmen should not be here, and Simon probably shouldn't be here either."

Simon said, "Most of that is true. This is all my doing."

Carlos volunteered his opinion. "I warned you about this dumb-ass idea of yours. Needless bullshit, picking up this little weasel."

"Despite that sentiment," Greve summarized glancing from Simon to Hart then back again, "we are here, and sadly my old friend is not. I am sorry, young man, that you are evidently unhappy to be among us."

"Unhappy is pretty far south of how I feel. If we can get back to Sao Paulo, that would go a long way to helping."

Lucy walked up to the small gathering, "Everyone planning on staying for the Jazz Brunch? We need a count."

"Not hardly," said Hart. "We're leaving."

"Shut the fuck up punk. You're not in charge," Carlos said.

"So?" Lucy patiently asked again.

"Hell no. We're leaving," Carlos replied.

Simon watched Hart forming a response in his mind. He moved quickly to intercept him but missed his window. "Listen, shithead," Hart declared, "consider yourself lucky I don't file charges for assault. You SHOT me!"

"Don't be such a pussy. You're none the worse." Carlos chuckled.

"What is all of this? Simon? Carlozihno? What is he talking about?" Greve wanted an explanation.

"Father," began Simon, "Carlos created a nightmare for us."

"Carlozinho, is this true?" Greve asked.

Carlos stared at Greve, then let his temper flare. "I have promises to keep too, brother."

"I'm lost." Carmen said, bewildered.

"Uh, me too. What's that supposed to mean?" Simon added.

"Your friend was a foolish waste of time in Sao Paulo. I warned you." Carlos' temper rose.

Lucy looked genuinely disappointed and disconnected. "Looks like my cue to bid you all goodbye. I hope to see you soon, Father." She hugged Greve and walked off to attend to her lunch.

Carlos began a deliberate pace towards the Jeep. "Brother," looking over his shoulder, " now it is truly time to go. There's a seat for you and her. The asshole stays."

"The hell with that crap." Hart glared at Simon.

"You'd be over in a millisecond. He's deadly," said Simon plucking out the misguided thought he read in Hart's eyes. "Be patient. Greve is a great man, with a valuable message. All I wanted was for you to see what I've seen."

"I'm sitting in the front row. How much closer do I have to be?"

"Granted, but you don't know anything yet. We haven't had the chance."

Hart looked over at Carmen, back at Greve, and then he did the math, "Carmen, these are the Jesuits—the guys that blow shit up. Right!?" He glared back at Greve. "Hey man, I almost died in an elevator, before Simon here decided to save my life by crashing me in the jungle. Is that what you're all about?"

"Father, I profoundly apologize for the disrespect of my friend," Simon said.

"Don't fucking apologize for me!" Hart shot back.

Greve offered a bemused smile on his face. "Young man, we have not blown up anything, nor would we ever."

Carlos dos Reis re-entered the conversation, "Is that a fact, brother?"

Disappointment and surprise suddenly streamed across Greve's face. "Carlozihno? You have something to tell me?"

"It's nothing you haven't asked for in so many words. You want change, but are afraid to put it into action. In the phrase you are so fond of quoting, be careful what you wish for, brother."

Hart interjected to Simon, "Hold on, these guys are related?"

"Hart! Shut up for one second," said Simon.

Greve spoke to Hart patiently, "Young man, this world is broken in so many places. It's hard to find the loose ends and even begin to put anything back together again. Even though all we can do is pick up one piece at a time, each effort must matter. It must be deliberate and conscious. We," he looked around, "will gather the people around us to regain control of our country and our world."

"So you blow things apart to emphasize your point?" he said to the priest. Somehow he had landed in the middle of a Brazilian vigilante film festival screening Death Wish 42—Third World's Revenge. Getting in the car might seem counter intuitive, or objectively stupid, but he still knew it was the wisest course of action to make his eventual escape.

"I will not debate with you young man." Greve turned away.

Simon grabbed Hart by the arm and pulled him aside, "You've got to shut the hell up. I promise to get you out of here, but please use your head!"

"He's the one that started with the whole manifesto conversation. Is this what you're about? Holy shit man."

Before Simon could respond the heavens decided at that precise moment to launch a torrential commentary on their little corner of the jungle. An organ-drenching rain squall enveloped the group in mid conversation. They were suddenly doused in great sheets of water.

Greve reached up and grabbed a large leaf off a nearby palm tree. Simon and Carmen ran for the nearest hut. Greve followed. Hart stood uncovered and alone for a moment, staring at Carlos who stood unflinching in the downpour. Sensing nothing productive would come from that he dragged his organ-soaked self into the hut.

"Father," Hart restarted after entering the hut, "before you continue to incinerate, bomb, or otherwise crush the opposition. I have a different view of the world."

"No one cares about what you think," said the frustrated Simon.

"You do! Right? You dragged my ass out here," came his quick response.

"My brother is not bombing anyone." Carlos had appeared behind Hart.

"You've been doing that," Carmen summarized for everyone.

"Lazarus," Carlos shifted topics, "it's now or never. You need to get back."

"He actually is your brother?" Hart looked at Greve in disbelief. "What a messed up dinner table that must have been."

"I hate to offer a cliché, but this shit has got to stop somewhere. We're not all serfs slaving away for kingdoms we have no stake in," offered Simon.

"And I imagine Father Greve was about to explain that to me?"

"No, I wasn't," he dismissed. "It's time to go." Greve gathered himself to leave despite the rain.

Hart could not quite balance the events. Counter to Carlos, Greve seemed so blatantly un-psychotic. He did want to get the hell out of there, but now he was conflicted about his rideshare option. Adding to the blender of events, Hart now realized his sense of smell had gone AWOL, and his creeping headache was intensifying. He knew the signs and dreaded the certainty. A bout of depression was not what he needed at this moment. He felt a spreading sense of gloom and isolation making its way up his consciousness. While leaving this place had been number one on his agenda, staying put now emerged as the best choice.

"So be it," Hart said. "Simon, let's plan to catch up on all this stuff soon. Dinner, for sure next time you come to town."

Carlos stuck his head back in the hut, glaring at Hart, but commanding Simon, "Bring the asshole. We can't leave him now."

"And miss Jazz Brunch Wednesday? Not a chance." Hart looked Simon dead in the eye with absolute sincerity. "Carmen and I are staying."

Simon simply invited Hart out the door with a wave of his hand and began walking. The jeep waited outside already idling with Willie Nelson's Brazilian spawn positioned behind the wheel. Greve sat in the passenger seat. Carmen was already situated in the back. An unhappy Hart slid into the SUV to sit between Carmen and his unrecognizably misguided, best friend. Lucy waved a disappointed farewell as they pulled out of the village. Hart reconciled that her luck was non-transferrable. He fought against a swooping, sinking feeling of fatigue.

"What about Gil, your surrogate father? Have you moved through your multiple stages of grief that rapidly?" He tried to work his way under Simon's skin one final time.

"No. But I'll have to let him go for now."

"Father," Hart started in on Greve, "Simon says Brazil is ground zero for Earth's new re-org movement."

"I didn't say it like that." Simon felt embarrassed.

"I admit I'm paraphrasing, but I might have a heart attack any minute and leave this astral plane never understanding the mystery that has engulfed me."

Greve was miles away focused on the road ahead. Carlos displayed no reaction whatsoever. Carmen fell silent, looking anywhere but in Hart's direction.

"So Willie," Hart now targeted Carlos.

"Jerk off, don't make this worse," Simon whispered.

"Oh, come on. No one is that bad ass in real life. He'd be in prison. His brother's a priest." Hart whispered back to a chagrined Simon.

"I could throw him out right here." Carlos slowed the vehicle scanning the side of the road.

Hart protested, "In the middle of nowhere? You can't just vote me off the island and drop me anyplace. Have some humanity. Take me where you're going then let me off in a town at least. I'll make my own way back to Sao Paulo. And what about Carmen? Carmen, anytime you'd like to chime in would be great!"

The rain suddenly stopped as quickly as it had started. They made their way down a narrow, twisting road lined on either side with dense jungle. The track they drove had breadth enough to accommodate the Jeep, but not an ant's width more. Carlos barreled down the muddy road. He jogged the steering wheel left and right slipping and sliding the tires like a Zodiac raft captain navigating ocean swells. Miraculously, the jeep maintained center in the barely discernable ruts, but the ride was anything but smooth.

Hart had a pronounced distaste of winding roads generated by a childhood of bad idea vacations to mountain resorts indulging his father's far and wide tennis camps and tournament cravings. As they bounced and twisted their way through the jungle Hart felt a telltale queasiness rising in his stomach.

Simon knew him well, "Dude, you don't look so good."

Hart couldn't muster a reply.

Carmen added, "You look green."

"Buck up pussy. Don't even think about it." Carlos kept jockeying the car left to right, right to left, bounce up, drop down, left, right, left, left, left, right. Left and up, right and…the urge became too powerful to contain.

"Huh, aaaahhhhh!" Hart gagged as a stream of vomit jet-sprayed out of his mouth onto and over Carlos' head splashing against the windshield. Hart leaned over Simon swiveling his body to aim the next shot out the window as fast as he realized what had happened. Seeing the window was not rolled down enough he quickly opened the door as Carlos simultaneously slammed on the brakes and skid stopped the Jeep straddling the ruts.

The momentum swung the door wide open hurling it hard against its hinges. The force whip snapped the door clean off. It passed directly by the drivers' side view mirror stripping it off the car before landing in a heap by the left front tire. Hart popped out of the car and into the bush continuing his gut twisting hurl-a-thon. Carmen bounded out of the jeep coming to his side. Why would she do that? Hart considered her display of pity unmanly and pushed her away while he continued to spray the flora and fauna with whatever contents remained in his stomach.

"I'm going to kick your ass for that." Carlos was beyond pissed wiping Hart's noxious heave off the back of his head. Carlos was the unanimous choice by all parties as the last guy in the car you'd want to catch a stream of fresh vomit.

"I'm sure it was not intentional, Carlohino," Greve said.

"Hey man, ease back. It wasn't on purpose," Simon too became Hart's protector.

Hart's inner dope decided to ventilate a burst of misguided testosterone, "Yeah, I actually did."

The only thing shielding him from certain death was his continued sporadic vomiting.

"Listen asshole, the police are probably looking for me, and on your trail right now." Hart said before wretching yet again.

Carlos walked over to the back of the jeep and pulled out a gallon jug of water. He poured it over his head then did the wet dog shake. He made is way over to where Hart remained doubled over.

"Carlos," admonished Greve.

Too late, Carlos grabbed Hart by the hair yanking him upright. Hart braced himself wondering about the pain involved with a broken jaw. The powerful man reared back with his right hand and slapped Hart so hard across the face he actually saw stars. He wanted to cry like a pre-teen in a playground fight. While gathering his wits he heard a scuffle taking place in front of him. Hart looked up to find Carlos inexplicably sprawled on his ass covered in mud. Carmen was standing a foot in front of the fallen tattoo parlor wiping traces of mud off her hands.

"That's bullshit. I'll be ready for that shit next time," Carlos grumbled as he got up and walked back to the car.

"And I'll be ready for that too," answered Carmen.

"I apologize. That was truly uncalled for," Father Greve had come to Hart's side. "Simon, bring the water."

Greve supported Hart by the arm while Simon brought over the gallon jug of Brazilian Spring water. "Carmen, you've been studying your heritage I see," said Greve.

"Thanks." Hart took the water and rinsed off his face, mouth, and hands.

"Jesus, Hart, uh, sorry Father. Get a clue." Simon was now afraid for his friends safety.

Hart's olfactory sense had now completely abandoned ship. He couldn't smell anything let alone himself. His head throbbed with a world-class Olympic headache.

"Why am I here against my will?" Hart asked.

"You should not be. Your friend must answer for that," Greve answered.

"Please tell me this isn't all about the rain forest? I love the rain forest, I love oxygen and I know that it comes from the trees. I know we're all trading satellite dishes for Brazilian rosewood but,"

"There is a great upheaval on the planet that will most assuredly lead to our annihilation. Do you believe in heaven?" Greve held the water jug for Hart.

"Father, I'm not dying. I just got car sick." Whether or not he believed in a designated Five Star resort community for afterlife care and comfort had little influence on Hart's answer to Greve, "I don't think about those things top of mind. If there's a Heaven I suppose there's a Hell, and this might be it. I'm not interested in anymore riddles," Hart wanted to manage his splitting headache and address no more mysteries.

"Humanity is suffering from a profound and alarming lack of empathy." Greve put down the water jug and reached for a rag in the back of the jeep to hand Hart.

Greve continued, "No problem can be solved by the same level of consciousness that created it. Our mortality, the mortality of every living thing is the common bond that brings us together to protect all human life, and our planet itself. We will make change outside of governments, outside of institutions, with the will of the people."

"There's a big upheaval coming," chimed in Simon

"Okay, okay, big upheaval. I hear you. What are you doing about it? Voter's rights, silent protest, gun control? Fatwa? Why is everything so vague and elliptical? Father, perhaps your truth is the right truth. People power? I don't have any idea." Hart trenched into his position. His anger, and his overwhelm hardened his resolve. "I have no reason other than the dart bruise in my neck, the ache in my jaw, and a splitting headache not to believe what YOU teach, whatever that may be, might be a path forward. But it's not MY path."

Simon thought he saw a glimmer of possibility in his friend. He stepped up in support of Greve, "Hart, if we want a new world, each of us has to start taking responsibility for helping create it."

"Not at someone else's command I won't." Hart looked around at his collection of captors. He glanced at Carmen hoping she would chime in and wondering why she had exhibited such an enduring patience with these people. Still he pushed on alone, "You are, all of you, entitled to your opinions and actions, however lunatic they may appear to me. However, none of you are entitled to decide mine."

"I quite agree. Make your own choices," said Greve.

Carlos emerged from the jeep munching on a Ghirardelli 73% dark chocolate bar. Cleaned up a bit, he felt ready to rejoin the conversation. He suggested flatly, "Let's get rid of him." He broke off another square and popped it into his mouth. Motioning towards Hart, "He's a hassle. Chocolate?" He offered Hart a square.

"Sorry about the vomit," Hart said. He took the square to get the acid taste out of his mouth.

"I've moved on. Chocolate?" Carlos offered everyone else a square then walked to the rear of the car and sat on the bumper.

"Leave my closest friend here in the jungle? What the hell's the matter with you?" Simon demanded.

Carlos smiled sarcastically, "Not leave him. Kill him, then leave him in the jungle." He peeled back the wrapper and bit off another square.

"Carlos get back in the car please." Carmen again rides to Hart's rescue.

"Thank you, Carmen," Hart said.

"Don't thank me. Your instincts are base and narrow, without a thought for anyone else."

"Hang on. What in the hell did I do? I'm the victim here?" Up to that point, Hart never truly felt his life was endangered.

"Uncle, please, it's enough," Carmen said to Greve.

Hart staggered a moment. "Uncle?" he repeated. "Is he? He's your Uncle?"

"It's a bit of a complicated journey," she said, "but yes, more or less he is my Uncle. Technically I suppose he is my half brother, but given the age difference I've always called him Uncle. His Father was my father, but my mother was his nanny. So you can figure out the connections."

Hart felt the disaffected gloom of his Dukkha smothering his judgment and impairing his reality. The ground suddenly shape shifted beneath his feet. He felt adrift, cut off from everyone and everything, alone in his space capsule.

Hart looked back to Carmen for some truth, "You don't really work at Maytag, do you?"

"In a fashion. Remember, I said I had never met Mr. LeVitta. I've known Bolo for many years. His friend Rita gave her position to me for the past couple weeks."

Hart was reeling, looking between Simon and Carmen, to Greve, and the chocolate-munching Carlos. "Simon?"

Simon sheepishly met Hart's eyes, "I met Carmen through Father Greve and Gil."

Hart was busy putting the family pieces together, "Wait, that means the psychopath is your brother too?" He asked Carmen.

She shrugged. "That was a surprise I didn't know about. My mother never told me."

Hart stared back Simon, "I thought you had the right road, and I had veered off into a ditch. So I followed you. I admit it. I followed you?! What a Gold medal-winning bonehead move on my part. You've become a mess, a progressive disaster that gets worse with every bump in the road."

"It wasn't supposed to." Simon took his friends shoulder.

"Too much damn talking." Carlos wiped his hands on his pants and tossed the wrapper to his chocolate bar on the ground. He hopped out of the jeep, heading straight for Hart.

Hart would have liked to have said a lot of things, but a chocolate-covered fist sealed his last conscious moment. It didn't hurt. It all magically went black in a jungle millisecond.

Chapter 25. | In the midst

"You're awake." Carmen leaned over a bleary eyed Hart emerging from unconsciousness, "How do you feel?"

"I can talk so I guess my jaw isn't broken, right?"

"It's pretty swollen. You're in Botucatu." Carmen politely provided Hart's new location.

He moved his jaw around to be sure it truly had not been broken from the punch. He felt only a dull ache, minus any sharp pain, meaning he had been spared. The ocean breeze wafted through an open window of the house, which sat on top of a hill overlooking a large soccer field. He sucked in the air hoping to energize himself and clear his head.

"I apologize for my older brother. He's an impulsive idiot." Carmen said.

"This probably isn't news to you, but your 'family' is seriously dysfunctional. Carlos is your brother? I thought he was your…" Hart pointed over to Greve.

"Same father different mother."

Hart held up one hand. "Stop! It doesn't matter. Your brother is a violent psychopath."

Greve stirred a cappuccino and turned towards Carmen and Hart. "He's my brother, so family is still family. Sadly, I fear you are right."

"Where's Simon?" Hart looked around the room.

"Big day for us. There are almost twenty-thousand people out there waiting to hear from Father Greve." Carmen appeared eager and excited.

"Really?" Hart assessed his options scanning the windows and attempting as best he could to get the lay of the land.

"It's for Carlos, and others like him that Father Greve stands up," Carmen offered Hart some form of explanation.

"Ex-cons and psychopaths? I'm sorry Carmen, but I guess I'm not seeing it."

"Please. Don't be childish. Look at the dividing lines. Look at the favela's. They're not exclusive to Brazil." Carmen nodded towards Greve. "Carlos and Father Greve grew up together," Carmen added.

"Simon and I grew up together too. That hasn't turned out so well for me either."

"Simon was only trying to show you."

"Can we leave him out of this for the moment? Are you about to tell me your brothers' tragic downfall and resurrection story? Because that would be a much more compelling tale than my pal Simon's."

"There's more here than meets the eye," offered Carmen.

"The only thing that truly matters is what meets the eye when the eye is open."

"Carlos is proof of the consequences of living a life without conscience, and without empathy. He is paying the steepest price for a lack of awareness."

"Is he dead?" Because, actually, I thought death was the steepest possible price?"

Greve standing off to the side of the room answered, "Absolutely not."

Simon walked into the room. "Father the crowd's raging out there."

"So this is your idea of grabbing life by the balls?" Hart suddenly became aware of the crowd noise from outside.

"Actually, yes. It is messier than I wanted it to be, but I'm grabbing and holding while you choose to do jack-shit."

"Simon, why do you keep taking these shots? Why are you so damn disappointed in me?" Hart asked.

After another moment Simon somberly looked Hart straight in the eye, "It doesn't matter if I saw you yesterday, the day before, or a year ago. I know you."

"And I know you too. Wahoo. Look where it got us." Hart said.

"Can't argue that. But right now, I am completely willing to give up on you. Really."

Carmen stepped over to Hart, "I would appreciate it if you would wait until after Father Greve speaks before bailing. Can you do me that favor?"

Hart pondered the request. What would it truly matter in the long run? One more surrendered hour tossed to the wind could not possibly jumble anything beyond the current state of disarray. Nothing had gone according to any plan he had imagined since stepping off the damn airplane in Sao Paulo. Yet he had remained unchanged through all of it. The likelihood of whatever Kool-aid these people had already swallowed affecting him in an hour, or even two, seemed more remote than anything that had occurred during the last twenty-four.

"Hart," implored Simon, "the world is coming to Brazil—the entire world."

"I'm completely aware of the Olympics. I was trying to help with all that myself." His Hail Mary letter and phone call to the Brazilian Olympic committee seemed like another lifetime ago.

"This isn't about making money. It's about changing minds. Changing the world. None of that interests you in the tiniest way?" Simon asked.

"We happy few, we small band of brothers? I've got a better shot at doing their laundry than altering the course of humanity."

"We are not a 'happy few' pal."

"Did you really believe you had to go through all this shit for me to simply sit down and hear you out?"

Simon sat down drained of his spirit. He looked up at Hart, "Buddy, I guess not. It's more like everything I had to go through."

Hart looked Carmen in the eye, "I'll stay, but please promise to keep the psychotic away from me."

"You don't know the half of that guy." Simon advised.

Carlos walked up at that precise moment. "Father time to go," He glowered at Hart, "stay the fuck out of my way you little shit."

Hart simply raised his middle finger. Everyone walked out of the house. They loaded into two golf carts one driven by Carlos, the other by another older man in shorts and a tropical shirt. He nodded a greeting at Simon.

"Another whack job Jesuit, or some convict pal of yours?" Hart sarcastically tossed out.

"Hello Rabbi," Simon said before turning back to Hart. "He's a huge Carmen Miranda fan," smirked Simon.

They drove down to the field stopping next to a set of stairs leading up to a stage setup at one end of a soccer field. Waiting at the base of the stairs stood a timelessly beautiful, elderly woman with a perfectly lean build that belied her age. Her piercing green eyes briefly glanced over at Carlos before landing on Greve. "Lazarus, I'm so proud of you." Manuela Dos Reis rushed up to Greve and wrapped him in her arms.

"Mother!" Carmen excitedly rushed to greet her.

Greve kissed Manuela on the cheek and stroked her braided, grey-black, ponytail before following Carlos up to the lip of the stage. As he climbed the riser stairs, becoming visible on the stage, the large crowd erupted in applause. He paused a moment as a stagehand placed a headset microphone around his ears. He then continued to center stage as Simon, Carmen, Manuela and Hart watched.

Greve gazed out at the crowd of perhaps twenty thousand people filling the soccer field. He exhaled, then looked skyward for a brief moment, "My friends, I have radical news!"

The crowd hummed with anticipation. "It will change everything without having to change a single thing. The world is a horrific place. Children starve while the family next door throws away perfectly good food. Young people are talked into fighting wars they cannot begin to understand and are left without arms or legs, having seen things from which no soul can find rest. Men, women too, take pride in providing a life of ease for their children by making money off the bent backs of others. People lie, cheat and steal with no apparent remorse."

Greve kept up his dialogue to the enraptured crowd, "There is little real justice, and seldom, true mercy. And, we will all die, every one of us. And most likely, it will not be pleasant!"

The crowd went stone-cold silent. A poised Greve held the moment.

Hart stared at Simon with a mystified 'I'm not getting this," expression. Simon hushed him with a raised hand.

Satisfied he had created the desired heightened dramatic impact, Greve shifted his outlook, "As bleak as our world may seem, in truth it is anything but. Buddhists say 'Nirvana in this very life.' Heaven is not found in some distant promise, some favored religion, not in material wealth, not in the bliss of drugs, or on a large flat screen TV. It is not in being right, in winning, or in having a comfortable bed, and a retirement plan. Heaven is a radically different way of seeing. Jesus was only one voice among many—Moses, Buddha, Mohammed, Krishna, Gandhi. Most of us prefer to worship the teacher, rather than follow the teachings, rather than change our way of life, even when our way of life no longer serves us. We continue to paint God in our image. Let us allow God to paint us in His."

A spontaneous wave of applause and cheers erupted from the crowd bathing Greve in the knowledge that he had made his connection.

Hart recalled the bombing in Sao Paulo and glanced over at Carmen again. She realized his addition skills had connected two dots. He leaned over to Simon whispering intensely, "Holy shit, Simon. What the hell have you gotten yourself into?"

With guilt written across her face, Carmen said, "Carlos promised it would raise the profile. Father Greve had no idea."

Hart glared at Carmen, "And you said I wouldn't understand because I'm a colonially judgmental American?"

"You are." Her gaze turned downward, then back directly into Hart's eyes.

"Is that guilt, and you agree with me now?"

Greve kept up his post abyss momentum, "There is right and wrong. We must punish the wicked and reward the good. That is exactly how our church, and many others, has thrived—by righteous indignation, fear and promise. But that is not the truth of any God. We must question without losing what is good and right. There is beauty and meaning in every path, in the paths of our neighbors, and in the paths of our enemies. When God's way of seeing becomes ours, the world will suddenly be a very different place, although nothing, not one thing, will have changed."

"That's the big new thing? Nothing?" Hart angled his commentary towards Simon.

Simon answered, "You know that part of a tennis match when you need to turn the burner up? Take a decisive action to change the momentum?"

"We're not playing tennis," Hart countered.

"Exactly."

"Hungry children will still call for your love and assistance, but the family who over-consumes will now too evoke your compassion. You will still ache for the young people who are talked into fighting wars they cannot begin to understand, but what keeps your heart breaking open will be the heartless men and women who sent them there. Those people who built their own families' comfort on the underpaid labor of others become the recipients of your concern and your prayers. You will feel for the person who had their possessions stolen, but you will look for the man who stole them to ask why. Our compromised planet brings tears of sorrow, but also tenderness towards those who continue to wound her."

"Carmen," Hart touched her arm, "You need to make sure they let me go, or all of you are going to be arrested for kidnapping. You know that, right? It's been three days."

"Simon insisted I meet you. We figured it would be a couple of days at most. Not a big deal."

At that moment Greve appeared to be winding his way to a thundering finale, "When we let go of opinions and ideas something else emerges; love. We are called upon to change something far more fundamental. We, all of us, must dare to live a life that is entirely informed by compassion—by our abundant capacity for genuine human empathy.

This then is my radical news for all of us: nothing, absolutely nothing has to change! Nothing but the way we see. Poverty, injustice, disrespecting our shared planet; all of that will be as it is. Small changes will not be enough to save us. And if we don't stop our rising fear and concern, we will truly, all of our own accord, turn our heavenly earth into a very real hell. But what if we are courageous? What if we are not governed by aggression, violence, and self-interest? What if we see life as it is, not as we wish it be, but as it truly is: light and shadow, good and evil. Underneath all of that lies a beautiful sea of gray in which all the colors of the universe reside. What if you let go of all you ever thought, and simply commit your life to attachment, affection and companionship: to love? Awaken Brazil. Awaken to the world of your possibility. Can we be the first of many to make our stand? Will we? That is a fight worth winning."

Greve took two steps back from the proscenium of the stage to a thunderous ovation.

"Well?"asked Simon waiting for Hart's miraculous and swift conversion.

Hart's mind wandered. It traveled back in time to life at twelve; the two friends driving down the Disney Autopia highway together—their speed and route governed by a higher power, every turn manageable and predictable. The entire ride, setup as a safe, foreseeable path from start to finish. Simon had now driven off the track. Yet, he still needed Harts' approval to keep driving. Had he been able to locate a scant teaspoon of compassion in his soul at that moment Hart might have generously offered his pal a great send off. Hart flashed on Siddhartha saying goodbye to his best friend Govinda at the Bodhi tree. 'May you walk this path to its end. May you find deliverance.' The words appeared clearly in his brain. Hart knew for certain that his friend who had been a compass, shadow, and barometer for his own life had now left him.

Hart's sub-conscious typhoon emerged, "What a bunch of crap Simon. I'm out of here."

"I understand," Simon said with resolute finality.

"I don't see anything revolutionary about something that's been spoken about by so many others throughout history, ad vomitus."

"No need to gush on, I can see that you're happy for me," Simon said.

"What a horrible disaster. What am I supposed to tell Leice?"

"Tell her I'm thriving."

Looking around and seeing nothing restraining his exit Hart felt his freedom. He grabbed his friends' hand. "Okay. I'm happy you found something to believe in and fight for. Truly. I hope it brings you peace and fulfillment, but I can't help being worried about you." Then he smiled and jabbed, "Carmen? I guess she's an acquired taste, like me, I suppose. It's the strangest date ever, but maybe that could have worked in some warped way." Hart delivered this final salutation as sincerely as he could. He then let the words lay there for Simon to interpret on his own.

"I'm gone." He glanced at Simon, who nodded.

Hart quickly turned and walked away, praying he could simply disappear among the crowd now dispersing all around the field. He didn't realize until that moment how much easier Simon had it than him. Simon may have hitched up to subjugation, or insanity, or both, but he had surely made his choice. And Hart was stuck sitting in a leaky boat watching the big one swim by him on its way out to sea. He had a solemn epiphany, now believing Simon ended up with the preferred end of the nirvana deal. He sank. 'Simon wins the orange robe of peace and fulfillment, while I'm stuck out in the sweltering jungle with a six inch loincloth, and a lifetime supply of Black Mambas.' Hart continued walking wrapped deep in his shrinking cocoon of depression, questioning each uncertain step forward.

"Stuck with myself once more." The distance between everyone around him seemed to expand. He scanned his surroundings, feeling thoroughly clue free on which direction to turn. He needed a plan, a destination. He read a banner strung up on one end of the field, 'Future Site Olympic Futbol.' The Olympics, he reminded himself, then noticed his change of heart. Screw the Olympics, he thought. Forget Maytag and the entire concept of clean. He hastily arrived at a plan of action. He'd simply follow the crowd out and chase up a ride to any town. He remained conflicted whether or not to go straight to the police and turn everyone in for kidnapping, or let this go down as some warped reckoning with his childhood pal. He could not picture Carmen in a jumpsuit behind bars. He could not fathom Simon there either. He had no problem picturing Carlos manacled and shuffle stepping off to jail. He imagined Greve would be placed in some sort of Jesuit detention center for the not-quite-psychotic, wearing a hair shirt for ten to twenty.

Hart continued his slow slide away, catching a backwards glance as Greve walked down the stairs from the stage along with his psycho brother.

Through his vantage point, descending the stairway, Carlos caught the departing Hart and glared at Simon. "Fuck's he going?"

"It's done," Simon confessed.

"I don't think so. Get him back." Carlos' expression shifted to anger in a heartbeat.

"I made a deal. I can't. That dart, like your 'harmless' bombs, was a terrible mistake Carlos. I regret it." Simon stood fixed.

"Me too. I'll retrieve the little prick. Then come back and deal with your waste of time." Carlos gleefully turned to chase down Hart.

Greve stood open jaw, "Carlozinho, it IS true!"

Manuela, standing at the bottom of the stairs bounced her gaze between Carlos and Greve, "What is true, Lazarus? Carlos, what have you done?" Manuela had already spent years mourning the lost path of her first-born.

"I'll do it." Carmen stared down Carlos and headed in Harts direction. Carlos shoved past her in an instant.

Seeing Carlos take off, Hart doubled down making his way deeper into the crowd attempting, to blend in and disappear. He hoped to grab someone's cell phone and dial whatever the Brazilian equivalent of 911 was to call for the closest Carioca Seal team.

A true, by the book, expertly executed, chokehold does not include choking at all. When used properly the victim simply loses consciousness within a second or maybe two. Unless the perpetrator is a real hack, the whole deal ends in a heartbeat with not much to do at all. Carlos came out of nowhere and performed a perfect ten-execution level on, what Hart later learned, was a blood chokehold. Hart was wide awake one second, gone the next. No fun, but thankfully no real trauma other than a little background headache to add to his already throbbing migraine.

Hart woke up to find himself still stuck in Botucatu surrounded by the same crew. Bleary eyed, his awareness slowly crept back into focus. Without skipping a beat the conversation carried forward as if he had merely stepped out for an iced latte.

"Take these, they'll help." Carmen handed Hart two aspirin and an actual iced coffee.

"Not my doing." Simon copped a weak plea.

"He knows too much about me. Can't have that." Carlos shrugged his shoulders.

Given his present predicament Hart decided the best course of action to be simple silence.

Manuela scowled, "Carlos, this is wrong. I don't know who this is, and I don't care, but you need to let him go."

Carlos recognized no authority from his mother, "You have nothing to say to me. You don't know the first thing about me, or any of this."

Hart glared over at Carmen with a 'what now' expression. She shook her head. Hart felt more confused, but his confusion was trumped by a serious fear for his own safety. He groggily looked over at Greve, "I can't make judgments for all of your followers Father, only for myself, but if he's the representative you need to raise your sights."

Then Hart glanced back at Simon before continuing, "A piece of me is elated for Simon. Another part of me wants to slap him silly, dart him, throw him in a cargo container, and ship his ass back home. I think forcing peace and deliverance with your mission is a delusion fueled by the power of your charisma enforced by your bomb-happy, maniac brother. If I were one of your disciples, like my old friend here, I would find peace and deliverance a mirage manufactured by exclusive devotion to you."

Manuela walked purposely over to Hart and lifted him to standing.

"I'm taking him out of here. Nobody make a move to stop me. I can still handle myself fairly well." She glared at Carlos while leading Hart outside.

Suddenly the air around them began to shudder and vibrate. They all heard a steady swooping thump, thump, thump. Three helicopters were descending directly above the field where the crowd continued to straggle out.

Hart perked up and spoke confidently. "Simon, you can still come with me."

As the first skids from the helicopter hit the ground six, uniformed officers leaped onto the field. One of them held a cell phone to his ear.

"We are leaving now," Manuela said.

Simon nodded to Hart and began to walk away as well. The next helicopter sat down on the grass. Out popped another six officers. The third one landed depositing an equal amount of men plus one snow-white, pale woman with flaming red hair onto the field. The contingent began weaving through the crowd in a coordinated ballet of potentially lethal force. The woman walked over to the officer holding the cell phone. Carlos' face, which had at first displayed concern and intensity, suddenly shifted to a furious anger.

"Carlos, much as I have enjoyed our time together —" Hart let go of Manuela's hand. He had been holding onto it as both a crutch and an insurance policy.

"That bitch," Carlos spat turning his gaze right at Hart. "Don't think so pal." He came after Hart.

Hart doe-eyed Father Greve and Manuela. "Help?"

"Carlos!" Manuela shouted.

"I might need him," He looked over his shoulder calculating the approach of the police squadron.

"As a human shield?" Hart now felt even more imperiled.

"No one shoots Americans anymore," flipped Carlos.

"So you see now Hart, the reason you are here," Greve offered. "Your moment arrives too brother." Greve nodded his head slowly at Carlos and stepped aside.

Protected by Manuela, Hart inched himself towards the helicopters. All the while the perimeter of police converged around them.

Carlos looked at his brother, "I believe in you Lazarus, but that's Dot over there. They're coming for me and no one else."

"Give yourself up, or at least give me up, then do as you please," Hart suggested.

"I believe in the work. I truly do." Carlos sounded convicted eyeing his brother.

"I believe in you, Carlozinho," said Greve.

Hart could not believe his ears. "That's the sage advice you have for him? I believe in you dude? Tell him something usable at least. Idiot, turn yourself in! Live to fight another day, let Hart go, he's a victim."

Hart now looked again to Manuela for help. To his dismay, the group had slowly begun navigating away from the impending dragnet until they heard the voice from the megaphone.

"Carlos dos Reis—Stay where you are." Detective Rosado's unmistakable voice rang out across the crowd.

Simon moved back into the picture, "That's enough." He said moving between Carlos and Hart. "Let him go."

"You pussy." Carlos slapped Simon across the face, knocking him sideways.

Hart jumped on Carlos to try and wrestle him down to the ground. He heard the police running towards them. Simon jumped back into the fray as they both battled with Carlos. Manuela leaped in trying to pull them all apart. Carlos clung to the ground by all fours like a leopard gathering strength for an attack. His family heritage handled both Hart and Simon in a split second.

First Carlos wheeled around, knocking Simon five feet back collapsing him into Carmen. Then he turned towards Hart. Not pausing for a millisecond. Hart turned and ran. Carlos gave immediate chase. Manuela followed as best she could.

The Police closed in on their position, "The American is the tall one," Rosado yelled in the bullhorn.

Brazilian Police carry out their manhunts unfettered by any American concepts of presumed innocence. During a Brazilian manhunt, the law is not expected to be courteous. They are under no compunction to issue the standard warning phrase 'halt or we'll shoot!' They simply blaze away as the perceived need arises. Thus began the hail of bullets headed towards Hart and his pursuer.

"Holy Shit! Don't shoot at me!?" Hart yelled, incredulously waving his arms.

A voice emerged from behind the police line. "Are you people out of your minds! What the god damn hell are you shooting at?" Bruce LeVitta yelled to no avail.

Carlos caught up to Hart. Both men were out of breath. Strangely, they held onto each other's shoulders for a split second of rest. The mystery of the moment: a comradely connection with the least likely being in his hemisphere did not escape Hart's notice. He also felt keenly aware, unlike other times in his life, that in this instance he could most definitely die.

Some people die too late, an unfortunate few die too early. In Hart's mind, this would be way too early. His death would not be the consummation of anything. By his own account, he had not accomplished near enough to have even the smallest cupcake of celebration. Dying at the wrong time would leave nothing but a promise not kept, potential squandered, opportunity wasted. All of this occurred to him as both men caught their wind. They both turned, catching sight of Manuela huffing her way up behind them. Wordlessly, they both decided to get the hell out of there. Now they ran side by side. Together. Had Hart possessed his full complement of wits he would've realized running was the most unnecessary, and very worst, of all his options.

"Filho, pare, por favor," Son, stop, please, Manuela yelled to Carlos.

No calculation he made could figure out the why of it. He truly hated Carlos without question; this was a violent man who surely deserved to die. Right? Still, he wanted to protect Carlos' humanity from the hail of bullets. That's the moment he felt it happen. A primordial emergence, from a pond of ooze lying fathoms beneath his surface. It wove through the shadows cast by his personal doubts, wound its way up the length of his ego, and gave a fond, parade wave, to the truth of his lack of direction. It comforted his loneliness, easily quenched his search for meaning anywhere in his life, and neatly extinguished the hollow echo of emptiness Hart had always felt at the mercy of life.

The throbbing in his brain disappeared in an instant. The gift of his Dukkha, suddenly and graciously, blossomed, then lifted. He felt it soar out of his body ascending before his eyes with a wink and a victory cigar. He wanted to shield the reprehensible, vile Carlos, the Shade, from a violent death at the hands of an unsympathetic world. While his body kept running in an autonomic continuum, Hart laughed to himself, 'what in the vast universe of possibilities was wrong with me? Was anything truly or uniquely wrong with me after all?'

In barely an instant, he felt a hot, hard punch to the stomach. The breath suddenly left his body. In an unfeeling haze he folded over, sliding his right hand to his navel. He reached for a deep inhale. The world slowed to a crawl. He turned and witnessed Manuela clutching her side then twisting down in slow motion only a few yards behind him. He grimaced. Then the ground seemed to rise up meeting him half way to catch his fall. Carlos dropped down next to him, swiveling his head and scanning around them. He looked hard in Hart's eyes for a single frozen moment, then vaporized into the scattering crowd.

Hart lie alone on the ground. How screwed up these events had turned out. Simon and Carmen raced over.

"This is screwed." Hart winced.

"Son of a bitch man, you're gushing blood. Oh my god!" Simon had no idea what to do.

"I saw you're mom go down, Carmen. I'm sorry. I like her more than your brothers," Hart wheezed.

"I couldn't run anymore. Sideache. Oh my god, he's shot!" Manuela appeared at his side.

Hart stared up at Manuela and Carmen. He suddenly felt lonely.

"We've got to get some help!" Carmen looked around.

Simon stood up yelling frantically, "Help! We need help over here!"

"Well, I guess this is something you will have to live with, isn't it?" Hart was not sure if Simon heard that.

Simon wept. Carmen picked up his hand, which felt comforting and futile to Hart.

"Pretty sure I need a doctor. Breathing is getting kind of tough in here. Like getting kicked in the balls, only more permanent," he wheezed.

Simon stood up screaming for a doctor. A policeman appeared and kneeled down to take a look.

LeVitta appeared, "Oh my god son! Rosado, god damn it, get some help over here!"

"Keep pressure on the wound," the officer volunteered, "a doctor is coming. Did you see which way the he went?" He looked directly at Hart, his gun still drawn. Hart thought to himself, this guy could've been the idiot that shot me and he's asking for my help?

"He's shot, you bastard. Get the hell out of here." LeVitta picked him up by his shirt back. He towered over the smaller policeman.

Simon sat next to Hart on the ground holding his friend's other hand. It made Hart remember being kids and huddling under the shade of his best friends frame.

Hart's voice faded, "Worst hang-time ever?"

He didn't think Simon heard him. Hart's mind kept working. Even as his body dangled by the tenuous, his thoughts cascaded in rapid fire. 'I'm leaving everything tragically on the table. It actually doesn't feel that bad—more like I'm packed for a field trip. I thought I'd be better prepared.

The tropics being the tropics, it began to rain.

Hart gulped, and stared straight ahead at no one in particular. "But I feel so ripped off."

Then he died.

Chapter 26. | When Buddha Smiles

Died might be too confining a term; too "in the box," with no wiggle room. It was true Hart had not issued a final ceremonial goodbye to anyone. No dire last words between amigos were exchanged. Greve did not show up to give him a comforting farewell Jesuit blessing, nor did Hart sense any enlightened epiphany about his actual final moments. Nothing he expected had occurred, save the unexpected surprise of the final chain of events. It had all been essentially low key.

Hart began a brief end-of-days, post-game foray into logistics. Did they catch and kill Carlos? How bad did Simon feel about his death? Were he and Carmen truly a great match as Simon had calculated? What did Carmen's messed-up family tree look like? Who was going to call his parents? He soon realized the preoccupation with logistics amounted to a gigantic waste of time he no longer had handy. He focused on what passed for the present.

He found himself sitting on a cushioned red bar stool next to a stainless steel countertop. It looked like a 1950's burger joint. It came complete with a decent condiment collection clustered on the counter in front of him. Above the counter, where the burger menu ought to be, dangled a red sign with white lettering:

The world is a perfect chain. All paths lead to the same destination.

Well that blows, thought Hart. Life comes with a manual like some Ikea chest of drawers; only you don't get it until AFTER it's built? As Hart contemplated his heightened irritation, an older, well-tanned man wearing a yellow cardigan approached him from behind the counter. Resting an elbow on the clean steel, his hand tucked beneath his pointed chin, the man smiled. Hart's jaw dropped open. He had all too quickly recognized the man staring benignly back at him from behind the counter as, Raymond Gil.

Gil apologized, "Sorry for the delay. I did not see you come in. You look surprised."

Hart made an attempt to get a handle on the moment. "More like nightmarishly disturbed."

"I would not be overly concerned about it."

Hart stuttered, "Really. From where you're standing that makes perfect sense, but for me this, I mean, I have a full recollection of the last breath. Well, I'm certain now, that I'm, but.."

"Welcome back," came the instant reply.

"I've been here before?"

"How did that go for you?"

"My life?" Hart stopped to contemplate, but felt flooded and overwhelmed. He began blurting out the collection of random thoughts flashing through his mind. "A disastrous mess! An epic screw-up! Did you ever know someone who you thought had gotten it all completely wrong? I mean, their whole life was spent driving down the absolute worst road possible, but at the end, the very last edible moment, you realized they had gotten it completely right, and you were the actual joker driving completely off the cliff. I never fulfilled anything of consequence. I guess I'm saying it didn't go so well."

"Sounds rather harsh to me," Gil said.

Hart thought Gil seemed to be playing coy, hesitant to reveal something of consequence.

"Not at all," Gil replied straight-faced.

"You can hear my thoughts? That's invasive," Hart said.

Gil smiled, "That simply no longer matters. We are all one and together."

"Oh please," Hart shot back. "Is that drivel supposed to make me feel better? Besides, I don't see much of a 'we.' Since you can't tell me if I've blown anything, is there some sort of review board, or reckoning commission to assess this stuff?" Hart observed the unchanging expression on Gil's face. He instantly regretted his ridiculous call for a supervisor. "Do we only get a few moments of grace? Did I have that? I do remember playing one, singular tennis match and feeling invincible. Simon and I kicked ass on Marty and Gene. Was that bliss?"

"Maybe, but your backhand was always a little weak. Don't you think?"

Gil waited with a beatific smile. Hart matched his expression, unsure of how to process the comment. "I am messing around with you." Gil paused, "You know, to ease the tension. Your backhand was always much better than you gave yourself credit for. May I ask you to take my hand?"

"I'd prefer not to." Hart shrank back from the counter.

Gil extended his open hand towards Hart's looking calmly and peacefully into his eyes, "Rise above yourself for a moment. It will not hurt."

Reluctantly accepting the challenge, Hart reached across the counter as the man gently folded Hart's hand in his. Gil's face dissolved into a thousand faces, all faces, every face Hart had ever known. Every soul he touched in any way passed through his consciousness. He experienced no concept of time. A second could have passed, or a millennium. Hart watched his first parakeet, Skeeter, appear on a pure blue horizon flying closer and closer passing directly through his eyes. He witnessed his grandparents' lawn bowling; leagues of friends and acquaintances appeared as mist wafting through his body. His abominable fifth grade teacher, Mrs. Ramses who, he was sure, had harbored a private hatred of his very existence, smiled at him. That stupid looking embryo from the last scene of A Space Odyssey floated by him too; 'So cliché,' he thought to himself. He wondered if everyone got that vision, and how did Arthur Clarke know about that so much in advance? He saw his face morph from an infant to his last moments of struggle for life on the bare ground in Botucatu. He saw Marjorie, Simon, Simon's mother Leice, Carmen. He passed through a thousand faces and souls of people he'd never known. He observed as if from a National Geographic duck blind, images of people hugging and weeping, making love, violently angry. At the same moment, he saw fear in the faces of people he barely ever knew, counter clerks from Starbuck's, newscasters reporting on war. There was birth, death and destruction, intermixed with joy and peace. Then one face appeared. It captured all faces, all events, all movement, all shadows, all light. He witnessed his own face fast and peacefully asleep. Finally he opened his eyes, or maybe they were already open, to see the man facing him across the countertop.

The man appeared for a moment as Raymond Gil, but then as if it he had been there the entire time, a smooth skinned, dark complexioned figure emerged. Smiling broadly and running his right hand over his bald head, the man's gaze penetrated directly into Hart's being, "You read the counter sign," he said.

Hart then knew exactly what he was about to hear. "Again?" He mulled it over for a beat. "I can do that." Hart answered before the man had uttered a sound.

"Yes, you can."

Then everything became dark just before it got light again.

And then…

Chapter 27. | Scattered showers with occasional sun

Hart shivered. The vibration ran throughout his body from bow to stern. He tracked a hot, searing warmth. It started in his left arm, flowed into his heart, then spread in one radiating pulse to the rest of his body. The world began to shake. 'Where, in the universe, had I landed now?' he pondered. The quaking grew more violent like the space shuttle passing through the troposphere on re-entry. Hart grew irritated—haven't I already been through enough crap? Even the afterlife has turbulence?

"Hart! Wake up!"

He heard an unmistakable voice. Not possible, he thought. I'm okay with dead. Aside from the bumps, there's nothing truly wrong with dead. I'll get another go round and work out all that shit I screwed up on the first time. He was actually looking forward to his next at-bat.

"Hart, wake up! What should I do? Should I slap him?" a woman's voice said.

Maybe he was going to an 'ever after' cocktail party before heading back to life.

"You can't slap someone with an IV in him. Jesus, Carmen!"

"I can hear you." Hart heard himself utter the words aloud.

"We know," the voice answered.

Simon watched Hart's face crinkle, trying to figure things out.

"It's time to come back, pal. You and I aren't done yet."

"My eyes are open," Hart thought. He reached deep inside himself expecting to find his inner dope laughing its ass off, holding a Corona and bowl of barbeque potato chips.

Hart sent a query to his eyelids. "You guys are open, right?" "Not sure," came the reply. Hart's lids slowly peeled themselves free. The sunlight streamed in from what felt like an IMAX 3D projector. It illuminated everything around him, including the relieved faces of his pal Simon and the ever radiant, if red-eyed, Carmen. His eyes went wide-screen.

"No shit, pal." Simon echoed his response.

Simon, who was one artery to the left from carrying an unbearable, lifetime burden, smiled. He leaned over his pal, covering both of them in the cool, protective shade of friendship and family. As the gurney continued rolling towards the waiting helicopter, Hart reached for Simon's hand.

Acknowledgements

It's oddly ironic that the last thing I thought about was this paragraph. Considering that the people appreciated herein were the most essential, first piece, of sustaining grace that allowed me to even write the book. It should have been first. Thank you is a weak sentiment for the patience and tolerance granted to me by my wife Nancy and daughters Tess and Dia. They allowed me the space to be surly, grumpy, distracted, and, in general, an extended pain in the ass during a substantial portion of the effort. Special appreciation to Nancy for allowing me to bounce idea after idea off of her, knowing her insightful talent at sifting through the worst to get to the best. Thanks to the talented Ilene who was supportive and insightful from the first paragraph to the last word. Deep thanks to my amazing, genius pal, Laina for subjecting herself to the first read, and artfully lifting the work with her suggestions. Thanks to Milo & Kaiya for lying silently on the floor each day in unconditional support of the process. Thank you to my pal DMW for being on the other end of the phone whenever needed. My gratitude and appreciation to Saral Burdette for her gifted contributions to the story in all matters of priestly importance. Amazing thanks to my editor, Leslie Wells for even taking this book on, then teaching me how to say what I mean in the most economic and elegant way possible. Sadly, I thank my recently passed former agent, Loretta Barrett, who was a relentless support system to me for many years. She was a grand soul who I will miss.

Lastly, thanks Pop. I hope you liked it before you left.